THERE BUT FOR THE

ALI SMITH

PANTHEON BOOKS · NEW YORK

Copyright © 2011 by Ali Smith
All rights reserved. Published in the United States by Pantheon Books,
a division of Random House, Inc., New York.
Originally published in Great Britain by Hamish Hamilton, published by
the Penguin Group, an imprint of Penguin Books Ltd., London.

Pantheon Books and colophon are registered trademarks of Random House, Inc.

Grateful acknowledgment is made to Nanada Music, B.V., c/o Tier Three Music
(ASCAP) for permission to reprint an excerpt from "Ding-A-Dong" by Dick
Bakker, Will Luikinga, and Eddy Ouwens, copyright © Nada International C.V.,
administered by Nanada Music, B.V. International copyright secured. All rights
reserved.

Library of Congress Cataloging-in-Publication Data
Smith, Ali, [date]
There but for the / Ali Smith.
p. cm.
ISBN 978-0-375-42409-0
1. Middle-aged men—Fiction. 2. Personal space—Fiction.
3. Social interaction—Fiction. 4. Dinners and dining—Fiction.
5. Greenwich (London, England). 6. Identity (Psychology)—Fiction.
7. Psychological fiction. I. Title.
PR6069.M4213T47 2011   823'.914—dc22   2010051377
www.pantheonbooks.com

Jacket design by Peter Mendelsund

Printed in the United States of America
First United States Edition
2 4 6 8 9 7 5 3 1

for Jackie Kay

for Sarah Pickstone

for Sarah Wood

ACKNOWLEDGMENTS AND THANKS

I'm indebted for sources of some of the stories about songs in this book to *America's Songs* by Philip Furia and Michael Lasser (Routledge, 2006). I'm also indebted for information used in the first section to Caroline Moorehead's *Human Cargo: A Journey Among Refugees* (Chatto and Windus, 2005).

Thank you, Cherry. Thank you, Lucy.

Thank you, Xandra, and thank you, Becky.

Thank you, Sarah and Laurie.

Thank you, Mary.

Thank you, Kasia.

Thank you, Andrew, and thank you, Tracy, and everybody at Wylie's.

Thank you, Simon.

Very special thanks to Kate Thomson.

Thank you, Jackie.

Thank you, Sarah.

The essence of being human is that one does not seek perfec-tion, that one is sometimes willing to commit sins for the sake of loyalty, that one does not push asceticism to the point where it makes friendly intercourse impossible, and that one is pre-pared in the end to be defeated and broken up by life, which is the inevitable price of fastening one's love upon other human individuals.

—George Orwell

For only he who lives his life as a mystery is truly alive.

—Stefan Zweig

I hate mystery.

—Katherine Mansfield

Of longitudes, what other way have we,
But to mark when and where the dark eclipses be?

—John Donne

Every wink of an eye some new grace will be born.

—William Shakespeare

The fact is, imagine a man sitting on an exercise bike in a spare room. He's a pretty ordinary man except that across his eyes and also across his mouth it looks like he's wearing letterbox flaps. Look closer and his eyes and mouth are both separately covered by little grey rectangles. They're like the censorship strips that newspapers and magazines would put across people's eyes in the old days before they could digitally fuzz up or pixellate a face to block the identity of the person whose face it is.

Sometimes these strips, or bars, or boxes, would also be put across parts of the body which people weren't supposed to see, as a protective measure for the viewing public. Mostly they were supposed to protect the identity of the person in the picture from being ascertained. But really what they did was make a picture look like something underhand, or seedy, or dodgy, or worse, had happened; they were like a proof of something unspeakable.

When this man on the bike moves his head the little bars move with him like the blinkers on a horse move when the horse moves its head.

Standing next to the sitting man so that their heads are level is a small boy. The boy is working at the grey bar over the man's eyes with a dinner knife.

Ow, the man says.

Doing my best, the boy says.

He is about ten years old. His fringe is long, he is quite long-haired. He is wearing flared jeans embroidered in yellow and purple at the waistband and a blue and red T-shirt with a Snoopy on the front. He forces the thing off the man's eyes so that it flicks off and up into the air almost comically and hits the floor with a metallic clatter.

This T-shirt is the first thing the man on the bike sees.

The Snoopy on it is standing on his hind legs and wearing a rosette on his chest. The rosette says the word hero on it. Above the Snoopy there are more words, in yellow and in the writing that's always used with the Snoopy characters. They say: it's hero time.

I'd totally forgotten about that T-shirt, is the first thing the man says as soon as the boy's jemmied off the thing that's been over his mouth.

Yeah, this one's good. But you know the orange one that says hug a beagle on it? the boy says.

The man nods.

Whenever I wear it, it's weird, but girls are always really nice to me, the boy says.

The man laughs a yes. He looks down at his feet, where both the grey rectangles landed. He picks one of them up. He weighs it in his hand. He feels the tender places round his eyes and at the edges of his mouth. He drops it on to the floor again and holds his hand away from himself in the air and flexes it. He looks at the boy's hands.

I'd forgotten what my own hands looked like, he says. Look like.

Okay, so we've done that now. So *now* can I show you? the boy says, do you want to know *now*?

The man nods yes.

Good, the boy says. Okay.

He takes two blank pieces of paper off the floor. He gives one to the man. He sits on the bed and holds the other piece of paper up.

So, he says. What you do is. You get a plain A4 sheet of paper and then you fold it in half. No, that way. Lengthways. And make sure the corners are even, so they're on top exactly.

Okay, the man says.

Then unfold it so it's like a book, the boy says.

Okay, the man says.

Then fold one corner, the boy says, the top corner, then fold the other. So it looks like that, like a book but a book with a triangular head. Then fold the folded point towards you down and crease. So it looks like an envelope. Then fold over one corner again so there's a little tab sticking out at the end. Then the same for the other one. But so that you get a blunt point, not a pointed point. Blunter is better.

Wait, wait, wait, the man says. Hang on.

Yes, a little triangle sticking out of the flap, the boy says. Then fold the small triangle back up on top of the flaps. Then fold outwards, not inwards, so that the triangle is on the outside. Make sure it's all even. Then take hold of the top and fold it down to make the first wing. Then flip over and do the same for the other wing. Make sure it's even or it'll be out of control.

The man looks at the plane in his hands. He creases it down, then opens it up. Outside, on its top, it looks like a plain folded piece of paper. Inside, underneath, it is packed tight into itself with surprising neatness like origami, like a small machine.

The boy holds up his plane and points it towards the far end of the room.

And that's the finished article, he says.

It flies evenly and direct, very nicely, from the boy's hand right into the corner.

Actually aerodynamic, the man thinks. Substantial, for a single sheet of paper. It feels much heavier than it did before it was folded. But it isn't, is it? How can it be?

Then he aims his own plane at the opposite corner by the door. It follows its flightpath exactly. It is almost insolent, the exactness of it.

The man laughs out loud. The boy nods and shrugs.

Simple, the boy says. See?

THERE

was once a man who, one night between the main course and the sweet at a dinner party, went upstairs and locked himself in one of the bedrooms of the house of the people who were giving the dinner party.

There was once a woman who had met this man thirty years before, had known him slightly for roughly two weeks in the middle of a summer when they were both seventeen, and hadn't seen him since, though they'd occasionally, for a few years after, exchanged Christmas cards, that kind of thing.

Right now the woman, whose name was Anna, was standing outside the locked bedroom door behind which the man, whose name was Miles, theoretically was. She had her arm raised and her hand ready to—to what? Tap? Knock discreetly? This beautiful, perfectly done-out, perfectly dulled house would not stand for noise; every creak was an affront to it, and the woman who owned it, emanating disapproval, was just two feet behind her. But it was her fist she was standing there holding up, like a 1980s cliché of a revolutionary, ready to, well, nothing quiet. Batter. Beat. Pound. Rain blows.

Strange phrase, to rain blows. Somewhere over the rainblow. She didn't remember much about him, but they'd never have been friends in the first place if he wasn't the sort to enjoy a bad pun. Was he, unlike Anna right now, the kind of person who'd know what to say to a shut door if he were standing outside one trying to get someone on the other side to open it? The kind who could turn to that child stretched on her front as far up the staircase as her whole small self would go, the toes of her bare feet on the wood of the downstairs hall floor and her chin in her hands on the fifth step lying there watching, and straight off be making the right kind of joke, *what do you call two mushrooms on holiday? Fun guys,* straight off be holding forth about things like where a phrase like *to rain blows* came from in the first place?

The woman standing behind Anna sighed. She somehow made a sigh sound cavernous. After it the silence was even louder. Anna cleared her throat.

Miles, she said to the wood of the door. Are you there?

But the bleat of her voice left her somehow less there herself. Ah, now, see—that's what it took, the good inappropriateness of that child. Half boy, all girl, she'd elbowed herself up off the staircase, run up the stairs and was about to hammer on the door.

Bang bang bang.

Anna felt each thud go through her as if the child were hammering her on the chest.

Come out come out wherever you are, the child yelled.

Nothing happened.

Open sesame, the child yelled.

She had ducked under Anna's arm to knock. She looked up at her from under her arm.

It makes the rock in the side of the mountain open, the child said. They say it in the story, therefore the rock just like opens.

The child put her mouth to the door and spoke again, this time without shouting.

Knock knock, she said. Who's there?

Who's there?

There were several reasons at that particular time in Anna Hardie's life for her wondering what it meant, herself, to be *there.*

One was her job, which she had just given up, in what she and her colleagues laughingly called Senior Liaison, at what she and her colleagues only half-laughingly called the Centre for Temporary Permanence (or, interchangeably, the Centre for Permanent Temporariness).

Another was that Anna had woken up a couple of weeks ago in the middle of her forties in the middle of the night, from a dream in which she saw her own heart behind its ribcage. It was having great trouble beating because it was heavily crusted over with a caul made of what looked like the stuff we clean out of the corners of our eyes in the mornings when we wake up. She woke up, sat up and put her hand on her heart. Then she got up, went to the bathroom mirror and looked. There she was.

The phrase reminded her of something Denny at the Evening News, with whom she'd worked on neighbourhood liaison pieces and with whom she'd had a short liaison herself, had told her some time ago, on their second and last lunchtime. He was a sweet man, Denny. He'd stood in front of her in her kitchen, their first time, and presented his penis to her very sweetly, rueful and hopeful both, a little apologetic about his erection and at the same time proud of it; she liked this. She liked him. But two lunchtimes was all it was, and they both knew it. Denny had a wife, her name was Sheila, and their two girls and their boy were at Clemont High. Anna made a pot of tea, put sugar and milk on the tray because she wasn't sure what he took, carried it upstairs, slid back into the bed. It was a quarter past one. They had just under half an hour left. He'd asked could he smoke. She'd said, okay, since it's the last lunch. He'd smiled. Then he'd turned over in the bed, lit the cigarette, changed the subject. He'd said did she know he could sum up the last six decades of journalism in six words?

Go on then, she said.

I was there. There I was, he said.

It was a commonplace, he said. By the middle of the twentieth century every important report put it like this: *I was there.* Nowadays: *There I was.*

Soon it would be seven words, Anna said. The new century had already added a seventh word. *There I was, guys.* She and

Denny had laughed, drunk their tea, put their clothes back on and gone back to their different jobs. The last time they'd spoken was some months ago, about how to handle the story with the local kids giving urine to the asylum kids in lemonade bottles to drink.

In the middle of the night, some months later, holding her own heart, feeling nothing, Anna had looked at herself in the mirror in the bathroom. There she was. It was the there-she-was guise.

There she was again, then, two evenings ago, sitting in front of her laptop one summer evening with the noise of Wimbledon coming from neighbours' TVs through the open windows of the houses all around. Wimbledon was on her own TV too. Her own TV's sound was turned down. It was sunny in London and the Wimbledon grass was still bright green, only a little scuffed. The TV screen flickered away by itself beyond the laptop screen. Pock noises and oohs and ahs, strangely disconnected from their source, accompanied the little noises she was making on her keyboard. It was as if the whole outside world was TV soundtrack. Maybe there was a new psychosis, Tennis Players' Psychosis (TPP), where you went through life believing that an audience was always watching you, profoundly moved by your every move, reacting round your every reaction, your every momentous moment, with joy / excitement / disappointment / Schadenfreude. Presumably all professional tennis players had something like it, and maybe so to some extent did everybody who still believed in God. But would this mean that people who *didn't* have it were somehow less *there* in the world, or at least differently there, because they felt themselves less observed? We might as well pray to the god of tennis players, she thought. We might as well ask *that* god as ask any other for world peace, to keep us safe, to bring all the birds that've ever died, ever sunk into dust via little mounds of feather and crumbling hollow little bones, back to life, perch them all on that sill right now, the small ones at the front and the large ones at the back, and have them sing a rousing chorus of Bye Bye Blackbird, which was a song her father used to whistle when she was a little girl, and one she hadn't heard for many years. No one here to love or understand me. Oh what hard-luck stories they all hand me. Was that it? Something about hard-luck stories, anyway. Just as she was about to look the lyrics up on the net new mail came pinging into her inbox with an electronic little trill.

The new mail was quite a long email which Anna nearly mistook for the please-transfer-money-to-this-account-because-I-am-dying-and-need-your-help kind. But she paused her finger above delete when something about it caught her eye. It was addressed to her with the correct first name but the wrong surname initial. *Dear Anna K.* It was both her and not her, the name. More: something about it made her feel super-eighted, instamaticked. It gave her a feeling something like the word summer used to. Most of all it reminded her of an old spinebent copy of a Penguin classic paperback by Kafka, yes, Franz Kafka, which she had read one summer when she was sixteen or seventeen.

Dear Anna K

I am writing to you because my husband and I are at the end of my tether and we are hoping to God that you will be able to help us.

Ten days ago we invited Miles Garth, who I believe you know to dinner here at our house in Greenwich. He is a friend of a friend, we actually hardly know him which is why this situation is so difficult and actually untenable as you can imagine. To cut a long short story Mr. Garth has locked himself in our spare bedroom. I am only relieved the bedroom is ensuite. He will not leave the room. He is not just refusing to unlock the door and go to his own home, wherever that might be. He is refusing to speak to a singe soul. It has now been ten days, and our unwanted tenant has only communicated by 1 piece of paper slipped under the bottom of the door. We are slipping flat packs of wafer-paper-thin turkey and ham to him under the said door but are unable to provide him with anything more dimensional because of the size of the space between the said door and the floor. (Our spare room door, in fact all the upstairs doors in our house are believed 18th century although the house itself dates from the 1820s you can understand my concern and the hinges are on the inside side. I have reason to believe he has jammed one of our chairs under the c18th door handle too.).

I/we have absolutely no idea whatsoever why Mr. Garth has chosen to barricade himself into our house, it is certainly nothing to do with me and it is nothing to do with my husband or my daughter. As you can imagine ten days is a long time at the end of the day. We have tried his work associates but nothing has worked.

We do not however wish to be unpleasant. We are at present using a softly-softly approach, also on the advice of the police advisers.

This is why I/we are contacting you as one of the few Significant others we can trace for Mr. Garth. We were fortunate to find this email for you in the address book in his phone which he did not take into our spare room with him but left with his jacket and his car keys in our lounge.

We have moved his car temporarily to the driveway of a friend but it cannot stay there indefinately (it was originally left I'm afraid illegally in a Residents Permit Space.).

If you can help my husband and myself at all in any way I/we would be very grateful. Our telephone number is at the bottom of this email. I would be very much obliged if you would contact us as soon as possible even if it is only to let me know that you have received this message even if you can't actually help in this instance.

Very many thanks indeed and I/we look forward to hearing from you.

Yours sincerely
Gen Lee
(Genevieve and Eric Lee)

Who was Miles Garth, again?
Miles.

Yes.

When we went to Europe.

Anna read it through again.

He is refusing to speak to a singe soul.

Later that evening she found that instead of thinking (as she did every night as the dark came down and every morning as the light came up) about work, and about the faces, one after the other, of the people she had failed, she was preoccupied with this notion, a lightly burnt soul, its scent of singed wool.

Before she went to bed she tapped out the following, and sent it.

Dear Mrs. Lee,

Thank you for your email. What a strange predicament. I'm afraid though that you might be on to a wild goose chase with me, since I don't really know Miles Garth or anything about him, having met him only very briefly and quite a long time ago now, back in the 1980s. I am not at all sure I can help you. But if you think I can, I'm willing to give it a try. What would you like me to do?

All my best,
Anna Hardie.

Now it was two days later.

Miles, she said to whoever was behind the door. *Are you there?*

Where exactly was Anna, then, who had travelled in on the packed train that morning next to a man in a Gore-Tex jacket who was watching porn on the screen of his phone? She'd crossed the capital past the posters on the tube station walls advertising *This Season's Atonement* and under the ads in the tube carriage with the picture of the kitchen bin with the speech bubble coming out of its mouth saying *It's My Right To Eat Tin Cans* and the words beneath which said *Deny Your Bin Its Rights*. She'd gone for a walk between stations and seen St. Paul's rise to the surface on

9

the riverbank like a piece of old cartilage. She'd ridden a train through a place that looked like the future had looked when she was a child. Now she was walking up a hot summer street of beautiful buildings and shabby-chic houses trying to remember what Greenwich meant again, which was something to do with time. When she got to the right address, a child wearing a bright yellow dress over the top of a pair of jeans was sitting on its top step picking little stones out of a fancy border of pebbles at each side of the door. She was whistling a repetitive strip of tune a bit like the Judy Garland song from The Wizard of Oz and throwing the stones at a drain in the road, presumably trying to get them down the grate of it. The drain cover and the road around it were dotted with little white stones.

Hello, Anna said.

I'm broke, the child said.

Me too, Anna said.

Really? the child said.

Yes, Anna said. Almost totally. What a coincidence. Aren't you hot in all those clothes?

Nope, the child said reaching up to the doorbell. Because I feel that I am not doing myself full justice if I don't wear them all.

But it was a white woman, dressed in summer whites and beiges, who answered the door. She pushed the child to one side and held her hand out to shake Anna's hand.

Genevieve Lee, she said. Call me Gen. Thank you so much for coming.

She led Anna into the lounge, still holding her by the hand. When she let go Anna folded her jacket and put it on the arm of the couch, but Genevieve Lee stared at the jacket there for an unnaturally long time.

I'm sorry. It makes me afraid, Genevieve Lee said.

My jacket does? Anna said.

I now have a horrible fear that people who take their coats off in my house might never leave my house, Genevieve Lee said.

Anna picked her jacket up at once.

I'm so sorry, she said.

10

No, it's fine, you can leave it there for now, Genevieve Lee said. But as you can tell. We really are at the end of our tether with your friend Miles.

Yes, well, as I said, he's not really my friend, Anna said.

I promise you, we can't take much more of our oh you tea, Genevieve Lee said.

Sorry? Anna said.

Our Unwanted Tenant, she said.

Oh, I see, Anna said.

No. Oh you tea, Genevieve Lee said.

No, I meant—, Anna said.

Also, oh you tea spells out, Genevieve Lee said, which makes it what Eric, my husband, and I call a positive thinking exercise.

Genevieve Lee was currently a freelance Personnel Welfare Coordinator for people who worked in Canary Wharf. When they had problems, financial, emotional or practical, their companies could contact her and she'd tell them what kind of help was available in both the public and the private sectors.

As you can imagine, work's been off the scale recently, she said. What are you currently doing yourself?

I'm currently unemployed, Anna said.

I can help you with that, Genevieve Lee said. The main thing is, it's very, very important to talk about it. Here's my card. What's your field?

Senior Liaison, Anna said. But I've just given it up.

Gosh, given it up, Genevieve Lee said. Presumably something better on the horizon.

There'd better be, Anna said, or I may kill myself.

Genevieve Lee laughed a knowing laugh.

She told Anna that Eric worked at the Institute for Measurement and Control and that he'd be back at three.

The child, who'd followed them in, was sitting in the retro-modern armchair at the window, batting her bare heels off the front of the chair.

Stop kicking that, Brooke, Genevieve Lee said. It's Robin Day.

Robin day? the child said. Today?

Brooke, we're busy, Genevieve Lee said.

You would think robin day would be a day that it would make more sense to be nearer in time to Christmas, the child said. It is a very good idea for a day and everything. But the fact is, it's the summer not the winter now, which is therefore probably why robin day hasn't caught on yet and nobody knows about it like we know about Valentine's day and father's day and mother's day and Christmas day.

Anna noticed again how surprisingly polite and old-fashioned the child sounded.

I'm sure your mother's calling you, Genevieve Lee said.

I can hear nothing that resembles what you suggest, Mrs. Lee, the child said.

Let me put it another way, Brooke. I think you're wanted elsewhere, Genevieve Lee said.

You mean I'm not wanted here. Words words words, the child said.

She jumped up and down. Then she did a handstand by the side of the couch, next to Anna.

That's from Hamlet, she said upside down from underneath her dress. A play by William Shakespeare, but you probably already know that. *Words* words words. Words *words* words. Words words *words*.

She kicked her legs in the air. Genevieve Lee got up and stood pointedly at the door. The child upended herself on to her feet and straightened her clothes.

Would you like to walk the tunnel later, right, maybe? the child said to Anna. It was built in 1902 and it goes underneath the river, have you ever walked it?

She told Anna that if she'd been here three years ago she'd have been able to see the actual Cutty Sark.

Because I don't mean see the *station*, she said. But you probably already know how the fact is it was originally a ship, not just a station, and before the fire on it, it was still there, therefore if you or if I had come out of the *station* called Cutty Sark, and we'd turned the right way at the exit, by which I mean turned to our left, we'd have seen the *ship* called it. The point I'm making being, the thing is, I didn't actually come to live here till last year. So I can't see it until it is restored to its former glory. But maybe you saw the real original when you were my age or a bit older, I mean before it burned down.

I missed it, Anna said. I never saw it in real life. I've seen it in pictures. And film of it on TV.

It's not the same, the child said. But it'll do, it'll do, it'll have to do.

She did a wild joyful dance in the doorframe.

Brooke, Genevieve Lee said. Out. Now. And leave my stones alone. They cost money. Scottish river pebbles, she said to Anna.

Very expensive, Anna said.

She winked at the going child.

Bye, she said.

Brooke was nine, apparently, and lived round the corner in the student flats. Her parents were research fellows or postgraduates at the university.

Obviously not ours, Genevieve Lee said. Very cute, though. Quite precocious.

Genevieve Lee poured the coffee and told Anna about the night of their annual alternative dinner party, which was something she and her husband, Eric, usually held at the beginning of the summer before everybody disappeared for the holidays. Once a year they liked to invite people who were a bit different from the people they usually saw, as well as the friends they saw all the time, Hugo and Caroline and Richard and Hannah. It was always interesting to branch out. Last year they had invited a Muslim couple; the year before they had had a Palestinian man and his wife and a Jewish doctor and his partner. That had resulted in a very entertaining evening. This year an acquaintance of Hugo and Caroline's, a man whose name was Mark Palmer, had brought Miles Garth with him.

Mark is gay, Genevieve Lee explained. He's an acquaintance

of Hugo and Caroline's. We thought Miles was Mark's partner, but it seems not. Probably for the best, because if they *were* partners there'd be an outstanding age difference between them, twenty years, more maybe. They apparently go to a lot of musicals together. Mark Palmer loves musicals. They tend to, don't they? He's in his sixties. He's Hugo and Caroline's friend.

Genevieve Lee went on to tell her that Brooke's parents, the Bayoudes, had been invited too, and had also come along, though they'd recently moved here not from anywhere in Africa but from Harrogate.

Anyway, we were all having a lovely supper, Genevieve Lee said. Everything was going really well, until after the main course, he just stood up and went upstairs. Well, we thought, naturally, that he was going to the bathroom so I waited the sweet course, which was complicated in itself, because I needed to torch the brûlées. But he didn't come down. Fifteen minutes at least. Possibly more, because we were quite happy, just drunk enough to be happy; that's another thing about him, he wasn't drinking, which always makes you self-conscious if you go to dinner or if you hold a dinner and someone's not drinking and we all, I mean everyone else, is. Anyway, I put the coffee maker on, did the scorching, served everybody else, left them to get on with it, popped upstairs and knocked on the bathroom door and asked him was he all right. Of course he didn't answer. Of course he wasn't in the bathroom at all. Of course he'd already locked himself in our spare room.

He really virulently disliked what you'd served for starter and main, then, Anna said.

Genevieve Lee got quite excited.

He's like that, is he? she said. Other people eating scallops and chorizo would have upset him that much?

Ah, well, I've no idea, no, I was just, you know, making a joke, Anna said.

It's no laughing matter, Genevieve Lee said.

No, Anna said. Of course not.

You have no idea how awful this is for us, Genevieve Lee said. There is lovely, lovely furniture in there. It is a really outstanding spare room in there. Everybody who has stayed there has told us so. This last thirteen days has been hell.

Hell on earth, yes, I can imagine, Anna said.

She looked hard at the wood of the floor.

So then Eric went up, Genevieve Lee said. He knocked on the bathroom door and had the same response as I'd had, no response at all. When the coffee was poured and we were all, all nine of us, actually getting a little worried about him, his friend Mark, the man who'd brought him here in the first place, went up. Then he came down saying he'd tried the bathroom and that its door wasn't locked, and that there was actually nobody *in* the bathroom, the bathroom was empty. So Eric went up to check, and then so did I. Completely empty. So we all assumed he'd just gone home, just left, you know, slipped out the front door without saying goodnight, although why he'd be that rude. And why he'd leave his jacket behind, which we realized when we were all saying our goodbyes and there it was just lying there on the couch.

Genevieve Lee gesticulated towards the couch. Anna looked at the couch. So did Genevieve Lee.

They both looked at the couch.

Then Genevieve Lee continued.

And Mark, who's gay, she said, he's an older man, was most upset. They can be hysterical, in a good way *and* a bad way. Anyway, after coffee, and a very nice orange muscat that Eric dug up in an Asda, which nobody could believe, everybody went home happy, except for Mark of course who was clearly a bit perturbed. And Eric and I went off to bed. And it wasn't until the morning that we saw that his car was still in the Resident's space and had actually already been ticketed—which I'm not paying for—and Josie, that's our daughter, came downstairs and asked us why the spare room door was locked and what the note she'd found on the floor meant.

What did the note say? Anna asked.

Fine for water but will need food soon. Vegetarian, as you know. Thank you for your patience.

It was the child's voice. It came from behind the armchair. She hadn't left at all. She'd crept back into the room without them hearing or noticing her.

I thought you said in your email you'd been feeding him ham? Anna said.

Beggars can't be choosers, Genevieve Lee said.

They don't want him to get too at home in there, the Robin Day chair said.

Genevieve Lee ignored this.

Clearly he's not all there, she said.

He *is* all there, the child behind the chair said. Where else could he be?

Genevieve Lee ignored this too, as if the child simply wasn't there. She leaned forward, confidential.

We're only glad to have been able to find a contact, she said. Mark hardly knows him at all, certainly not well enough to persuade him to open the door. He's a bit of a loner, your Miles.

Anna told her again about how she hardly knew Miles Garth, that the only reason she knew him at all was fluke, in that they'd both won a place nearly thirty years ago on a European holiday for teenagers from all over the country, a competition organized through secondary schools and sponsored by a bank. She and Miles had spent two weeks in July of 1980 on the same tour bus, along with forty-eight other seventeen- and eighteen-year-olds.

And kept in touch for years afterwards, Genevieve Lee said.

Well, no, Anna said. Not really, hardly at all. I kept in touch with six or seven people from the group for a year or two, then, you know. You lose touch.

But a beautiful memory, one that meant everything to him all those years ago, Genevieve Lee said.

Nope, Anna said.

A painful break-up, the first time his heart broke, and he's never been able to forget, Genevieve Lee said.

No, Anna said. Honestly. I really don't think so. I mean, we were vaguely friends. Nothing else. Nothing, you know, meaningful.

Which is why he's carried your name and address with him all these years, for no meaningful reason at all, then, Genevieve Lee said.

Genevieve Lee was getting red in the face.

If there's a reason, I don't know what it is, Anna said. I mean, I can't imagine where he got my email address from. We haven't been in touch for, God, it must be well over twenty years. Way before email.

Something very special. On your trip thing. Happened.

Genevieve Lee was shouting now. But Anna's job had trained her well when it came to other people's anger.

Sit down, she said. Please. When you sit down, I'll tell you exactly what I remember.

It worked. Genevieve Lee sat down. Anna spoke soothingly and kept her arms uncrossed.

The first thing I remember, she said, is that I got food poisoning at a medieval banquet they laid on for us in London right at the beginning of the fortnight. And I remember seeing Paris, the Eiffel Tower, Sacré Coeur, for the first time. I remember there was nothing to do in Brussels. We found an old closed fairground and wandered around it. I hated the food in the Heidelberg hotel. There was a wooden bridge in Lucerne. And all I remember about Venice is that we stayed in a very grand hotel that was very dark inside. And that a bomb went off in a railway station somewhere else in Italy, in the north, while we were in Venice and it killed a lot of people, and that there was a small mutiny among some of the boys in the group because the hotel staff were sharp with them after this happening, you know, told them to make less noise. I remember there was quite a row about a beer bottle or a beer can being thrown out of a hotel window. I can't remember if that was Italy or not.

From France to Germany Genevieve Lee had been passing a pencil she'd picked up off the little table next to her from one hand to the other. By Italy she had started tapping the table with the pencil.

So, Anna said. I had a look through my photos after your message came, but I don't have many, only twelve, I obviously only took one spool, and there's only one photo with Miles Garth in it. I mean, *I* know it's him, *I* can look at the photo and be sure it's him, but you can't see his face, he's looking down in it so you can only see the top of his head. There's a group photo, of all of us, they took one outside the bank before we left. It's too far away to see anyone very clearly, but he's there, at the back. He was tall.

I already know he's *tall,* Genevieve Lee said. I already know what he *looks* like.

I remember he tied little bits of french bread on to bits of denim thread he pulled off the frayed ends of his jeans, Anna said, and we used these to try to catch the goldfish in a lake at Versailles. That's what he's looking down at in the photo. He's tying a knot round the bread. And—that's all.

That's all? Genevieve Lee said.

Anna shrugged.

Genevieve Lee snapped the pencil she was holding in two. Then she looked down at the pieces of pencil she held in each hand in surprise. She laid the bits of pencil down neatly together on the table.

That's when they'd gone upstairs.

That's when Anna had stood with her fist up ready to—to what, exactly?

Miles. Are you there?

Silence.

Then—bang bang bang—the child, hammering on the door.

Tell him who you are, for God sake, Genevieve Lee hissed at Anna then.

Miles, it's Anna Hardie, Anna said.

(Nothing.)

From Barclays Bank European Grand Tour 1980, she said.

(Silence.)

Tell him about when you fished for the goldfish with the bread and that, the child said.

Miles, I think the Lees would really like you to open the door and leave the room, Anna said.

(Silence.)

I think the Lees would like their house back, she said.

(Nothing.)

Tell him it's *you*. Tell him it's *Anna K,* Genevieve whispered.

Anna looked at her own fist still stupidly raised. She rested it against the wood of the door. She lowered it. She turned to Genevieve Lee.

Sorry, she said.

She shrugged.

Genevieve Lee nodded. She made a tiny precise gesture with her hand to indicate that Anna was now to go downstairs again.

At the foot of the stairs the two women stood, nothing left to say. Anna looked through the door at the lounge. It was like a contemporary chic lounge in a theatre performance would be. She looked at the geometric arrangement of logs next to the fireplace. She looked at the ceiling, at the huge beam of wood which ran all the way from the back of the lounge and above her head into the hall.

An amazing piece of, uh, wood, Anna said.

Genevieve Lee explained it was believed to be a piece of a ship which had fought at Trafalgar, and it was why the lounge had never been renovated and extended. As she explained all this, she visibly calmed. She opened the front door, held it open. The day's heat came into the cold old hall.

Though we'll be upgrading to Blackheath, she said, soon as the market picks up sufficiently. Eric will be home at three. I know he'd like to talk to you.

You mean, you want me to come back here again at three? Anna said on the doorstep.

If you would be so kind, Genevieve Lee said. Just after would be ideal. Ten past.

19

The thing is, Anna said, if I go now I can catch the less expensive train home, but if I stay it'll cost me twice as much.

We appreciate it, Genevieve Lee said. It's very kind. Thanks very much indeed.

She went to shut the door.

Just one thing, Anna said.

Genevieve Lee paused the half-closed door.

It's the Anna K thing, Anna said.

I'm sorry? Genevieve Lee said.

In the email. Dear Anna K. And again, up there, Anna said. You called me Anna K. It's not my name. My name's Anna H. Hardie.

Genevieve held up her hand. She backed into the hall. She came back with a black jacket. She took a mobile phone out of its inside pocket and held it up.

It's in the memory, she said.

Then she dropped the phone into the jacket pocket again and threw the jacket through the door straight at Anna so that Anna couldn't not catch it. She spoke sweetly.

You are now responsible, she said. When this is all over I do not want, and will not accept, I'm making it clear right now, any accusations about usage of any bank or credit cards which happen to have been left in a jacket which happened to be left in my house.

Then she shut the door, click. Anna stood on the doorstep.

Eric and Gen. Gen and Eric. Jesus. She'd invite them to her own special annual dinner party, the one she annually gave for generics. Who knew what was going on between Genevieve Lee and Miles Garth, or Eric Lee and Miles Garth, or their daughter, or whoever, and Miles Garth? Who cared? Who cared whether Miles Garth had invented the perfect rent-free way in a recession to be regularly fed, at least for a while? Who cared why he'd chosen to shut himself in a hateful room in a hateful place? She was going home. Well, to what passed, for her, for home right now.

She turned on her heel on the pavement in the direction of the station.

The child was at her side, skipping.

Tunnel? the child said.

Should you not be in school? Anna said.

Nope, the child said. Closed early. Swine flu. You talk in a really funny accent.

Thanks, Anna said.

I like it, the child said. I don't dislike it.

A long time ago I was Scottish, Anna said.

Been there, the child said. Done that. I mean, I liked it there, man. I didn't dislike it. Therefore, I'd go again. There was a great number of trees in it.

She handed Anna something. It was a piece of pencil, the pencil Genevieve Lee had broken in two, back in the lounge. The child held up the other piece.

Thanks, Anna said. But you got the end with the point. That's not fair.

Yeah, but you are an adult and can afford to buy a sharpener at, like, a stationer's, or in a supermarket, the child said skipping ahead and talking to the rhythm of her own skipping. Or just *take,* a sharpener, and put it in, your pocket if, you wanted it, and therefore then, you wouldn't have, to pay at all, because you know, pencils should always, come with sharpeners, because what use, is pencils without, a sharpener? We should all, be able to, help ourselves to, free sharpeners.

Now that's what I call anarchy, Anna said.

And that's when she remembered.

(Europe. Land of InterRail. Place known as Abroad. Visited by Cliff Richard and some boys and girls twenty years ago on their double decker bus, though right now, at the very start of the 1980s, Cliff Richard is singing about a girl who's missing, has maybe been murdered, used to room on the second floor, left no forwarding address, left nothing but a name on a payphone wall.

Europe. Place of the Grand Tour for fifty British teenagers from up and down the country—of which Anna is the one from furthest north and the only Scottish one—who've each won a place in a publicity event organized by a British bank by writing *a short story or an essay of not more than 2000 words* about *Britain In The Year 2000,* which is twenty years from now.

1980. Year that Anna Hardie, a prizewinning writer about what life will be like in twenty years' time, unbends the leg of a paper-clip and threads it through one of her ears in Versailles, France, infecting the ear, giving herself a slight fever and having to start a course of antibiotics three days and a couple of countries later, in Brunnen, Switzerland, where the views of the mountains and the lakes, and of the mountains in the lakes, are stunning.

But first: London, Paris, Versailles. The fifty prizewinning writers about the future are on their fourth day. On day two everyone woke up to find that he or she was now one of

the party-people, or

the weirdo swots, or

the total outsiders.

Already Anna has been goosed, for the first time in her life, by a seventeen-year-old weirdo swot (who, in twenty years' time, will have become an internationally renowned Professor of Theoretical Physics). At the time of it happening she has no idea that this is what's happening; the inexplicable pain between her buttock and her thigh and the red-haired blushing boy-man with bad eczema behind her seem in no way related, though later in the fortnight she will see him stand close to the back of one of the other girls and see the other girl leap in the air away from him, and then she will understand. Already the nastier of the party-people have got another of the weirdo swots drunk by spiking his drink at supper in the Paris hotel, have held him down drunk in one of the bedrooms and have shaved off one half of his little RAF-war-hero moustache. He is wandering lopsidedly about in the summer haze at Versailles Palace today, a single-winged recording angel. Why would he not just shave the whole thing off? she wonders. Is it so that the people who did it to him will be made to face their meanness every time they see him? Or because he doesn't want to lose the half he's got so he can reconstruct the other exactly? Anna doesn't know. She hasn't spoken to him. (She has hardly spoken to anyone.) She knows his name is Peter, and that he had announced to everybody at the Medieval Banquet on day one in London that he was especially looking forward to Versailles, to seeing the historic mirror room where the peace treaty was signed at the end of the First World War. Ironic, the thought of him seeing his own war-wound in every one of those huge tarnished mirrors.

Anna is one of the total outsiders.

This is because she is the only Scot on the tour and all forty-nine of the others are loudmouthed scary confident articulate English people. (It might also be because she had food poisoning after the Medieval Banquet and spent a lot of the first evening of initial group formation by herself, in the hotel room in their hotel in Bayswater, throwing up.)

Right now she is sitting tearing little bits off the french stick that came with the packed lunch and putting them into her mouth. She is at the side of a huge lake with an elaborate fountain in the middle of it. Are its gold horses struggling like that, their hooves and mouths and manes all panic, because they're scared that they'll sink to oblivion, or because coming back to the surface after being down in the deep is so terrifying?

There are eleven days, including today, left.

Today is only partially over.

Roughly one-third of today is over.

What if the bus the fifty future-writers are all crossing Europe in crashes on this tour and they all die and she never gets home again?

If she had her passport she could go home. She could just go back to the hotel in Paris, pick up her bag and go. She could leave a note at reception saying somebody at home is ill, or that she's had a bad dream about the family and because her dreams are so strong and intuitive she has decided she'd better return home immediately even though nobody has phoned for her or anything. No. That's pathetic, and regardless of pathos and regardless of dreams, all the passports are in the safe-keeping of

Barbara, the Bank's Accountant, one of the five accompanying staff members (ten future-writers per staff member, presumably). Anna tries to imagine her passport, rubberbanded to a wedge of the other forty-nine passports, probably alphabetically, somewhere safe, maybe *in* a safe, the hotel safe. Or does Barbara the Accountant carry them everywhere with her in that briefcase? Anna in her passport photo—taken in the photobooth at the post office at home, at the beginning of June, and never did a photobooth seem so blessed, so lucky, even its little curtain enviable, just in being back there in that place called home—is wearing a Siouxsie and the Banshees T-shirt; she is dark-eyed, she looks stern, disaffected, miserable and you better not dare ask why, and this is the self that has to last her in the world until she is the ancient age of twenty-seven, when she will be a totally different person, when everything will be different, life will be easy, will make sense, will all have fallen into place.

She is wearing the same T-shirt today. She can see herself and the masky face of Siouxsie undulating in the posh French water.

She had not known she was this shy.

She had not expected, out in the world, to find herself quite so much the wrong sort of person.

She and the roommate she has been allocated, whose name is Dawn and who is pleasant enough to Anna but is definitely one of the party-people, have nothing to say to each other.

She hasn't said more than eleven words to anyone for twenty-four hours, and they weren't even all full words.

(G'night.
G'morning.
Hi.
S'this free?
Yeah.
Thanks.
Bye.)

Look at the blue of the sky above her. Look at the dark of the sky in the surface of that lake. Look at the gold of those fixed, lashing horses. This is paradise. This is success. It said so in the papers which reported that she was the most northerly winner of a place on this tour. So she will be good. She will write it on a postcard and send it home to her parents who are so proud of her. *It is amazing here. I am so lucky. We eat in hotels every night. I saw the Eiffel Tower, and a really beautiful church. Today is Versailles. It is like paradise also you can hire a boat and go rowing, ho ho, bye for now love Anna xox* She will write what she really wants to say on the postcards she sends to her best friend from school, Douglas, and she will send one from every place the tour visits. No, they will be wittier than that, they will be all song lyrics pretending to be conversational. If she puts her mind to it she will be able to think of a lyric line which will translate as: I am the only fucking Scot, the only fucking person from anything like home, on this tour and everybody else is English and they just don't get it. *Dear Douglas. Could this be the plastic age? Just buying some reflections of my own sweet self. Meltdown expected. Anna xox. PS, they don't want your name, just your number.*

No, she will be even wittier, she will choose specifically Eurovision hits. *Ding-a dong every hour, when you pick a flower.* She will find a picture of the belltower of that big church and send it on that. Douglas will think that's really funny. *Ding-a dong, listen to it. Maybe it's a bigot. Even when your lover is gone gone gone, sing ding dang dong.*

Along from her at the lakeside there is a gangly boy. He's one of the tour group. Yes, he's definitely from the group; he's got the blue folder next to him on the grass. She's seen him, she remembers now; he's one of the popular ones. Is he one of the nasty popular ones or one of the less nasty? And has she been humming that tune out loud, the Eurovision one she was just thinking about? She must have been, because that boy has started to whistle it, and he can't have been thinking of that completely random song, which is years old, and a private joke between her and Douglas, at the exact same moment as *she* thought of it.

He starts whistling something else. It's the Abba song about I have a dream. He doesn't look the Abba type.

He sings the lines about how if you see the wonder of a fairytale you'll be fine in the future. He has a quite good voice. He's singing quite loud, loud enough for her to be able to hear him clearly. In fact it's almost as if he's singing for her.

Then, next, does he really sing this?

I believe in Engels.

That's unbelievably witty, if that's what he's just sung and she hasn't misheard. That's the kind of thing only a really good friend of hers would have known to do to get her attention.

Then the boy speaks, and it *is* to her.

Come on, he says.

He seems to want her to sing.

She gives him her most withering look.

You're joking, she says.

I only joke about really serious things, he says. Come on. Something good in everything you see.

Don't know it, she says.

You do, he says.

I don't, actually, she says.

You do, actually, he says, because Abba songs, as anyone who knows knows, are constructed, technically and harmonically, so as to physically imprint the human brain as if biting it with acid, to ensure we will never, ever, ever, be able to forget them. In twenty years' time Abba songs will still be being sung, probably even more than they're being sung now.

Is that what you wrote your Britain in the year 2000 thing about, then? she says. The Generation Maimed In The Brain By Abba?

Maybe, he says.

No way, she says.

What was yours, then? he says.

I asked first, she says.

Here's how mine starts, he says. There was once a girl in a dated-looking punk T-shirt—

It is *not* dated-looking! Anna says.

—sitting by the side of the water at a French historical palace—

Very funny, Anna says.

She was very funny, he says. Or *was* she? Nobody knew, nobody

26

ever found out, because she was so determined to keep herself to herself. If only she'd joined in with the Abba song Miles was singing by the water at Versailles that day, then everything would have been, as if by magic, all right. Unfortunately, something stubborn, which had taken hold in her constitution at a very early age—

I'm not stubborn, she says.

Unfortunately, something supercilious, which had taken hold in her constitution—, he says.

I'm not that either, she says, whatever it is. There's just no way I'm going to be caught dead singing Abba.

I'd never sing Abba, he says. I'm not singing Abba, I'm singing revolution. Unfortunately, something conservative, small c *and* big C, had taken hold in—

I am no way either of those, she says. And your story's completely pathetic. I'm actually not joining in because I actually don't know the words of it.

Making them actually up myself actually, he says. Anyway actually it's you who started with the actual Eurovision pop, not actually me. There was once a girl twenty years in the future who was totally unable to communicate except by rolling her eyes and saying only the word actually. There. Now. You tell me the first line of your story.

You tell me the real first line of yours first, she says.

He has moved to sit closer to her.

What's your name? he says.

Anna, she says.

Your name is almost Abba, he says.

This makes her nearly laugh out loud.

There was once, and there was only once, he says. Once was all there was.

That's your beginning? she says. Really?

He looks away.

That's quite good, she says.

Thanks, he says.

Except, you say there was once and there was only once, and

then with that next line you say it again, so you end up saying the word once three times, which means once doesn't end up meaning once at all, she says.

There was once a girl who was too critical for words, he says. Or maybe just critical enough for words. What's *your* beginning, then, critic?

The future's a foreign country. They do things differently there, she says.

Yeah, I know, but what's your beginning? he says.

Then either he winks at her or he's got something in his eye.

It's, like, from the LP Hartley book, she says. Like a new version. You know. The past is a foreign country. From the book The Go-Between.

Uh huh, he says. Though I think the original line written by LP Hartley is assonantally better than yours.

You can go and assonate yourself, she says.

Well, okay, I will, he says, but it won't have the same effect as when they assonated Presidents Lincoln and Kennedy.

This time she does laugh out loud.

Anyway, he says. Actually. What was it about, your story, anyway actually?

It's about this girl who wakes up in the year 2000 after being asleep for twenty years, Anna says. And the catch is: in the year 2000 pretty much everything's exactly like now, except this. When the girl tries to read words it's like they're all printed upside down. She wakes up and she goes to the kitchen and gets out a packet of cereal and it looks exactly the same as a corn-flakes packet now. Except she notices that the writing on it is upside down. She can still read it and everything, but it's a bit weird. She turns it on its head, but that doesn't work, because the words are printed in the same order as they would be if they were printed the right way up. Then she tries to read the newspaper and she realizes it's the same—the words are all printed upside down. And then she's in a panic and she thinks she's losing her brain, and she goes to get her old copy of her favourite book off the shelf, a book she read twenty years ago, like, now, and it's The

Go-Between by LP Hartley, and she opens it, and its words are all the right way up and everything, and she breathes this big sigh of relief. But then she goes out into town. And the writing on the front of the bus is upside down. And all the shop names are upside down. And no one else thinks it's a big deal or anything. And then she gets suspicious, and she goes specially to the bookshop she always went to, you know, twenty years ago, in 1980, and she takes a new copy of the same book, The Go-Between, down off the shelf. And sure enough, on the cover the title is upside down, and on the back the summary thing they write about the story is upside down. And she opens it, and every page is printed upside down. And then half a day passes, and by lunchtime she's used to the words being the wrong way up. Her brain just processes it. And by the end of the story she isn't even noticing they're upside down any more.

She stops speaking. She is suddenly embarrassed, at saying so much out loud, and exhausted too. It is more than she's said all in one go since she left home.

Oh, that's good, the boy is saying. That's really subversive. Subversive sleeping beauty. I mean how would you wake her? Kissing her won't do it.

It isn't a line; he isn't being flirtatious. He actually looks preoccupied.

He is very witty, and definitely clever; he is probably one of the ones on this trip who are going to Oxford or wherever it is they're all going. But he doesn't sound rich or like he goes to a posh school. Also, he has already made her really laugh. She wants to ask whether he knows anything about the people who shaved off the boy's half-moustache. He doesn't seem like he'd be the kind to do that sort of thing.

He is dark-haired, big-nosed. He'd be good-looking if it wasn't for his nose. He looks the quiet type. Maybe he looks more the quiet type than he actually is. He looks a bit tired this close up. His hair is longish, not too long. He is wearing a blue vest-top. He's quite broad-chested. His arms and shoulders come out of the vest-top gangly and pale, like he doesn't fit himself. But the way he moves just then, to flick a little greenfly or something off the leg of his jeans, is both gentle and exact.

She stops looking at him because he starts looking at her.

What are you doing? he says then.

She shrugs, nods at the Timetable on the top of her Tour folder.

Waiting for whatever it is we're supposed to be doing next on the list, she says.

No, I mean, what are you doing with *that,* he says.

He is pointing at her head, at her ear. While they've been talking she has unbent the paperclip from the Useful Information sheets in the folder and, without really thinking about it, has been poking its end into her ear piercing.

Oh, she says. Making an earring.

Out of a paperclip? he says.

I only brought one earring with me. I mean from home, she says. I don't want the hole to close up.

When people do that on TV in dramas, like unravel a hairpin or a paperclip, it's because they're going to unpick a lock or something, he says. But then you stuck it into your earlobe. That's so 1976.

I'm so. Twentieth century, she says.

It's probably still really new wave, to do that in France, he says. No, I mean, probably still really *nouvelle vague*. Hey, listen. If your second name was Key—

She looks sideways at him.

You'd be Anna Key in the UK, he says.

He is laughing at her now.

Then she is laughing too, at herself.

Wish I was in the UK right now, she says.

Your earrings really mean that much to you? he says. Wow. No, I like it here. I like places of disrupted history that have managed, all the same, to come out of things looking pretty good. I'm enjoying all the tourifications. But you. You'd rather be there than here.

Anna nods.

You're not having a good time, he says.

Anna looks away from him, looks at the water.

Well, he says. You could. Just go. Just go home.

Yeah, right, Anna says. Well, I would if I had my passport. I'd like to at least have the choice.

Let's see it, he says.

What? she says.

Your passport, he says.

They took them, Anna says. They took mine. Did they not take yours?

Come on, he says. Here to help. Show me your passport and I'll help you cross the border.

He puts on a stern face, points at the french bread sticking out of her packed lunch bag, holds out his hand.

You want this? she says.

Passaporte, he says. I've eaten mine.

You're being such a tube, she says.

But she hands him the bread.

Right, he says. Come on.

He stands up.

Where? Anna says.

Fishing, he says.

They spend the afternoon throwing bits of bread at the water and watching for the mouths of the fish to appear, to open and close as if detached from any actual fish-bodies, at the surface. On the way back to Paris, when everybody crowds scrumming for seats on to the bus, he catches the edge of her jacket in his hand when she passes his table. He moves over into the empty seat next to him. She sits down.

This is Anna Key, he tells the two other people sitting at the table. Anna Key in the UK, and Anna Key when she's not in the UK too.

This time on the bus when she gets her book out of her bag, it isn't because she feels bad. Everybody talks round her all the way back to Paris like she belongs, like she's never not been there. She even joins in with a couple of the conversations.

In her room in the hotel, before supper, she sits on the bed and takes the list of prizewinners' names out of the information folder. There is only one Miles. Miles Garth. Next to his name is the word Reading. It is the place he's from.

There was once, and there was only once; once was all there was.

She wonders if that was really his first line. She wishes she'd asked him how the rest of it went. She tells herself to remember to ask him the next time they speak.

That evening, when she comes down to dinner in the hotel, some of the same people she sat next to on the bus ride back have kept her a seat. She makes friends with a girl who didn't seem shy but, she finds, *is* quite shy, and who, it turns out, is from Newcastle. They both talk about nothing for a while, then nod at each other in the knowledge that they can now safely hang out with one another whenever they need to for the ten days left. Meanwhile the boy, Miles, is across the other side of the hotel dining room, standing chatting at the staff table. She sees, from this distance, how it's as if there is a kind of agreeableness in the air round him. She watches how he and the people sitting near him at that table all laugh at something someone's said. She bets herself it was him who said it, the funny thing.

After dinner she is waiting in the queue for the freaky, creaky old hotel lift with the dangerous metal door when out of nowhere he's beside her, leaning on her shoulder very lightly.

I went between, his voice at her ear says.

Eh? she says.

I penetrated to the heart of the machine so as to appropriate the machine, he says.

Eh? she says again.

Eh is for Abba, he says. B is for Banshees. C is for covert criminal activity.

He holds something up. It's a passport. It's open at the photo page. The photo is of her.

I penetrated to the heart of the forest, he says, sacrificed myself, and brought back—you.

32

He hands her her own passport. He smiles. He nods just once. There you are, he says.)

Now, thirty years later, walking down a road in Greenwich in London with a small girl skipping ahead of her, this is what Anna remembered, all at once, of that gone time: the particular smell, like wood polish, in the house and in the clothes of her old schoolfriend, Douglas; the way that the lift door in a hotel she'd once stayed in, in the city of Paris, on that European tour, wasn't a real door, was just a gold-coloured concertina-like iron grille through which you could see the concrete between the floors as you went up; a certain raw combination of hope and disaffection; a knowledge as vivid as an actual taste in her mouth, of what the time she'd been alive in had felt like; and clear as anything a voice, and the words: *there you are.*

She was walking along a road she didn't know, carrying two jackets. One was hers. The other was stylish, expensive, covetable, light in the cloth, bulky at the pocket. She put her hand inside the jacket pocket and felt Miles Garth's mobile and wallet in there.

In the middle of the night, not long after she'd left her job, she'd sat in front of a Marx Brothers film which happened to be playing on TV. In it Harpo was unexpectedly old. Some violent henchmen who were looking for a diamond necklace hidden in a tin of tuna held the ageing Harpo against the wall and searched him, emptying the pockets of his old coat out into the room behind them. The pockets went unthinkably deep; among all the junk the henchmen pulled out and piled up behind them were a coffee pot, milk jug and sugar bowl, a car tyre, a hurdy-gurdy music box, a sledge, a couple of prosthetic limbs and a small dog which shook itself to get its dignity back before it padded off across the room. A henchman slapped Harpo very hard across the face. Harpo was a genius. He smiled a delighted smile and slapped the henchman back. The real joke was that the henchmen were determined to make Harpo Marx, of all the people in the world, talk. They tried to do this by torturing him. But every horrible thing they did to him seemed only to please him more.

What what what? the child said. You're sinking. What are you sinking about?

They were passing a wall low enough to sit on. Anna put the jackets down on the wall between the two street signs. Crooms Hill. SE10. Burney Street. SE10. Above her head there was a sign saying Our Ladye Star of the Sea Church, with an arrow pointing the way. The old-fashioned spelling of Ladye in modern street sign Helvetica looked like a mistake.

She sat down next to the jackets. She looked at her watch.

What I'm sinking, she said, is that we're not going any further unless you've got permission. Are your parents near enough to ask, or have you got a mobile or something?

We live there, the child said.

She pointed across the road towards a church.

In the church? Anna said.

The child laughed.

Behind there, she said. Kind of over there and behind.

How close? Anna said.

We've a mobile but we hardly use it, the child said, because my mum says what *is* the point of being on a train and shouting down a mobile, I'm on a train, because it makes it like *not* being on the train at all. She thinks you should *be* there on a train when you're on one, therefore not be on a phone instead.

I'd like to meet your mum, Anna said. She sounds great.

She is great, the child said nodding. There is a history project in year six on mobiles. Motorola 1990 was the first one. It all happened ten years before I was born.

Uh huh. And will they be home or are they at work, your parents? Anna said.

They work at the university, the child said. It's over there.

Well, can you run and tell your mum or dad where you are and who you're with, Anna said, and come back either with your

34

mum, or your dad, or with a note addressed to me saying that it's okay and that you've got permission and that they know you're safe?

The child put her hands on the wall, levered herself expertly into the air, let herself expertly fall.

I *can,* the child said. Though they trust me. I am not stupid. And your name is the same as mine. So what I tell them is I'm going to the tunnel with Brooke and then to the Observatory to see the Shepherd Galvano-Magnetic Clock.

Maybe, but listen, my name's not Brooke, that's you, Anna said. I'm Anna. Tell them I'm a friend of, of, the man who's locked himself in the room at the Lees' house.

Yeah, but when you first came, the child said, when we were at the Lees' front door, you said you were called the same as me.

No I didn't, Anna said.

I said, *I'm Brooke,* the child said, and then you said, *what a coincidence, I'm Brooke too.*

No, Anna said. The thing is, when we met on the steps, I didn't know you were saying the word Brooke, I thought you were saying the word broke. And I'm broke. So I said, me too. It's a pun.

Like, broken? the child said.

No, I meant it in the sense of having no money, Anna said.

What exactly is a pun therefore? the child said.

What exactly is a pun *there* for? Anna said.

The child thought this was very funny.

No, she said when she stopped laughing. What I want to know is, what constitutes a pun.

Constitutes? Anna said. Blimey. Constitutes. Well, um, pun. Well, they're like if a word means differently from what you expect. Like, take me hearing the word broke when you said the word Brooke. That was a sort of involuntary pun.

Involuntary, the child said.

It means it happened without us meaning or choosing it, Anna said.

I know it means that, the child said. I was just saying it to see how it felt in my mouth to say it.

She sat beside Anna on the wall, crossing her legs like Anna, looking ahead like Anna.

Okay, Anna said. So.

And what is the *point* of a pun? the child said.

Um, Anna said.

And is it like if someone at school says to you, listen you, you're history? the child said.

It depends, Anna said. Who said that to you? Like a teacher, for a project or something?

No, I mean, the child said. Because, obviously, it is a different meaning from me actually *being* history, when I am not even famous and I am only nine years old and will not be ten till next April, and have therefore not yet had much time to do anything to make me historic. I know that it doesn't mean that I am like President Obama. I know it means something not good. But it would be good if I knew what it was called, because then I could say, the next time he says it to me, if he says it again, you can just stop using that pun at me right now.

Anna nodded.

I see, she said. I don't think it's a pun. A pun is more like—say you were at a musical at a theatre and it wasn't a very exciting musical, and you were a bit bored. Instead of saying there's no business like show business, you might say there's no business like *slow* business.

The child's face filled with delight.

I am going to go to a musical again, probably soon, she said. Show slow. Brooke Broke. I bet you are broke because you are redundant because of the recession, or are you a student or a postgraduate?

No, I had a job, but I gave it up, Anna said, because the job I had was rubbish.

Like community service like picking rubbish up on the heath? the child said.

No, Anna said. In my job I had to make people not matter so much. That was what my job really was, though ostensibly I was there to *make* people matter.

Ostensibly, the child said.

You know what that means? Anna said.

Yes, but I can't think what exactly at this exact moment in time, the child said.

It means, uh, well, I don't know how to explain what it means, Anna said. It means what things look like on the outside. Ostensibly my job meant one thing, but really it meant another.

Like lying, the child said. Or like punning?

Well, you tell me, Anna said. This is what my job was. First, I had to get people to talk to me about stuff that had happened to them, which was usually pretty horrible. That's why they were having to tell me it in the first place, so that I could help them. Then, because there was pressure on me, I had to put pressure on them, to fit these true stories, their whole life stories in some cases, on to just two-thirds of one side of, do you know what A4 is?

A4, like paper? the child said. Or a road that is smaller than a motorway?

Paper, Anna said. So. Because I didn't like this job, I told the people I worked for that I was going to leave. But they told me how good I was at the job, then they gave me a promotion which meant I made a lot more money. But my new job was to make people redundant, the ones who were doing my old job and weren't good enough at getting people's life stories to be less long. So, in the end, I left.

Your job was immortal, the child said.

I think you mean immoral, Anna said. But you might mean immortal.

It's a pun! the child said.

Such good pun we're having, Anna said.

The child squealed with laughter.

I've got one, I've got one, the child said. In a minute we will be going through—the punnel.

Ha ha. Only if you get back with a parent or a note that says we can, Anna said. Go on. I'll wait here.

Will you? the child said.

Yes, Anna said.

And therefore definitely be here when I get back? the child said.

Therefore, yes, Anna said. Careful crossing the road.

Okay. See you, the child said.

The history child. She skipped off across the road, down the street opposite and round the corner. Anna watched her disappear. Then she wondered to herself. Did that child really just *skip* across that road? Did I imagine it? Have I just made up an idyll of childhood to make myself feel better, because that's the kind of thing a child would do in an imagined idyll, skip rather than run?

She thought of all the children, literally thousands of them, the same age as that child, crossing the world by themselves right now.

She told herself, let it go.

She told herself she was no longer responsible.

She leaned back in the sunlight. She looked up. The summer sky was blue and full of swifts, lucky birds, world-travellers born with the knowledge hardwired into their nervous systems, by nature, of the routes they were about to fly over terrain they'd not yet even seen. The trees in the distance were lifting and waving their leaves, making the light and the dark of summer. These restless, thrashing new summers, the windy summers, the global-warming summers, were grey and sticky and flyblown, not like the summers she remembered from childhood, summers sweet and complete and enclosed, each held like a story already told, like a set of Chinese boxes holding all its predecessors all the way back to the first ever box, the first ever perfect summer, there inside it.

Ding-a dong, listen to it. Maybe it's a bigot. Imagine remembering that after all these years. She should get in touch with Doug, send a Christmas card this year, ask him if he remembered it too. Where was Doug these days? She wondered if his parents were still living there, where they used to live. Then she wondered if his parents were still living.

Ding-a dong every hour, when you pick a flower. A world before

Interim Dispersal Measures and *Significant Knowledge Transfer.* A time before weapons sales initiatives were called things like Peace. Words, words, words. Freedom. Identity. Security. Democracy. Human Rights. *Deny your bin its rights.*

She shook her head, because her head had started to hurt. The word redundant, which she'd heard in the mouth of that preternaturally articulate child, was beating inside her head. It made her think of a tablecloth, a placemat. It was a cheesecloth tablecloth and it had places on it where the food which had been spilled on it hadn't washed fully out, had stained permanently. The tablemat, between her knife and fork, had a brown surround and an illustration of huntsmen on horseback jumping a hedge. This is where she was, at the dining-room table at dinnertime, and she was a small child and it was the day her mother had come home from her work at the Telephone Exchange and told them all that she was to be "made redundant" by Grace.

Who was this Grace, who could upend dinnertime, bring her mother to the verge of tears and her father to such paleness? Anna had wanted to know. But Grace wasn't a person at all. Grace was a system—Group Routing And Changing Equipment— which meant that there would be less need for telephone opera-tors, which was the thing her mother had always been, because people would from now on be able to dial abroad direct and would be put through automatically.

Anna sat on a wall in Greenwich nearly forty years later in the summer of the year 2009 and looked down at her shoes. They were trainers, and they were scuffed, and Genevieve Lee had looked at them in something like horror when Anna went up her clean stairs in them. Imagine if people decided at birth never ever to throw away any of the shoes they wore over the whole course of a life, and had a special cupboard where they kept all these old shoes they'd walked about the world in. What would there be in such a shoe museum, when you opened its doors? Row upon row, perfectly preserved, the exact shapes we took at certain points in our lives? Or row upon row, rack upon rack, of nothing but old soiled leather, old stale smell?

There was person after person, sitting in front of Anna, still in Anna's head. They were from all over the world. They arrived by air, by sea, by lorry, in car boots, on foot. If they tried to enter the country invisibly their heartbeats could be detected (like the thirteen Afghanis and the two Iranians hidden in the lorryload of lightbulbs had been) by the special new detector sheds of which the Agency was very proud, and the brand new probes that could detect whether someone was breathing where he or she shouldn't be.

A lot of the people Anna had seen had trouble speaking, either because of translation problems, or because a rain of blows had made them distrust words. Or both. Translation was sometimes itself a little rain of blows. How could what had happened to them be possible in one language, never mind be able to be retold in another?

In any language, it was almost always about what home was.

Anna had written it down in as shorthand a form as possible, what one man could remember of seeing his mother's head being used by the border guards as a football. (This man was finally judged not credible.) Anna had written it down in as shorthand a form as possible, about the rooms one woman passed in the corridor, in which she could hear other people also being tortured, on her way to and from being tortured herself for seven months, daily, on different parts of her body by electric shock applied by the use of two small live electric wires which came out of the wall, like electric wires do, behind the chair she was made to sit in each time. For instance, hearing the voices of others being tortured was not as salient as being tortured yourself. The shock that came not from being tortured but from realizing that the wires were the exact same simple domestic wires that everybody who had electricity had in his or her house was not as salient either. (This woman had been pending judgement when Anna shifted career position.) Anna had written it down in as shorthand a form as possible, which was easy in this case, what the woman who had been a university professor said, *it is like my chest stops and the words will not, just will not,* who had proved unable to finish that sentence and say what it was that the words wouldn't do, and about whom it was decided by Anna's superiors that she couldn't possibly be as clever as her summary indicated, being so demonstrably inarticulate. (This woman was finally judged not credible.)

You are really good at this, the area head had told her. You have exactly the right kind of absent presence. Best of all, your reports are 95% word-length perfect.

Somewhere over the rainblow.

Anna Hardie was no longer responsible for the word-lengths which resulted in truth, credibility or redundancy.

She was out of there.

What would it be like, to be crouched, hidden, for thousands of miles in a dark lorry full of lightbulbs? Everything round you, to the sides of you, towering above you, would be light and fragile, cardboard and glass, and you would know, too, that each of the thousands of bulbs in the truck, heading blindly for a light-socket somewhere, was held more secure, padded up in its box inside a box inside a box, and on its way to a surer destination, than you.

You would know yourself to be worth less than a lightbulb.

She put Miles Garth's jacket over her head like she'd seen the tennis player do with the towel. It was hot in there, but momentarily soothing.

Then, after that moment, she felt stupid. She wondered if she looked, to passers-by, like someone in a special kind of deep purdah, or like an old-fashioned nun whose headdress thing was on the wrong way round, or like a mad person. You could only really put a jacket over your head if you were with friends and it looked like a jolly jape.

She wiped the sweat off her face into the silk lining of the jacket, then came back out into the world. Greenwich was full of people and nobody was looking at her; nobody had even noticed her putting a jacket over her head. But probably a CCTV somewhere had made a note of it.

To be noticed is to be loved. Who was it who'd said that, again?

A novelist from the last century. Anna could spot, without even trying, three CCTV camera points from where she was sitting. She waved at the closest of the three, across the road on the wall of a derelict-looking office building. Hello. How like a brand new, insane sort of narcissism it would have seemed, this mad filming of ourselves all the time, had we had a preview of it even just twenty or thirty years ago. What a paranoid, jealousy-maddened love affair just walking down any street in a British city in 2009 resembled.

The inside of that jacket had smelled nice.

There was no sign yet of the child.

She checked her mobile. It was ten to three. She held it in her hand, weighed it, felt its lightness. Imagine. This phone. A historical object.

She took Miles's mobile out of the jacket pocket. It wouldn't switch on. Its battery would be dead. She put her hand back in and felt for the wallet. *Vera Pelle, Made In Italy.* Three credit cards, two debit cards, Royal Bank. An AA card with his name on it and the word Roadside. Six first-class stamps. A membership card for the Tate. Three twenty-pound notes.

The man in the picture on the driving licence was nobody she recognized. He was balding. Even on the rather poor reproduction you could see furrows in the forehead.

But when she saw the reproduction of his signature there on the licence, the little loop on the l in Miles, the slope of the G and the r and the way the t and the h ran together in Garth, she knew him again immediately. Even more, when she saw his handwriting she saw clearly in her head, in the same hand, the address of her own original home, the home of a total stranger now and as long gone and as ever-present to her as her own dead parents.

She was eighteen and home from university and a letter had come. It had said in it that he was playing or singing in a band called The Shakespearos. He had drawn a cartoon of The Pink Panther playing an electric guitar on the back of the envelope.

And—yes!—he had even come to visit her at home once, Miles Garth; she *had* seen him again, the next year, 1981, was it?

He'd come all the way up the country because he was going camping in Ullapool and had been passing through her town and had called in. Her mother had made him a salad, with summer new potatoes, because he didn't eat meat and they were having mince. At one point she'd left the room. When she'd come back—she remembered it as clearly as if it had happened in a story—she could see him sitting there so English and polite on the couch in the patio. She'd watched him for a moment through the kitchen partition. He didn't know she was there. He'd been given a cup of tea and he'd felt the base of the cup with his hand and had realized it was wet and that some of the tea had spilled on the tiles by his feet. But because her mother was speaking to him, or her father was talking about something, tomato plants, this is what he did. He unzipped his ankle boot. He did it decorously, without looking down, without stopping listening, and in a way that meant neither of her parents noticed. Then he levered his foot by slight shifts and shakes out of his boot. He put his socked foot down where the tea was spilled, felt for it, and mopped it up with his sole. Then, still without looking down, he felt for the mouth of the boot with his toes and put the foot back into it again. He did this without ever once having looked away from whoever was speaking.

She sat in the future and turned the driving licence over in her hand. Valid till 17-03-32. She flipped it over again to the little bleached photograph. When this furrowed stranger was a boy in a foreign country, he had gone out of his way for her. He'd reinvented her. He'd moved up and made space for her on a bus. In her home he'd been kind to her parents.

Thirty years later that last memory revealed itself clean as a new potato in the soil it's just been unearthed from.

She wiped her eyes on the sleeve of Miles's jacket, which let her know she'd been crying, which was something she hadn't done for quite some time. This knowledge, in turn, made something deep inside her chest crack open and shell off.

Bang bang bang.

Listen to that. Feel that.

That noise was her.

She'd definitely register now in any heartbeat detector shed.

Film that, you cameras. Let's see how much it's possible to know about what's really happening by filming me sitting here today. Go on, prove I was there. Show us what it meant, that I was.

Anna stood up. She faced one of the CCTV cameras. She put her fist in the air.

But then she felt a bit stupid doing it, standing there so alone. She pretended she'd been stretching her arm. She stretched the other one too. Ah. There. That's better.

She sat down on the wall again.

Imagine the relief there'd be, in just stepping through the door of a spare room, a room that wasn't anything to do with you, and shutting the door, and that being that.

There'd be a window, wouldn't there?

Were there any books in there?

What would you do all day?

What would happen if you did just shut a door and stop speaking? Hour after hour after hour of no words. Would you speak to yourself? Would words just stop being useful? Would you lose language altogether? Or would words mean more, would they start to mean in every direction, all somersault and assault, like a thuggery of fireworks? Would they proliferate, like untended plantlife? Would the inside of your head overgrow with every word that has ever come into it, every word that has ever silently taken seed or fallen dormant? Would your own silence make other things noisier? Would all the things you'd ever forgotten, all layered there inside you, come bouldering up and avalanche you?

Did he want to know what it felt like to *not* be in the world? Had he closed the door on himself so he would know what it feels like, to be a prisoner? Was it some wanky kind of middle-class game about how we're all prisoners even though we believe we're free as a bird, free to cross any shopping mall or airport concourse or fashionably stripped back wooden floor of the upstairs room of a house?

Did he inhabit his cell for the good of the others, like a bee or a monk?

Or was he, say, a smoker and was it all an elaborate ruse to make himself give up?

Then she laughed out loud. Miles Garth, whoever he was, was making her join in all over again.

Yep iep iep iep!

The child was back. The yellow and blue force of her collided, breathless, with Anna still sitting on the wall.

Knock knock, the child said.

Come in, Anna said.

Ha ha!

The child buckled over on the pavement in happy merriment.

Come on, come on, the tunnel! she said. She says we can go!

Where's the proof? Anna said.

I have it here in my head, the child said.

No, I'll need something more substantial than that in this wicked day and age, Anna said.

Well, I *am* allowed to go to the tunnel with you, and that's a fact, the child said. And my mother says it is a fact. She's at home right now. She's writing a paper about how nature says that God is dead.

About what says what? Anna said.

Do you get it? It's a pun! It's a pun! the child said. She told me it to tell you. Do you get it? She says it is a really good one, pun I mean.

We're still not going to any tunnel, Anna said.

Then she asked the child about the window in the room the man had locked himself into.

It's not just any tunnel, it's the Greenwich Foot Tunnel, the child said.

She walked Anna back up the street and into the crescent, past all the front doors, then down some steps in an alleyway round the back of the row of houses where, next to their neat little walled-off gardens, there was a parking lot and a patch of grass.

She pointed at the houses.

That one, she said.

Three windows along on the first-floor level there was a non-descript shut window with a slant of blind across the top.

There were other people at the backs of the houses. There was a head-shaven man cleaning a motorbike, and a woman in a slit-skirt business suit taking photos with a BlackBerry. There was a teenage girl, about fifteen, perched on the end of a pile of planks and what looked like market stall scaffolding by the wall. She was listening to an iPod, rolling a cigarette and glancing over every few seconds at the man cleaning the bike. There was a Japanese-looking girl and boy, both about twenty, both dressed very fashionably, sitting on folding chairs outside a little tent. They called hello to the child, who said a polite hello back. The boy was sitting with a dishevelled-looking old man. The girl was doing something with a camera the size of the palm of her hand.

It is a wise man not found anywhere on the world wide web, the Japanese girl told Anna.

It sounded like something you'd find on a slip of paper inside a fortune cookie. Anna nodded a thank you. Maybe the girl meant the dishevelled-looking man. He didn't look that wise. He looked more homeless. The Japanese boy was sharing hot water he'd boiled on a small gleamingly clean Primus stove with him.

They gave me their umbrellas, the man told Anna. For when it rains. To keep. They're retractable.

He put his hands in his pockets and brought out a compact umbrella in each hand.

Let it rain, he said.

The child knew the teenage girl over on the planks. She took Anna's hand and pulled her over to the girl. The girl took one earphone out.

Oh yeah, the girl said, you're Anna K. They're so waiting for you. She's in a state because you didn't get him out of there this morning.

She put the earphone back in.

Anna mimed taking an earphone out of her own ear. The girl blinked. Then she did as Anna asked.

Thanks, Anna said. Will you do me a favour and tell your dad I'm sorry I couldn't make it, and that I wish them both all the best?

You mean, me talk to them about something? the girl said.

I don't mind how it's conveyed, the actual message, Anna said.

The girl put the earphone back in her ear, got her phone out and started texting.

The child jumped up and down. She took Anna's hand and pulled like a dog on a leash.

Which window? Anna asked the child again. Then she went over past the Japanese girl, who was filming the backs of the houses. She got as close to the house as she could get, right up against its back fence. She leaned over it, put her head through the head-sized gap between the rows of razor wire. She brought her arms carefully through.

She cupped her hands round her mouth and she shouted up between the coils of blade.

Miles. It's me. I'm here.

There was once, and there was only once. Once was all there was, even though it was the year 2000 and it was the future and they were an advanced race wearing silver space suits (for that classic 60s "Apollo" look) and driving around in point-nosed cars exactly like the ones that featured twenty years before on TV shows like the one called Tomorrow's World. Even so, even here, now, in the future, there was no getting away from that faraway nostalgic look in everybody's eyes.

It was very annoying, the boy thought.

The boy was a paragon of modernity. He had the expensive shoes with the rocket-jet-propellers coming out of the heels that made it possible to fly to the record shop, to which, had it been twenty years ago, he'd have had to walk. He had his special injection packets lined up in the fridge-freezer for cancer and heart disease and flu and the common cold and pretty much everything that could go wrong with you. He had the extra limb that everybody could now have if they wanted (he'd chosen to have his new limb protrude from his forehead. This was so he could hold a book when he was tucked up in bed and turn its pages without untucking his hands, which were keeping warm under the covers—innocently under the covers. He was a good clean boy. Though he wasn't a saint. And anyway now, obviously, all pubescent sexual desires and urges were taken care of with 25mg per night of Junior Calmit, which you could buy at any good chemist's, and was made by Shake n' Vac, who had done a manufacturing about-turn shortly after floors became self-cleaning).

In short, he had every mod con.

But he looked at his mother, who'd been married to his father for all those years, and all he saw in her eyes was a curly-haired eighteen-year-old called Albert, which wasn't his father's name, and who'd once, when she was sixteen and on holiday in the Isle of Man, whistled a tune every time he passed underneath her chalet window all that summer fortnight to let her know he was there and he was waiting for her.

He looked at his father, and all he saw in his eyes was a double image of a dark and deep and still pool in the river near where his father had grown up; it was back before the rivers were ruined, and in both those pools and both those eyes there was a silver fish the length of his father's arm, and his father, aged twelve, who'd sat night after night waiting to catch that fish, was, God damn it, still sitting in the long grass at the side of that non-existent river right now in the far future.

He tried the eyes of some people he knew less well. He looked at their next-door neighbour. She had been hit by a bicycle when she was a young woman back in the ancient 1970s and her leg had been shattered, and even though she had a perfectly good new leg now all there was in her eyes was the fast flash of an after-noon of dancing at the wedding of her sister, when she'd been so fast and light on her originals, the feet she'd been born with, that it was as if they were winged.

He looked in the eyes of the neighbour who lived on the other side. This man's eyes were terrifying because there was nothing in them but swastikas, and the images at the back of his eyes were, the boy decided, a place he himself would never choose to look again.

He couldn't look in his grandmother's eyes, because she had died and been buried without the necessary inbuilt computing system they'd launched in the year 1990 so that you could access the inner photo albums of the departed and leaf through them—

just like, in the past, you'd have done if you'd gone to their house and a relative had handed you the album.

No one had yet solved the way of communicating with the dead. But when they did solve it, the boy thought, what would be the point anyway? All the dead would ever probably say, no matter what you asked them, would be, "Ah! once!"

The boy had known a girl who had died. She had been in the same year as him in the Young School. They'd sat together at the same Project Table; he had done Extinct Mammals (tigers and otters) and she had done The Old English Sycamore (the name, once, for a tree). Last year the girl had gone to bed one night and the next morning nobody had been able to wake her up.

It was a total mystery.

There weren't many mysteries left.

Most of all the boy wanted to look into that girl Jennifer's live eyes and see what was in them. There was no other girl's eyes he wanted to look in, which was annoying and irrational. There would have been no point, obviously, in looking in her dead eyes, even if he could. They would just say, "ah, once," etcetera.

But before she had died she had been young, like him, and not yet been onced by life.

Today the boy was taking his grandfather, who was a morose old man and didn't get out much, up in a Pensionglide. They went up the public launcher on the side of the hill. Pensioners' free airspace was from 10am till 12 noon, when less traffic used the skyway. There was a pretty good tailwind, and the Pensionglide went like a dream. His grandfather was in the back seat and the boy was in front, staring out at the blue of the sky and the stream of other pensioners going back and fore on the horizons of the turn of the century.

"Grandad," the boy said, looking ahead into the eyes of the sky itself. "You are meant to be old and wise, and I need badly to talk to someone older and wiser than me, but I'm afraid to look into your eyes in case I see the same old story I keep seeing in everybody's eyes."

Then he realized the old man behind him was laughing. The

51

old man was laughing so hard in the back of the Pensionglide that the little plane began to rock dangerously from side to side.

But he wasn't laughing at what the boy had said, because he couldn't hear what the boy had said; the boy's words had been blown away in the wind (and anyway the old man wasn't connected to his HearHelp).

"They forgot to give me my Senior Calmit, boy!" he shouted. "I never took my Senior Calmit! They forgot to give it me! I feel FANTASTIC. I haven't felt this good in YEARS. Look!"

His grandfather pointed down at his own lap in the cockpit. He looked back at his grandson with his face full of delight.

"Christ! I wish your grandmother were alive today. I wish she were here right here and right now, son! I'd hold her on my knee and I'd sing her such a fine old love song!"

When they landed, and after his grandfather had badly but very energetically demonstrated a dance by the early film star Fred Astaire, flinging his walking stick from hand to hand and up into the air in front of a crowd of cheering pensioners on the runway, the boy returned his grandfather to the Old School gate to sign him back in. As they drew near, his grandfather grew morose again and began to shake.

"Please don't grass on me," his grandfather said. "They'll double-dose me if they find out."

Grass on me was old-speak for tell tales or betray.

"Grandad, they probably already know," the boy said. "If they haven't seen it on their monitors they'll have tracked it via their Spirit Levels."

But if they knew they gave no sign of it, and the boy said nothing, and when the grandfather saw that the boy wasn't going to say, and that he'd got through the gates without being admonished or injected, he thanked the boy with his eyes.

The boy looked into the old man's eyes and saw something amazing all right. He didn't yet know it but he would spend the rest of his life looking back and looking forward in search of it, the still-unpolluted source that feeds into every ruined river.

This story is true and happened once in the future long ago.

BUT

would a man in shutting himself in / be asking things to stop or to begin?

Mark's mother, Faye, had been dead for forty-seven years. Her most recent attention-getting device was rhyme.

Mark walked through the park. He had forgotten how charming it was here. *Would he be testing whether he'd be missed / would such inversion mean he'd not exist?* this was interesting, because usually she was much ruder and cruder than she was being this morning. Also, it was quite unusual for her to ask questions. Questions demanded an answer, didn't they? They asked for a response. Unless they were rhetorical questions; true, she often used those ("a rhetorical question is one which does not expect an answer or one whose answer is implied": The Essentials of English, book of choice of the older boys at St. Faith's for spanking the younger boys with, leaving a particular broad-natured pain ever afterwards associated with grammar). Mark went the long way, round and up through the woody place, to get to the Observatory, thinking it might be less steep. No, it was still notably pretty steep. He waited to get his breath back sitting on a bench opposite the place where one of the Astronomers Royal, or was it Astronomer Royals, had dug a well a very long way into the ground. According to the notice, the Astronomer Royal had sat down there under the surface, literally inside the hill, it looked like, watching the sky through a telescope. The well was fearfully deep.

Then Mark walked round the side of the main house, stood

for a minute or two in the little Camera Obscura, and right now he was standing just along from the Talking Telescope, leaning against the railing that overlooked the park he'd just traversed *traversed ooh I can think of lots that's worse / than meeting someone for a quick traverse* there, that was more like her. He looked down the slope at the trees in their rugged neatness, the paths that met and crossed themselves, so elegant the way they seemed both planned and random, elegant too the white colonnades and all the grand old whitened buildings down at the foot of the park. The new business towers of the city shouldered each other beyond the river at the back of the view like a mirage, like super-imposition. Greenwich. Then and now. He hadn't been here for a long time. He should come here more. He loved *it's no surprise to me that you're so keen / a place beloved of many an old queen* and straight away as if to spite her he thought hard about the actual old Queen, the literal historical Virgin Queen, and the first thing that came to mind was something that had happened when she was the young Virgin Queen, where had he read it? He couldn't remember, but the writer, whoever he was *I hate to be reminding you again / that writers are not fucking always men* described Queen Elizabeth the First quite unforgettably, dancing in the great hall in her favourite palace right there, right here in Greenwich all those hundreds of years ago, she was young and beautiful, pale and thin from having been ill, in fact she was convalescing after a lengthy illness, an illness that had at one point been bad enough to endanger her life, and she was enjoying the first real spurt of energy she'd had for months, had been out hunting, had come back flushed and happy and very much wanting to dance. So the hall had filled with courtiers and musicians and she'd dressed up; she looked, the writer said, like a great tulip as she bowed and turned, but her secretary, Cecil, pushed through the ranks of the dancers all round her, he had urgent news, and he told the Queen of England in her ear that her cousin, the Queen of Scot-land, had given birth to a son. The Virgin Queen paled with shock, then flushed with shock; she stopped dancing; stood rigid. Then she, who was usually so controlled, so imperious, who was world-renowned for her imperturbability, turned and ran from the hall and all her panicked ladies-in-waiting followed bewildered in a great rush, their dance finery rustling as they ran, and when they reached her private rooms they found her collapsed and sobbing in a chair. "The Queen of Scotland is a mother of a fair son, and I am but a barren stock" *cause that's all girls are good for ain't it birth / Gawd knows they haven't any other worth* but the point of this story, Faye, is: the next day regardless she was fine again, unruffled, greeting statesmen, doing her queenly political deals much the same as ever, because even when she met her worst fears, even when she met her demons, she was what you'd call a survivor, that old Queen. Out of sheer strength of character she survived, didn't she, the vicissitudes of history.

There.

That'd annoy her.

It did.

Silence.

Mark heard birdsong, could hear birdsong for several whole seconds, could hear the murmur of the people queuing up behind him at the meridian line, could even make out some of the things they were saying, before she roared back into his right ear with something of the force of a wind tunnel nearly knocking him off balance *just wait you little bastard history / that made a fucking dunghill out of me / is waiting round the corner just for you / to turn you into tulip fodder too.*

Silence of the grave my arse, he said out loud.

The couple with the small child, who had been standing quite close to him and had smiled genially at him when he arrived, picked up their child and backed away. They stopped and put down the child further along the railing.

He was still waiting to see if there'd be any comment from her about his *my arse*.

No.

Nothing.

Fine, he thought.

He felt the usual: bullish, and a little disappointed. Me and my shadow. He stuck his finger in his ear and waggled it about to try and shift the wind tunnel effect. It was frustrating. Jonathan, gone for more than five years now, never said a word to Mark. It was only and always Faye. These days it was like being assaulted by a bag lady, an old tramp in a torn coat that's come through fifty wars, who shouts like she long ago lost her hearing.

This is going to sound weird but does she ever "speak" to you in any way? he'd texted David when mobiles were new and exciting, in a flurry which had simulated, for a little while, regular contact. David, with the annoying casual savvy of the younger sibling, had texted a whole long message back in roughly the same time it had taken Mark to remember which button to press to make a space between the words this and is. Evn f she did i woulnt answr blve me lfs so much bttr without it U R INSANE mark well spos ive knwn *that * snce I sw u that brkfst tm whn i ws 7 & u wr 12 & u apolgizd 2 th *toast * cz u hd chsn *cornflkes* ! ;-) David would never be so uncool as to use a semicolon properly in a text, or an apostrophe. Mark missed David. They weren't much in touch now because David's wife didn't like Mark. This was because Mark had taken her side when she'd split up with David, had made sympathetic noises throughout the many drunken telephone calls and had even let her move into his spare room for some of their time apart, all of which left her feeling humiliated at encountering Mark in any way after she and David got back together again.

Regardless of time, memory, family, history, loss, it was an October mid-morning in Greenwich Park today. The sky held the mild threat of rain and the day was warm, about nineteen or twenty degrees, far too warm for this time of year, a flaunting of warmth before the battening-down for winter. How adaptable human beings were without even realizing it, slipping blindly from state to state. One morning it was summer, the next you woke up and the whole year was over; one minute you were thirty, the next sixty, sixty next year quick as a wink, how fast it all was. How quickly and smoothly, yet how shockingly, when you thought about it, the seasons and the years gave way to each other *banal philosophizing for God sake / how long's this sermonizing going to take / you sound like an old vicar on the make* he blocked her by thinking hard of the beautiful image he'd sourced back in the spring for the autumn-winter edition of Wildlife. He'd suggested it for the cover, but no one ever listened to mere worker-bee picture researchers (they'd gone with penguins, again). It was a picture of a little gold-coloured bird singing in a field in winter somewhere in Italy. It was a close-up; the field frosty, the bird the colour of summer and so lightweight that it could balance itself on the bend of the stalk of a dead flower. But the really interesting thing about the picture was that you could see the song coming out of the bird's mouth. You could actually see birdsong. Because the air was frosty the notes the bird had just sung hung there momentarily in the air like a chain of smoke rings and the camera had simply caught them before they disappeared.

Winter. It made things visible.

But today on this balmy day, even though he knew winter was so close, winter was actually unimaginable *if I had known, when I was twenty-four / that you'd grow up such a godawful bore / well—what rhymes with back-street abortionist* never mind winter, autumn itself was unimaginable, even though this was actually meant to be autumn, even though the leaves had already, this early in October, left the first of their gold-coloured edgings along the pathways down there *yawn yawn yawn yawn yawn yawnyawn yawnyawn yawn / YAWN YAWN YAWN YAWN YAWN YAWN YAWN YAWN YAWN YAWN* but could you call it autumn if it was as warm as May? Could he really be nearly sixty, and still feel so like thirty? Yes, he felt thirty at the most, like someone trapped at the age of thirty inside the body of an old horse, at any rate trapped inside a slower body, a slowing brain, a newly paper-thinning skin, a maddeningly failing eyesight *you self-indulgent bastard take a hike / at least you know what failing eyesight's like / look at me I'm about three minutes long / like the way a whole year gets rammed into three minutes in that irritating I Just Called To Say I Love You Stevie Wonder song.*

That didn't scan at all well. She was upset. Interesting, though, that she'd taken to iambic pentameter. A very cultured lady, Faye. She'd been making her bed in his ear, pouring her lovable poison into it now, for longer than she'd actually lived on this earth.

Ironic, Mark said out loud. Actually very sad.

The couple along the railings exchanged worried looks and shifted a little further off. It didn't do to speak to yourself, or your dead, out loud. It was inappropriate. Mark turned towards the grassy slope where, historically, for centuries, the boys had dragged the girls up to the top only to drag them down the steepness of it at the kind of full speed that threw clothes and modesty into disarray and called for a lot of screaming. Over the centuries spectators had gathered at the top and the bottom of the slope just to watch this happen.

This world, Mark said under his breath, is insane. I'm sorry. Here's something you might prefer to hear. The song called Let It Snow Let It Snow Let It Snow was actually written in the hottest days of August. But it's not a great story because I've forgotten the names of the people who wrote it. Here's another one. This is how Jerome Kern came to write I've Told Every Little Star.

(Mark knew, obviously. He knew she was dead and gone, bone and dust in a box in the ground on top of the boxes of dust and bone that were what was left of her own parents, in a grave he never visited any more, in a pretty spot in Golders Green cemetery.)

So Jerome Kern was in bed, Mark said under his breath. It was early in the morning, he'd woken early, and so had his wife, her name was Eva. And lying there in the early morning light they heard a bird outside their window sing a tune over and over. It was a really pretty tune, they both thought so, and Kern told his wife that when they got up he'd compose a song round it. So he hummed it to himself to memorize it and went back to sleep. But when he'd wakened, and breakfasted, and sat down at the piano, of course the tune was completely gone, he couldn't remember it at all.

(Mark knew that probably the rhyming, which was new, was because this summer he'd looked out some of his old books from back then, the books she'd given him. Possibly it was also because he'd bought online and had been playing on repeat the Ella Fitzgerald / George and Ira Gershwin collection. Faye had had the original LPs. He remembered, now, the shine of them, their paper sleeves, even the feel and the smell of the big square hard-paper box they came in.)

So, Mark said under his breath over the fine view of old / new London. The next morning Kern got up early. He sat in the dark at the window with a piece of paper and a pencil and waited for the bird to come back. And he waited and he waited, as the morning light came up, because he knew that if that bird had come once there was a chance it would come again. And then, sure enough, he heard it again, the bird was there. The bird sang the tune and Kern wrote it down. Then when the bird had fin-ished singing and flown away Kern went downstairs, closed all the doors between his sleeping family and the piano room and roughed out, there and then, the main body of what would become I've Told Every Little Star.

(Mark had woken one spring day in his late twenties, on the folding bed in his Kensington basement flat, to a voice in his ear.

Though he hadn't heard her voice since he was less than thir-teen years old, he'd known immediately. Though she was saying very unlikely stuff, as if from a really bad script, or as if she were a posh person pretending to be cockney or were playing the role of a clichéd angry-young kitchen-sink character of the 1950s, it was definitely her. *Well, old man, wake up, I mean I don't mind and I know you're a queer one pardon my French but even a lah-di-da layabout who thinks the world owes him a living's got to make ebloodynough to pay the rent, and I mean just look at my fingers, worked and to the bone are the words for it, d'you hear me?*

I hear you!

He'd opened his eyes, overjoyed.

No one.

There was no one in the room but him.)

The bird was a Cape Cod Sparrow, Melospiza Melodia. It spawned not just a song but a musical too, about some people who, yes, write a song inspired by hearing a bird sing. Music In The Air; he wrote it with Oscar Hammerstein. And they all lived happily ever after, until they died. And when Jerome Kern was in hospital dying, Oscar Hammerstein came to his bedside, Kern was in a coma, they knew he'd die very soon, and the song Hammerstein sang to his dear friend Kern in the last minutes of his life was I've Told Every Little Star, because Hammerstein knew how very fond, among all his compositions, Kern was of that song.

The end. Oh, no, wait. Interesting fact about Melospiza Melodia, and it's that if it is well fed, the bird, and hasn't had to worry too much about finding food, it actually produces offspring that sing less than the offspring it produces if the parent bird has been hungrier. And the other thing about songbirds I was remembering to tell you is that it's now thought by some experts that they sing in their sleep as well as sing while they're awake. As if their sleeping selves are a kind of being awake, or their wakened selves are a kind of being asleep.

There. That's it.

The end.

Mark nodded to himself. Then he nodded at the couple and the child to show he wasn't mad and he'd meant and taken no offence, both. He didn't wait to see if they'd nod back. He pushed himself off the railing, turned towards the Observatory building and the ragged line of tourists and schoolkids in the yard waiting to straddle the meridian line, and all the people, one after the other, doing just that and having their picture taken by people holding cameras or phones well away from themselves. That was how people focused these days.

I'm standing on time! a girl said and toed the line. How cool is that?

I'm standing on not-time! her friend said jumping backwards away from the meridian.

Someone was talking, a youngish man in a T-shirt and fleece. He was a teacher, presumably, from the words he was using: last warning, confiscate, crisps.

If you take them off her, are you going to eat them yourself, do you know what I'm trying to say sir? a girl said.

No, Melanie, because crisps are sprayed with chemicals then fried in huge vats of fat, and I like to eat healthily, the man said.

These *are* healthy, sir, the girl with her hand in the crisp packet said. It says on the packet less fat and natural ingredients in it sir innit.

The three girls standing with the crisp packet girl all burst out laughing. In it innit! they said. Innit in it!

Because we learned on Tuesday, didn't we, the teacher said, that it's random. And about longitude and latitude and fixed points, he said. To know where you are when you're at sea and there are no landmarks. But who can tell me why it was decided to put it here? Jacintha, mobile off. Off. Off or confiscated. You choose. Thank you. Someone tell me why the experts at the time chose Greenwich. Rhiannon? Why Greenwich?

Because they had to put it somewhere so they could get on with the other important calculations about time and, and things like time and the sea and that, cause they needed something better than the thing called reckoning with that throwing logs tied to rope off moving ships, and on land too because like, that, Yarmouth being ten minutes ahead of Greenwich and in other places it could be noon in London and half past eleven in the place you'd just travelled to on a train, a girl said.

Thank you, Rhiannon, the teacher said. Very good. Except it's dead reckoning.

Ow! Rhiannon said when the girl standing behind her poked her hard in the back and said the word dead. Please sir, one of the bad girls said. The earth's wobble is what happens when Rhiannon Stoddart walks to the shops.

And Greenwich, the teacher said, was where the experts who met decided to put it because of the important work they'd already done here. Now, the meridian runs north to south and if you stand on one side of it, you're officially in the west, and if you stand on the other it's the what? Matthew, if you make a racially unpleasant comment like that again there'll be serious trouble. I mean it. I'm talking exclusion, Matthew. Now apologize. Not to me, to Bijan. Okay, Bijan? Right. Where were we? On one side the west, and on the other? Come on.

The kids stood bored and hangdog, yawning and squirming, their sweatshirts knotted round their waists. Above them, the domes of the Observatory: they all looked up when they were told to. The original domes, the teacher told them, were made of papier-mâché. A murmur went round the boys about the domes resembling big and small breasts. The teacher admonished. Two girls made outraged-sounding noises. They pointed at the notice which apologized that the time ball wasn't functioning today. One of the girls called out. Sir, when exactly did *your* time balls drop?

Nought degrees, the teacher was saying. Who can tell me about nought degrees?

If it's not degrees you want to know about, sir—, one boy said.

Yes, Nick—? the teacher said.

Then what is it, sir? the boy said.

This made Mark laugh. The group of girls saw him laugh and stared at him, then laughed nastily themselves, but at Mark.

I don't follow you, Nick, the teacher said.

If you follow Nick, sir, we'll report you to the authorities, another boy who was standing far out enough on the edge of the group not to be heard by the teacher said.

His friends sniggered.

Then this same boy, while the teacher talked on about what universal day was, and how many degrees made a day, an hour, half an hour, a minute, cast an unmistakable sheep's-eye glance at Mark. When Mark caught the stare and didn't look away, the boy spoke with an insolence that was cutting.

That old man, look at him, he wants it.

The friends round him sniggered again.

But even well after the sniggering had died away the boy continued to hold the stare. In it there was a perfectly judged balance of rejection and invitation. The boy was an expert. He looked all of thirteen. He was far too young to be acting so knowing. Mark stilled a wild laugh in his chest. He shook his head at the boy, but to make sure the boy wasn't offended he winked first. When he shook his head the boy looked down and away, and Mark did too, and moved off, out round the school party, back down through the gate and towards the park.

The slope down was painful to the knees, more painful than the climbing of it had been. Greenwich, the teacher was saying behind him as he went, and Greenwich, and again Greenwich.

Greenwich then: the word, white on black on the label of the 45 in his hands, Mark just thirteen years old himself: London American Recordings   1963   Then He Kissed Me   (Spector, Greenwich, Barry)   The Crystals.

Greenwich now: the word that had caught his eye when he was in a café skimming their copy of one of the weekend papers on Sunday, Observer, Guardian, whichever, and when he looked properly he saw the picture and recognized the woman, the one from the dinner party.

The column was the Real Life column, where real people told the paper about a real experience; usually something like Dolphins Carried My Baby To Safety or I Woke Up One Day Not Remembering Who I Was or My Life Was Ruined By An Over The Counter Cold Remedy or I Was Mugged By My Own Brother. Mark had waited till all the serving people were out of earshot and then had torn the page out, folded it and put it in his pocket next to that chap Miles's note. That night in the bath he decided: on his next day off, Thursday, he'd go to Greenwich and slip the page under Miles's door in case nobody else had thought to show it to him. And it would be nice, too, to spend his day off in Greenwich, see the place again, maybe visit the park.

But when he'd got to the Lees' house and knocked on the front door this morning there'd been no one home. Well, presumably Miles was in, but *he* wasn't about to open the front door to anyone, was he?

He had the article in his inside jacket pocket now, folded, along with Miles's note, well, he was assuming it was from Miles, it couldn't really be from anybody else, though it wasn't signed. He'd found it in there, a plain piece of foolscap folded twice, when he'd got his wallet out to buy a train ticket the Sunday after the dinner party. The handwriting was new to him. It was intelligent, slightly forward-slanted, neatly spaced down the page rather like a poem might be though it wasn't one. It was quite clear. Only one word was difficult to decipher.

He stopped on the slope. People went past him; a couple of people speaking French. Mark took both folded pieces of paper out of his pocket.

Below the words REAL LIFE: An Uninvited Stranger Lives In My Spare Room, was the picture of Mrs. Lee in profile, standing beside a door, looking rather tragically down at its handle. The caption read: *Genevieve Lee recounts what it's like living twenty-four-seven with an uninvited stranger.*

I had always loved living here
in our gracious old historic
Greenwich town house. From
practically the first day my
husband Eric and I and our
young daughter moved in, it
seemed to me to be asking to
be a really sociable space. I don't
think it's an exaggeration to say that
among our friends we're renowned
for our hospitality. Until June
this year we were forever having
people round for interesting
soirées and sending them
home happy after a meal I'd
have taken great pains to cook
to perfection each time.

We had no way of knowing that
this one dinner party, however,
would turn out so dramatically

differently from the others. That
particular evening in June
I had planned a menu including
a seared scallops with chorizo
starter, a main course of lamb
tagine and a dessert of crème
brûlée with home-made
chilli-vanilla ice cream. One of
our guests brought his own
guest, a man who seemed perfectly
genial and normal and didn't in
any way arouse our suspicions
or give any clue as to what was
about to happen. He wasn't
poor, didn't seem in distress,
and the fact that he was a
vegetarian, though it was a
surprise, was absolutely no
problem.

In the middle of the party this man,
we'll call him "Milo," left the
room and went upstairs. While
we merrily continued with our
dinner party downstairs he was
actually barricading himself into
one of the rooms in our house.
The next morning we woke up to
a fact that we have lived with
since that day. A stranger is
living in our house against
our will.

It has now been three months,
and it is simply an experience
unlike any I have hitherto

had. The man has made himself
incommunicado for an
unfathomable reason
in our spare room with my
rowing machine and my husband's
wine-making kits and DVD
collections of sci-fi classics
of the fifties and sixties,
a room which we were about to
turn into a badly needed study
for our daughter who has
important school exams this
coming year. He never speaks
and only once in the whole time
has sent us a written message,
about the food we provide free for
him; it is one of the little ironies
of the situation that for "Milo"
the dinner party he came
to as our guest has never
ended. Looking back now it is
also ironic to remember
myself hearing the creak of his
footsteps on our stairs as I
prepared the dessert that first
night not knowing what was really
afoot.

It is strange having a stranger
in the house with you all the
time. It makes you strangely
self-aware, strange to yourself.
It is literally like living with
a mystery. Sometimes I stand
in the hall and listen to the
silence. It sounds uncanny

and feels like I imagine
being haunted must feel like.
Sometimes the water flushing
or "Milo" moving about
in the middle of the night
wakes me or Eric and we
have the realization, all over
again, that we are not alone.
Sometimes I sit outside the door
behind which "Milo" is sitting
and just say over and over to myself
the word: Why? Perhaps in
some ways metaphorically we
are all like this man "Milo"—all of
us locked in a room in a house
belonging to strangers.
Except that this is our house
which makes it all seem
unfair and unnecessary.

A friend asked if we aren't
tempted just to go ahead and
use brute force and break down our
beautiful and authenticated c17th
door and send in the police or
someone who would simply
remove "Milo." I am a peaceable
person who abhors violence of
any sort so I am uneasy when
I consider we may have to resort
to force. But we do not know
when our home will feel
like home again. Even
though we knew our family
unit to be strong we never
expected it to be so thoroughly

tested. Who knows what the
future holds? Every new day
I wake full of the possibilities of
change. I am determined to
remain philosophical about it,
and keep urging my family
likewise. But all the same,
I for one know that I will
never see dinner parties
in quite the same light again.

Mark folded it up again and put both pieces of paper back in his inside pocket. "Milo." Miles gloriosus. Sweet mild-mannered Miles in a room five steps wide and seven steps long, and in there now for months.

(Three or four months back, one Saturday in June, Mark goes to a matinee of The Winter's Tale at the Old Vic. The play has been sold out for weeks but he manages to get a last-minute seat in the back of the stalls. The production is good; Simon Russell Beale believably madder and madder as Leontes, and the young woman, whoever she is, as Hermione, quite captivating, and as the afternoon passes and the story unfolds the play seems actually to be working. He sits up in his seat, excited. It's a hard one to get right, The Winter's Tale, but when it's right, he knows, the coming-to-life of the statue at the end is one of the most moving things theatre can produce.

It happens: the wronged queen comes back from the dead. She moves, she steps forward, she takes the hand of her husband, she turns towards her lost-and-found daughter Perdita, about to speak for the first time ever to her child, and someone's mobile phone goes off at the front of the stalls. Beebedee beebedee bedee beep. Beebedee beebedee bedee beep. Beebedee beebedee bedee beep.

The actress playing the queen takes her daughter's hands as if nothing had happened and continues her speech through it.

Minutes later the play ends.

Perfect timing, Mark says to the stranger on his left, the man he happens to be sitting next to, as the curtain comes down.

It was, the man says.

God, Mark says shaking his head.

But I mean it, the man says. It really was. I've often heard phones going off in the theatre or the cinema, but that was the best time I've ever heard it happen. Right at the moment when, there on stage, someone really needs to speak to someone, there it is, the same need in the audience watching it happen on stage.

Well, Mark says thinking to himself that the man he's chosen to speak to is an idiot to need such things explained. I take your point. But.

Ah, the man says. But?

There's a world of difference, Mark says, between Hermione and Perdita and what they've got to say to each other and whatever that person in the audience was going to hear in his or her ear, Hi I'm on the train, or Can you pick me up at half past five, or Can you pick up some cat-litter or Nurofen or whatever.

Reason not the need, the man says. Need not the reason. We don't know. We simply don't know. All we know is—someone wanted to speak to someone else. That's more than enough. Doesn't matter how quotidian it is, it's still all we have at the end of the day.

He says all this mildly.

He says the word quotidian with no self-consciousness.

The way he says the phrase *at the end of the day* somehow makes it not a cliché, makes it mean that days end and that it might matter that they do.

You don't think it ruined it? Mark says.

I think it made it better, the man says.

Astonishing, Mark says.

Yes, the man says. The play can still astonish, even though we think we know it, no matter whether we're seventeenth century or twenty-first. And I always feel a bit sorry for the daughter, who never gets to speak back. What's that last thing she says, when she believes the statue's still a piece of art and not her mother at all?

She's happy to be a bystander, a looker-on, and she'll gladly be exactly that, for twenty long years, she says, if she can just stand there for each of those years and appreciate this semblance, this combination of stone and paint that resembles the mother she never knew. Then, suddenly, from nowhere, it's not a statue at all, it's real, it's her real mother, miraculous, alive, right there in front of her. And then the play's over, and we never get to hear what she thinks.

So that phone going off, Mark says. Perdita phoning Hermione.

Another way to see it, the man says.

Mark laughs. The man is delightful. By now they've moved with the crush of the crowd out of the dark into the light and the foyer. They go out through the same exit. They stand for a moment in the surprising warm of the evening. It is lovely. It is summer. The man, Mark notices, is wearing a very nice dark linen suit and an expensive-looking shirt. He smells nice; Mark realizes that this man's aftershave has kept him company through all the madness and all the seasons all the way to the reconciliation.

He turns to Mark, almost as if he is going to bow. He smiles. This is him saying goodbye. Off he goes. His back is a proof of his completeness. He disappears in among the meaningless backs and fronts of other people.

Mark stands in the sun for a moment and into his head comes the moment in the play where the mad king asks the Delphic oracle for the truth, and the feather pen stands up on the table with no one holding it, by stage-trickery, by magic, and begins to write by itself.

Then he runs and catches the man up at the pedestrian crossing. He is out of breath from the short run. He asks the man, between breaths, if he'd like to go for a drink.

Why not? the man says.

He holds his hand out.

Miles, he says.

Mark, Mark says.

They shake hands.)

The Observatory was behind and above Mark now. He turned and looked at it and loud as day, loud as Faye *but why would someone choose to disappear / and why would someone choose to do it here?*

Here was where, not that long ago, men who didn't yet know the half of it sat in a freezing shed with the roof open to the sky all night, night after night, charting the light given off by stars— stars that were maybe already dead. Here was all about the visible-invisible borders, the thin lines between here and gone, then and now, here and there, random and meant, big and small. Infinite riches, little room. Here all the clockmakers in history had been confounded, until one of them finally clocked it—ha!— and found that the solution to keeping time when you were at sea lay in the very smallness of things, that a tiny watch mechanism was better than a thirteen-foot-high pendulum in the middle of the ocean any day.

He waited for a comment to come from Faye, something about size mattering.

Nothing.

Silence.

He imagined Faye locked in a little room. Imagine trying to contain an erupting volcano in a bedsit. Imagine that Icelandic singer, what was her name, Björk—but squashed inside one of your average kitchen units. The force would be explosive.

The force had been explosive.

For all the years you've lived, for all that jizz, Faye said cocky in his ear, *you've no idea what real explosion is, have you, old man?*

Finished with the rhyming, then, Faye? he said.

I'll rhyme when I like, she said. *And scan.*

(Well, it's for fun, mainly, the man called Terence tells the child. But it's for serious too. It's a very clever thing.

Are you lecturing me, by the way, would you say? the child says.

You asked, the man says laughing. I'm answering.

The child is his daughter. She's just asked what the point of rhyme is. They're all standing round the table looking to see which little folded piece of cardboard says whose name. In the place where Miles is supposed to sit the card says the words Mark's Partner.

Hugo picks it up and looks at it, looks at Mark, raises his eyebrows, puts it down.

There is wine already poured in glasses at each of the set places. Mark panics. White wine gives him terrible migraine and there's nothing on the table but white. There are five bottles of red, opened, full, over there on the sideboard. But the bottles have an untouchable air. And he doesn't want to ask; already there's been a fuss about drinks because Miles is driving and has refused to drink. We can organize you a taxi, the woman whose house it is, Jan, keeps repeating. No, really, Miles keeps saying, I'd prefer not to.

Terence and Bernice Bayoude; these are the names of the child's mother and father. Mark says the names over to himself a couple of times. There is no name card on the table for the child; the child wasn't expected. The people who are giving the dinner party are pretending that there's no problem about her being here but being arch and polite about setting her a place and finding a seat the right height for her.

Milton calls rhyme a troublesome modern bondage, Bernice says.

Gosh, aren't you clever? Jan says.

What's that about bondage? the reedy-looking man who came with the blonde woman says.

Preface to Paradise Lost, Bernice says. He calls rhyme the invention of a barbarous age.

Well, you've upped the stakes, Bernice, Jan says. Nobody's ever mentioned Milton at one of our dinner parties before. Esoteric, is that the word for it, Hugo?

It's also for helping memory, the father says to the child, since it's much easier to memorize something that rhymes.

Well I know that, I mean, duh, the child says. Obviously.

Don't say duh, Bernice says. Do say obviously.

Mark laughs. Bernice shoots him a glad look, a little secret handshake in a room full of strangers—which is what this room is, for Mark too, a room full of strangers except for Hugo, who, though he isn't one, is doing his best to act like one.

And not just memory, Terence is saying, but it also makes people feel safe, comforted, because when things rhyme it reminds them of their childhoods, and over and above that it's also like rhyme is saying, hey, things are good, they're all right, they're in some kind of harmony, they may even be funny.

You *are* lecturing me, the child says. I resist all attempts at lecturing and indoctrination.

Terence turns, shrugs his shoulders at Mark and Miles and Bernice.

Damn, he says. Another self-made freethinker.

And when I look back on this evening in a week and a month and a year and a day, I will remember every single thing about it, the child says.

No you won't, her father says.

I will, actually, the child says.

Physiologically impossible, Brooksie, her father says.

Yes, but you can't tell me what I'll remember and what I'll forget, the child says.

That's true, Bernice says. But. The whole point is, we *can* forget. It's important that we forget some things. Otherwise we'd go round the world carrying a hodload of stuff we just don't need.

In any case I intend to remember it all, the child says. I shall therefore go out of my way to do this particular thing.

Terence takes her by the collar, pulls her back, picks her up, swings her into the air and sits her on his knee.

That's a different matter, Brooksie, he says. Memorizing is conceptually and physiologically different from remembering.

Duh, the child says.

She gives the word her most intelligent inflection.

Brooke, her mother says.

Obviously, the child says.

She says it as though it means duh.

The conversation about rhyme and memory has arisen because a moment ago Mark asked the child what books she likes reading. Mark is usually more uneasy around children, who always make him feel like his best behaviour isn't quite good enough, because they are so true, like little truth detectives. But this child is a charming and quite unthreatening one. Have you ever read Struwwelpeter? he'd asked her. The story of Augustus who would not eat any soup? Or A Book of Nonsense? Have you ever read Edward Lear's limericks? There was a young lady of Norway. Who casually sat in a doorway.

Then while the child and the others have this conversation, Mark sits in amazement as his own mind unfurls and one after the other like little falling-open scrolls he finds line after rhyming line inside his head. Augustus was a chubby lad. Fat ruddy cheeks Augustus had. When the door squeezed her flat she replied, what of that? That courageous young lady of Norway.

My head is full of poems from fifty years ago, things I haven't thought for years and didn't even know I still knew, he says to Miles.

'Twas brillig, and the slithy toves, Miles says sitting down across from him.

I know that one, Hugo's wife Caroline says. Hello Mark. I'm glad they've put me next to you.

Did google twitter in the blog, Miles says.

Yes, Caroline says. It's amazing, isn't it, how very visionary he was. Imagine inventing all those words, words we use every day now. Brilliant.

She holds her full glass of white up for clinking.

To you, she says. And to—Miles, was it?

It was and is, Miles says.

I'm glad. How long have you two been together? she says.

About three and a half hours last Saturday and (glancing down at his watch) twenty minutes tonight, Miles says. Oh no, we stayed and had a drink last Saturday too. Four and a half.

We're not actually what you'd call together, Mark says.

Oh, she says.

She puts down her glass. She looks a little affronted.

Everybody is sitting down now except the woman whose house it is, Jan. Mark goes round the table naming everybody to himself. Start with Caroline on his right, then Hugo, uh, Hannah the blonde, then Miles. Then, is it Eric, the grey man? then Bernice, then the child, then the space where Jan will sit, then Terence, then directly on Mark's left what's his name, reedy man, microdrone, Richard.

Richard is the person Mark most hoped he wouldn't be put beside, apart from Caroline obviously (duh). Through in the sitting room, all through drinks, Richard had talked about his job.

Well, it's police we're doing the main selling to at the moment, he said. Though we're pretty much open to bona fide offers from anywhere.

Loves his work, Rich, Hugo said.

What's not to love? This thing markets itself, Richard said. Hardly like work at all.

What's a microdrone? Bernice had said.

Richard then described the versatile smallness, the engine size, the battery voltage, the weight that means they're not illegal and don't need clearance from Civil Aviation, the adaptability, the camera type, the HD quality, the facial recognition range (fifty-five yard), the mph (fifteen, in this particular model, though others are even more phenomenally nippy), the flying range (five hundred yard), the flying time (thirty-minute, we're working on that), the relative silence, the way they can be operated from inside a van or even in some cases from home, the training time (fifteen-minute) involved for the first-time user, and the way that even if some yob wings them with an air rifle they'll still function pretty well all said and done.

What he hasn't said is how cute they are, Richard's partner Hannah said. I want one for our boys. Like little toys.

Actually classed as toys, Richard said. Which is why they don't need clearance. Fantastic for football matches, protest meetings, you name it.

And then there's Project Anubis, eh, Rich? Hugo said.

Yes, Richard said, well, no point in being naïve about it, it's a nasty old world out there and it strikes me all sensible people will feel the same way as I do about it and if they don't they ought to. And what I always say is, what a relief it'll be when it comes to conflict, combat, and it's robots who'll do the work and so on. Efficiency is one fantastic thing, but the psychological liberation is a whole other massively important knock-on effect. To kill without actually having to. Hand to hand combat, gone in the wink of an eye.

I don't understand, Terence said.

I always think when we have this conversation, and we have it every time we all have supper together, Hugo said, that it'd be a lot more useful if our great minds were put to the task of sorting our genetics out. I'm only forty-five but I'm telling you, it's making me think, being forty-five.

Well, as long as something's making you think, Bernice said.

Touché, Hugo said.

Project what did you call it? Bernice said. Anubis?

Yeah, Anubis, it's just one of several levels of drone development, Richard said. Obviously the targeting specificity has been in development all along, alongside the surveillance aspect, and drones are already used widely in conflict situations. But right now we're emphasizing the surveillance aspect for the domestic market.

Project Anubis, Terence said.

Anubis is the ancient Egyptian god of the dead, Bernice said.

Is it? Richard said. Ah. Right.

Jackal-headed, Bernice said.

And they look so like toys, Hannah said and looked delighted. Unbelievable!

Unbelievable, Bernice said.

Nasty old world out there, Richard said. No point in pretending otherwise.

The Bayoudes exchanged glances.

Now at the table, while they wait for the first course and Mark sits and worries about what he's going to do with the wine in front of him, microdrone man asks him what he does for a living.

I'm a picture researcher, currently, Mark says.

Right, Richard says.

For BBC magazines. You know, thematically stranded in association with programmes and so on, Mark says. I source pictures for them.

Is that a very taxing job, then, Richard asks, or can you more or less do it with your eyes shut?

No, you do actually need your eyes to be open for it, Mark says.

Oh, yeah. I remember now, Richard says. You're the, uh, Hugo and Caroline's friend.

He clears his throat.

That'll be how you know Hugo, he says. I'd thought, before, you know, it might be the am-dram game.

The what? Mark says.

Likes a bit of a drama, Hugo, Richard says.

Hugo looks wounded. Mark can feel Caroline pretending not to listen on the other side of him.

Wildlife photography, only one of Hugo's many exotic hobbies, Richard says.

Hugo's pictures of barn owls are legendary in the business, Mark says.

I occasionally take a picture that's of occasional use to publications, Hugo says. And Mark and his employers occasionally see fit to use one or two. I'm a lucky boy. What does your, uh, Miles do, Mark?

You'll need to ask him, Mark says.

How about you, Miles? Hugo says.

He says it civilly but it sounds like a threat.

I'm so sorry, Miles is saying as Eric puts a plate down in front of him. I can't believe I didn't think to tell you. I'm vegetarian.

81

Ah, Jan says coming through with three more plates. That might actually be a bit of a problem, Miles.

What a shame, Caroline says. And the main course is lamb. From Drings, and everything. What a shame, Jan.

What about just taking the sausage off and putting it to one side and then you can eat the fish? Hannah, who's sitting next to Miles, says.

He's vegetarian, Hannah, Caroline says.

Yes, I know, Caroline, that's why I suggested it, Hannah says.

I do wish you'd let me know, Mark, or let Hugo know so he could have let me know in advance, Jan says.

I wasn't actually party to the information that Mark would be bringing somebody, Hugo says.

My apologies, Mark says. I'm so sorry.

No, my fault, Miles says. Mine entirely. I'm an interloper. Happy just to eat salad to atone. Happy not to eat at all if it's a problem. Happy just to have an enjoyable evening sitting here.

And then he was killed by a Viking who brained him with a bone that came from an ox, the child at the other end of the table is saying. He was the Archbishop of Canterbury and they made him a saint. It is why the church of St. Alfege is called his name. It happened here, in Greenwich, in the year ten twelve.

In the year twenty-five twenty-five. If man is still alive, Terence sings.

Adorable, Caroline says.

She smiles at Bernice. Adorable, she mouths the word the length of the table.

I'm not responsible for any adorability here, Bernice says. I'm the bad cop.

If woman can survive, Terence sings.

And the church has survived and is still there, the child says, though it has been rebuilt on the place, the exact place the original church where they brained him stood.

Ours are so grown up now, Caroline says. Theirs are still small, she says nodding at Hannah then at Richard. Lucky them, that's all I can say. I have fond memories of life BCG. Before computer games. D'you like children, Mark? Oh, excuse me. I don't mean that to sound like it sounds.

Um, Mark says.

I mean, I don't know that you don't have any. I was just assuming. I didn't mean to sound patronizing.

It is possible now for you lot to adopt, isn't it? Hugo said.

What lot, sorry? Mark says.

Miles is talking to the child about the restoration of the Cutty Sark.

The original, he says, was really fast. She was a tea-clipper, but built when tea-clippers were no longer relevant or really needed any more, but she was so adaptable and fast that she could even outrace the newfangled steamships.

But what I wonder is, the child said, why is it a she?

Would you rather we called it a he? Miles says.

No, the child says. I just wonder why it is, that's all.

I don't know, Miles says, but I'll try and find out for you. I think ships are generally shes. And you know what Cutty Sark means?

Miles tells the child its origin. Everybody round the table pretends to be entertained while he does.

So the man in the poem is a bit merry, a bit drunk by the time he goes home, Miles says, and in the dark he passes a lot of people dancing round a fire, and one of them is a really good dancer and she's wearing a very short shirt, so the man watches her, and shouts out well done short shirt! except it's in Scots he shouts it, weel done Cutty Sark!—she's so good at dancing and he's so drunk he can't help but blurt it out, out it comes. But the girl, well, she and her friends happen to be witches, and they're angry they've been spied on, and they chase the drunk man as if they're going to kill him, and even though his horse is good and fast he only escapes by the skin of his horse's tail.

Ha, the child says. Skin of his tail.

Her tail, Miles says. The horse was female.

That's why the ship is a she, Hugo says. Same as the horse. Females, always a bit fast.

83

Everybody laughs.

Why is that funny? the child says.

I hope they never reopen that bloody ship, pardon my French, Jan says. The traffic round here, I don't know what it's like where you live, Mark and Miles, but it's really been getting me down lately.

The child assures Jan that the ship will definitely be reopened to the public as soon as they remake it because nowadays you can do pretty much anything including remake something historic after it's burned down.

Yep-iep, her father says. You can do pretty much anything nowadays. Take film of people who don't know you're doing it and even shoot them dead from a helicopter that's classed as a toy. Anything.

Why has everybody stopped talking? the child says into the silence.

Ah, Miles says and winks at the child. A time to be silent, a time to burn things down, a time to restore them, a time to get drunk, a time to race away from things as fast as you can on your horse, a time to brain the archbishop, a time to make some headway with the starter.

Mark looks down at his plate. He looks at his full wine glass. He looks at his empty water glass. He looks at Miles's plate. On it is what looks like salad and blue cheese, which is what they've also served to the child who is now poking at her plate with a knife and looking suspicious.

A discussion starts about something Caroline has seen on a screen at a train station.

And then I thought, Caroline says, that now that we can do that, morph a tiger first into the shape of a man's foot and then into the shape of a trainer, I mean now that we have such tamed and, I have to say, beautiful images of something like a tiger and we can do exactly what we like with them, well why would we ever again be bothered about the extinction of real tigers? I stood and watched it happen and it struck me, we don't and won't need to see a real tiger ever again now, not now that we've got images like that, not really.

That's moronic, Hugo says.

Caroline rolls her eyes.

Everybody laughs.

Personally I wouldn't mind if they became extinct, Hannah says. I hate the way they're always killing deer and zebras and things on the wildlife shows.

The thought made me quite sad, Caroline says. But I mean, I looked at the pictures and, I have to say, I thought it. I mean, we don't, do we? We don't need real tigers any more. We've finally tamed the wild.

That's what they want you to think, my darling moron, Hugo says.

Don't call me a moron, darling, Caroline says.

Way the advert worked on you is the real point, Richard says.

Ah but no it isn't, though, Caroline says. I can remember that it was an advert for trainers, but I can't remember which make. So it didn't work at all, actually, not the way they wanted it to.

Hannah asks the Bayoudes if they've ever seen a real tiger at home. Not in Yorkshire, they say. She asks where they're from originally. They tell her they were living in Harrogate and working at the University of York, which is where they met. They work at the local university, they tell her. Bernice got a teaching post here in the arts faculty and Terence has latterly been accepted as a research fellow.

We had some luck, Bernice says. It's not easy to get academic jobs in the same place. Terence had a salary in York, so you might say we're missing that. But we're okay. We're together. We miss York. But we like it here a lot.

You're the only ones in the whole borough, then, Jan says.

Personally I like it here very much, Eric says sitting down.

It is the first thing he's said. Everybody turns and looks at him in surprise.

Miles passes his own water glass over to Mark's side of the

table. Hugo watches him do it, then reaches over for Miles's name card. He holds it in his hands, at arm's length, as if he needs glasses to read it. Then he puts it back where it was.

What is it you do again, Miles? Hugo says. I asked you before but we were interrupted by your vegetarianism.

Everybody laughs.

I'm an ethical consultant, Miles says.

Ah, Hugo says.

Mm, Richard says.

Ooh, Jan says.

What on earth's an ethical consultant? Hannah says.

Miles smiles at her.

You're the brave one, he says.

Am I? Hannah says.

She beams. Then she stops beaming when she sees the look Richard is giving her.

What it means is, I work for firms who want to ensure they're ethically sound, or who would like to present themselves as more ethically sound, Miles says.

Ha, Hugo says.

Ho, Richard says.

I comb their profiles and make suggestions about where, depending on the brief, they could make themselves greener, or specifically help communities they're local to, or capitalize on what's already ethically sound about themselves. Or I highlight potential for all of these. Or, if it's just presentation we're talking, I suggest possible rebrandings.

Gosh, Caroline says.

He's an ethic cleanser, the child says.

Everybody round the table bursts out laughing.

I don't know why everyone's laughing, the child says. I'm only repeating what he told me earlier.

Freelance, I take it, Miles? Hugo says.

What's the per annum on that, roughly? Richard says. Pre-recession, let's say.

That word, Jan says. Banned at this table.

This is delicious, by the way, Jan, Caroline says.

From the way people keep saying it, Mark gathers that the woman's name maybe isn't actually Jan, is maybe more like Jen. He tries to remember what Hugo called her when he insisted to Mark that he come tonight. He panics inside. Has he called her Jan out loud? He tries to remember if he's said her name to her.

My bonds and shares, Terence is singing. May fall. Downstairs. Who cares? Who cares?

You like to sing, then, Terence? Hugo says.

Gershwin, the child says.

You said it, Terence says.

He and the child high-five. But at the word Gershwin Mark's head fills with an unexpected music, a blast of Phil Spector production on He's Sure The Boy I Love, so loud that it drowns the party out for a moment. When he can hear again, Jan or Jen is praising Hugo for something. She's praising his singing voice.

That song at the end of the first half, Jen says, right before the interval, the one about the war being over in their dreams, do you remember? I'll never forget it. It was really moving. Wasn't it, Caro?

Hugo has apparently played Siegfried Sassoon in some kind of play, a play where he had to sing a song at the end of the first half. Mark takes a sip of water. It is new to him, the knowledge that Hugo can sing, the knowledge that Hugo acts in plays. He thinks of himself and Hugo in the bird-watching hut, Hugo behind him, deep inside him, saying, you are coming, aren't you? Working on it, Mark said laughing, any second now. I mean weekend after next, Hugo said sounding offended even through the effort of love. You are coming to Jan and Eric's?

Terence Bayoude, it seems, knows a great deal about musicals. Richard says it's amazing the things people get taxpayers' money to study these days. Terence tells Richard that his research fellowship is in metallurgy. Richard looks annoyed. Jen tells Terence again that Hugo's got a great voice and that the Bayoudes should hear him on stage. Mark begins to wonder if Jen is maybe sleep-

87

ing with Hugo too. He watches the shape of Jen's mouth and the flick of her eyes for how these respond to Hugo all through Terence talking about how microphones and film changed the shape of the standard popular song early last century by making it easier to sing short notes yet still be heard at the back of the balcony. That actually made it possible, he says, for songwriters to use more syllables. But his real passion, he says, is dancers. Then Jen asks him about the anal imagery in Busby Berkeley, about which there was an article in last week's Guardian.

Everybody laughs.

What's anal, again? the child asks.

Caroline blushes.

Oh God. I'm so, so sorry, Jen says to Bernice. I didn't think.

Terence tells the child that anal is the adjectival form of anus and that the anus is the opening at the end of the alimentary canal.

I knew that, the child says. But then what's the problem with saying the word?

Then Terence tells everybody round the table that Busby Berkeley wasn't a choreographer to start with, but came to it via the First World War, where he'd been a drill inspector.

I'm not musical at all, Richard says.

He hasn't a musical bone in his body, Hannah says.

Brained by the musical bone of an ox, the child says. Ha ha. St. Arpeggio St. Alfeggio.

Her father laughs.

Where did you get a word like arpeggio from? her mother says. As if I didn't know.

Is it stage musical or film musical you're keen on, Terence, or both? Jen asks.

I just don't get music, Richard says again.

Tell us some more facts like that one about Busby Berkeley, Terence, Eric says.

Everybody turns and stares at Eric.

Don't encourage him, Bernice says. He's anal enough about it already.

The whole table falls silent again.

Woah! Bernice says and hoots with laughter.

Well, Terence says. James Cagney and George Raft and John Wayne. The tough guys of Hollywood, well, they were all trained as dancers first.

That'll be the day, Richard says.

Discipline, yes, Hugo says, it's a very particular discipline.

And Fred Astaire, Terence says, had it written into his contracts that if he was being filmed dancing then his whole body was to be shown at all times, never just his feet or hands or head, never anything but the whole body.

Richard drops his knife. It hits the side of his plate quite hard.

Fascinating, Jen says nodding.

Hannah yawns out loud.

And Ruby Keeler, you know, the early tap dancer? Terence says.

No, Hannah says like a teenager, we don't.

Keeler was the first really famous tap dancer, Terence says ignoring her. And when we see footage of her, dancing, these days, and we compare her to someone like Astaire, it's easy to think she's not very good, quite clumsy, because she's so all over the place and clunky-looking. But in reality her dancing style came direct-descendant from the Lancashire Clog Dance. In fact it made Astaire's possible. She was the first popularizer of the form.

How do you know stuff like these things? Hannah says.

I read them, Terence says. In books.

No, but *why* do you know them? Hannah says.

Why? Terence says.

I always think it's so funny what people know and why they do, Hannah says.

Why does anybody know anything? Terence says.

I never know why anybody knows anything, Hannah says. But I'd have thought you would know about, you know, your own culture, before you knew other things about cultures like Lancashire and places like that, I mean.

Have you not met any or very many black people before or are you just living in a different universe? the child says.

Silence thuds down round the table.

No, Hannah says, I didn't mean it like it sounds, like that. I was just surprised that he knew so much, knows so much about music and, and when his job is metal, and musicals.

All art aspires to the condition of music, Bernice says. That's Walter Pater. All art aspires to the condition of musical. That's Terence Bayoude.

Jen and Caroline and Hugo make knowing noises.

And I didn't understand any of that last comment at all, Hannah says.

She looks desperate.

That was lovely, Jen, Bernice says. Thank you very much.

Miles, Jen says, there's couscous as accompaniment to the tagine, and I can have a look in the fridge and see what will go with it, but it might be a bit haphazard, I hope you won't mind. Or would you like me to make you an omelette?

Anything vegetarian will be really lovely, thank you, Jen, Miles says. Please don't go out of your way for me.

I'm only concerned that I've still got enough eggs, Jen says. But please don't let that concern you for a moment. Eric?

Jen and Eric stand up and start gathering plates. Then Eric comes back from the kitchen and fills everybody's glass with red, except Mark's, probably because Mark's white glass is still full and it looks like he isn't drinking. Mark can't think how to ask, and then the moment when he could have asked is gone.

The internet, Hannah is saying. If I need to know anything. That's what's so great about being alive now. But if it was just me, on a desert island, with just myself. Sometimes I have this dream, I've had it loads of times actually, it keeps coming back, where I'm at school even though I'm too old to be at school—

Are you naked in it? Richard says.

Everybody laughs except Hannah.

—and all the kids are much younger than me, and the exam paper is put down in front of me, she says, and all the little kids start writing the answers, and I sit there and I look at it and my mind goes completely blank, like an empty space, like the empty blank page I know I have to fill, you know, cover, with things I don't know, and I'm sitting there and it's not just that I don't know how to answer any of the things in the exam, it's that I *don't know anything.*

She looks close to tears. Miles jogs her elbow gently.

The next time you have that dream, he says, and you're sitting in front of that exam paper, tell yourself in your head that you *do* know. Sit at the desk and look at the paper and tell yourself about, uh, tell yourself you know—

A song, the child says.

Yes, a song, Miles says.

But I'm not musical, Hannah says crossing her arms and shaking her head. I haven't a musical bone—

Yes, but you'll know a song, there must be a song you like, Miles says.

I don't know *any,* Hannah says.

What's a song everybody knows? Miles says to Terence.

Everybody knows Somewhere Over The Rainbow, the child says.

Oh yeah, I know that one, Hannah says, from the film and everything.

Right, Miles says. When you're in that exam room the next time, say to yourself, I'm all right, I know Somewhere Over The Rainbow.

But I don't know anything *about* it, Hannah says. And if I look down at the exam paper, it'll say, like, who wrote the rainbow song, and tell us everything you know about the rainbow song, and all I know is that it was from a film and I still won't be able to answer anything right.

This is what we'll do, Miles says. Terence is going to tell you three facts about that song. And the next time you have that dream, you'll know three things about it and you'll be able to instruct your subconscious to write them down.

Hannah sniffs, blows her nose.

I probably don't even have a subconscious, she says.

Okay, Terence says. Three things about Somewhere Over The Rainbow. Uh. Right. It was written by Harold Arlen and Yip Harburg, Arlen did the music and Harburg the lyric. There's two things.

There's no way I'll be able to remember that when I'm asleep, I can hardly remember it right now when I'm wide awake! Hannah says.

Okay, Terence says. Okay—I know. The first two notes form an octave leap.

He sings them.

Fucking pansy, Richard says under his breath.

And the way they do that, Terence says, makes the word *somewhere* leap right into the sky, out of hopelessness to hope.

Hannah's face fills with panic. She turns to Miles and shakes her head.

Something more anecdotal, Miles says to Terence.

Anecdotal, Terence says.

He widens his eyes.

What's anecdotal? the child says.

Like when you tell a story, Terence says.

There's that really good story about it, about the little dog that always runs away, the child says.

Yes, Terence says. Yes. Good one, Brooke. So. Listen. You know the middle bit of the song? The bit about some day I'll wish upon a star?

He hums it. De da de da de da de da.

Hannah nods.

Terence tells her that Harold Arlen, the man who wrote the tune, had written the first part, the over the rainbow part, but couldn't think of a melody to link each verse, or to act like a bridge between them.

And Arlen had this little dog, Terence says, like a fox terrier or that kind of dog, who was quite badly behaved and kept running away and getting lost.

His name was Pan, the child says.

So, there was Harold Arlen, Terence says, standing there and rubbing his forehead, worried, one minute saying, I can't think what to do with this tune, then the next minute whistling for that little dog to come back—

Terence whistles the tune of the some-day-I'll-wish-upon-a-star part of the tune exactly like he is whistling for a little dog to come back.

Everybody at the table laughs out loud, even Richard.

I won't ever forget that! Hannah says. That's brilliant! Tell me another one like that.

Okay, Terence says. Brooksie. What else? Something else.

The man who, when they were boys, sat next to the other boy in school because of the alphabet, the child says.

Yep, Terence says. Yip.

Yep yip! the child says. Yip yip yooray!

She claps her hands above her head. Bernice laughs.

Yip Harburg, Terence says. The man who wrote the words. He wrote the words to so many songs we all just know, just like that. He was born a poor Jewish kid in New York, his parents were sweatshop workers, and he grew up in a house where he and his sister slept on chairs pushed together at night, they were so poor.

Snore, Richard says.

No, listen, Hannah says. And his parents made sweatshirts, go on, Terence.

He lit the gas lamps on Broadway as a boy, Terence says, it was his first job. And in the school he went to, they sat their kids in alphabetical order. One day he took out some poems he loved—

Could this be, sorry Mark and, eh, your friend, the gayest conversation I've ever heard in this house, or possibly any house? Richard says.

Don't, Hannah says. It's for my *dream*.

One day, Terence says, he had a book of poems with him in school and he was reading them, and the kid sitting next to him said, they're not just poems, you know. They're more than poems. And this kid took Harburg home with him, and played him some 78s on a gramophone, because the poems he'd been reading were the lyrics for Gilbert and Sullivan songs. H for Harburg. G for Gershwin. He was twelve years old and he'd been sitting next to the twelve-year-old Ira Gershwin, right there, next to him, at school. And they both grew up to be . . .

To be what? Hannah said.

So is Ira Gershwin something to do with the more famous George Gershwin? Caroline says.

She was his wife, wasn't she? Jen says coming in with plates balanced on her arm.

He was his younger brother, Mark says.

It comes into his head how much Faye loved songs. He had quite forgotten how much.

It does sound like a girl's name, though, doesn't it, Ira? Caroline is saying.

There's no way I'd ever call a daughter that, Hannah says.

Then she tells them all the story of the daughter of a woman she knows at her Parent Teachers Association who woke up one day in the middle of a field in Cornwall wearing new clothes. She didn't remember buying the clothes. She had no idea what she was doing in a field in Cornwall or how she'd got there. The last she remembered was being out for a drink on a Saturday night after work. The next thing it was Tuesday morning. And she was in a field miles from home. And she was dressed in new clothes. And when she looked at her credit card she'd bought them on that. But she didn't remember any of it.

Selective memory after shopping spree, Hugo says. Endemic among women. Sorry. Is that a bit sexist?

Yes, Miles says smiling.

Think so, do you, Miles? Hugo says.

He closes his eyes at the same time as he turns his head in Miles's direction.

It's not funny, Hannah says. It's true. It really happened in really real life.

Oh my God, Caroline says. Had anything . . . happened to her? You know, anything (she nods towards the child)—bad?

That's the thing. It didn't seem to have, Hannah said. But she didn't know. She couldn't know for sure.

Had anything good happened to her? the child says.

Much more interesting, Miles says.

Ha! Bernice says.

Easy to go to the bad, Miles says. I'm always much more interested in things going to the good.

Room's full of pansies, Richard says not quite under his breath.

Pansies, the child says, are for thoughts. Rosemary is for remembrance.

She couldn't, Hannah says. Remember. Anything. But, the thing is, nothing *at all* seemed to have happened to her.

So it's a pointless story, Richard says.

Hannah looks crushed.

No, it's a philosophical conundrum, Bernice says. How would you ever trust yourself again, or anything about yourself, or the world, or you in the world?

I know, Hannah says. It's *awful.*

You just would trust yourself, I think, the child says.

Bernice smiles across the table at her.

Optimist, Terence says.

Bet it was her husband's credit card, Hugo says. Or is that sexist, Miles, and is it offensive, and are any of the women round the table offended by it, or is it just you who can't take a joke?

Not very, only mildly, maybe about as sexist as a quite benign 1970s sitcom, Miles says. But yes, I think it definitely is.

As a what, sorry? Hugo says.

He narrows his eyes. He is getting quite drunk. Caroline cuts in, suddenly earnest, about the Viewfinder she's bought on eBay, exactly the same as the one she had when she was a child, which is why she bought it.

It was lovely to feel the little click of the black lever thing, it felt exactly the same as when I was small, except, of course, smaller, she says. I also got online a set of the Viewfinder pictures of the Eames house for Hugo, they're like designers—

They're not *like* designers, they *are* designers, Hugo says.

Caroline rolls her eyes.

—and some Womble pictures for me, she says, because that's what I had when I was that age. And when the package came and I opened it and took it out, the Viewfinder, it felt much smaller in my hands. Funny to think of my own hands, you know, so much smaller. I never thought it would be the Wombles that would reveal that to me. Sometimes we find out in the strangest ways how fragile we are, don't we? Mark, do you know what I mean?

Mark has been feeling a steady mental pressure on him coming from Caroline all night. He doesn't know whether he is creating it or she is. He suspects they both are. He knows Caroline most probably doesn't really know about Hugo and him; he knows at the same time that her subconscious will know everything there is to know. Now the whole table is waiting to hear from him about fragility.

He takes a deep breath.

He starts telling a story about when he was taking a taxi between a couple of small towns, for work, and about how the taxi driver had a picture of the Virgin Mary tucked into his sunshield, and four differently scented Magic Tree air fresheners plus another Glade air freshener, all in the one car. He is about to tell them what the taxi driver said to him, that he'd pick up anyone, anyone at all, he'd pick up gays, blacks, Jews, Asians, Muslims, druggies, he wasn't judgemental, except there was a pervert he knew about, who dressed in women's clothes, and there was a paedophile, and he knew where each of them lived in this small town, and he reserved the right not to pick them up because he didn't want people like that in his cab, and also he refused to take gyppos, the so-called travelling people could find their own means of so-called travel, far as he was concerned. As he said it Mark, belted in in the back seat, had watched the holy water glint inside the plastic bubble next to the Virgin Mary and had wondered if the holy water was selective too, and if that's what God was these days, and whether everybody now simply had a private god who sanctioned his or her own choices about who he or she would pick up in a cab.

But here at the dinner table, with everybody listening, he loses confidence halfway through and finishes his story at the fifth air freshener.

Plus a Glade air freshener. For luck, he says.

Hugo looks bored. Richard looks furious. The women laugh politely.

Didn't like the smell of people, that person, Bernice says.

Or the smell of himself, maybe, Miles says.

Both, Bernice says.

Richard picks up on the detail about the Virgin in the sunshield and he and Hannah take turns telling, all the time giggling like children, the story of their local lady vicar coming round to visit them to talk about something Hannah is doing with her Christian Young Mothers group at the church, and how embarrassing it was when this vicar suddenly just started praying, there in their lounge, in front of the tea and the biscuits, sitting there offering thanks to God.

Mark can't concentrate on it because he has seen Miles do something strange; he has slipped the smaller of the two salt cellars, after using it lightly over his omelette and couscous, down under the table. Nobody else has noticed. Now they're all talking about the free market.

A false balance is a bomination to the Lord, but a just weight is his delight, the child says in a sonorous voice.

He doesn't mean Greenwich Market, Brooke, Bernice says. He means the trade market, the global business market.

The whole world, Richard says. It's, well, a more or less borderless world. And that's as it should be.

Except for the borders where they check your passport for hours, the child's small voice says from the other end of the table.

Yes, but everywhere needs some defence against people just coming in and overrunning the place with their terrorisms or their deficiencies, eh, sweetheart, Richard says.

97

That's right, Terence says. Got to keep all those bad refugees out. The ones looking for a better life.

Couldn't agree more, Richard says. Humankind has needed fortifications since the start of humankind started.

And all this time since the start of the start of humankind we've needed little helicopters with cameras in, so we can see over our neighbours' fortifications, Terence says. It's a triumph of civilization.

Ha! Hugo says.

Don't knock civilization, Richard says. Personally I think it ought to be against the law to knock civilization.

It probably is, Terence says. I may need a lawyer sooner than I thought.

Nasty, British and short, Miles says.

You what, Miles? Richard says.

Team of solicitors I occasionally work for, Miles says.

Ha ha! Bernice says.

I don't think I get your meaning, Miles, Richard says.

Who's been to the theatre recently? Jen says. Anyone? Holidays. Terence! Bernice! Where are you going on holiday this year? Or maybe you've been? Where did you—

Oh, I'm really proud of being British, me, Hugo says. I'm very big on the choice of toothpaste we have these days. That's what I call global choice. It's great, living in such a multivalent universe and having so much choice. I am what I listen to on my iPod. And I love it that so many databases can find out at the flick of a button just exactly what my favourite toothpaste or music is, as well as all the other things they can know about me, like my date of birth, how much money I have, how I spend my money, who I phone, where I go, things like that. We've really used our talents well as a species, when it comes to freedom.

It'll be Iraq, Caroline says, any minute, here we go again.

She rolls her eyes.

The fact is, the child says, that there were astrolabes in Baghdad, where the Iraq war was, probably before anywhere else in history, and definitely in 1294.

What's an astrolabe, Brooke? Eric says.

It means an instrument for finding the positions of stars and planets, Mr. Lee, the child says.

Then she recites the names of the Astronomers Royal out loud. Flamsteed, Halley, Bradley, Bliss, Maskelyne, Pond, Airy . . .

Mark leans behind Richard to talk to Terence.

Is there a book you can recommend to me, maybe, about the Gershwins, or about that man you were talking about who wrote the songs? he says.

Easiest thing in the world, Terence says. With great pleasure. I can think of about four good ones off the top of my head.

They're making a secret assignation, Richard says. Talking arty behind my back.

Oh no, don't talk arty, Hannah says. I hate it when it comes round to the talking arty bit. I hate it.

No, you see, I have to say this, because the thing is, I've said it before and I'll say it again, I *like* going into the supermarket and seeing all the toothpaste there so new and clean and waiting, Caroline says. And I don't see why something that gives me pleasure and makes me feel safe has to be a problem, why it has to be a problem that I like the feeling it gives me.

Warhol, Hugo says. If you see something duplicated over and over you'll want it. You won't be able to forget it. You'll fall for it. You fell for it. Moronic. That's what Warhol's doing. He's pointing out the moronic.

I like there being a choice of toothpastes, Caroline says. It makes me feel, well, real. But apparently I'm a moron who doesn't understand or like modern art. Well, I don't. I'm coming out, Mark, and I'm telling the whole table. I'm not a snob. I like to see a beautiful thing if I go to an art gallery as much as the next person. But contemporary art, I don't like it, and most of the time I don't understand it. Most of the time it's so pointless.

There's some good children's literature out there, though, isn't there? Jen says.

Almost on cue, the child sitting next to her puts her head down on her arm on the table. A moment later she is completely asleep.

Caroline, meanwhile, won't be dissuaded, is red in the face, is shaking her head.

I mean, the songs and films you were talking about, Terence, they have an entertainment value at least, she says.

Depending what you class as entertainment, Richard says.

But it doesn't *change* anything, Caroline says.

Actually, that's debatable—Terence begins, but Hugo and Caroline cut him off.

Moron, Hugo is saying sweetly.

And neither does that woman artist's pointless awful bed and pointless garden shed, Caroline is saying, or the pointless skull encrusted with diamonds, and that pointless artist who had the lights coming on and off in the room. It doesn't make anything happen.

Well, Miles says. It does.

What does it make happen? Caroline says.

It makes the lights go on and off, Miles says.

He picks up Hugo's glass of red, raises it at Eric and then at Jen.

A toast to our hosts, he says. To the Lees.

To the Lees of happiness, Bernice says.

To the Lees! everybody shouts. Hugo is quite drunk, doesn't notice his red is gone and raises his white glass. While they're all drinking, Miles puts Hugo's glass of red down in front of Mark.

Then he leaves the room.

Caroline continues about how pointless art is.

No, Hugo says shaking his head too, I can't believe I'm going to have to have this argument again about it. And the very fact that everybody goes on and on about the same people, as if art didn't exist outside the tabloids. Emin and Hirst and so on, they're old hat already, they get in the way of what their art does, and part of me is starting to believe they've become such a cliché precisely so that people can say exactly the tripe you've been saying and you're about to say, and so there can be some kind of debate, not that I'd call it much of a debate by the way. But I won't have it said, when there's so much new art that's so interrogatory, that subverts the things that need subverting, that challenges all the right preconceptions.

Here we go again, Hannah says.

The secret of life is art, Bernice says. That's what Oscar Wilde said.

The secret of arty talk is death, Hannah says and draws her finger across her neck and makes a choking noise.

I don't care what he says, Caroline says pointing at Hugo who has taken on a piqued, supercilious look. All those words you use all the time, darling, about it, like enhance and retro and articulate and interrogate.

Money and power, Richard says. The real magic words.

Yes, Caroline says, and that's why I'm almost glad there's been a recession, sorry Jen, because maybe it'll shake up some of the stupid money there is in things like financial markets round the art he's always going on about. The kind of art you go on about, where people put themselves in glass cases in a gallery and get looked at, or sell all their belongings, or someone casts the hole in a doughnut in plaster and calls it The Hole From Inside A Doughnut, or fills an old tree trunk with concrete and calls it whatever, it's all a con. Art. No art has ever really changed anything. That's the bottom line. Full stop. Show me something that a work of so-called art has ever really done, anything in the world, except give people a migraine.

Hannah yawns audibly.

Art is stupid, she says.

But what about that boy, Mark says, in Germany, the boy who set up the resistance movement with his sister, I can't remember their names, in the Second World War?

Everybody turns to look at him. It is quite frightening.

The boy was in the Hitler Youth, he says, and he was reading a book one day, he was really enjoying it, until his troop leader found him reading it and gave him a severe warning because it was by a, a Jewish writer, it was a banned book. And the boy was so incensed that this really good book he'd been reading had been banned—was the wrong kind of book, the wrong kind of art, if you like, written by the wrong kind of writer—that he thought twice, he began to ask questions about what was happening, and then, it turns out, he went on with his sister, Sophie Scholl, their name was Scholl, to do this stellar work, to try to change things, make it possible for people to think, I mean differently. And they fought back, and they did change things. They did a lot of good before they were caught. And they were killed for it, his sister and him, the Nazi authorities took them to court, tried them, and they spoke out bravely, and were sentenced to death for treason, the Nazis cut their heads off, I believe.

Yeah, and after they did, they found out that their skulls were, like, encrusted with diamonds, and then the lights in the room they were in went on and then off by themselves, Hannah says and makes a spooky ghost noise.

Mark, shaken, realizes he has just made the terrible mistake of not just seeming to be but actually being sincere. It finally strikes him that this conversation about art probably takes place every time these people meet for dinner like this. As if to consolidate what he's just thought, Jen makes a little performance of checking that the child is asleep before she leans forward and says with deliberate sincerity:

But of course you must have seen some terrible times yourself, Mark, if you were gay before it was legal to be gay, were you?

Oh yes, I was, Mark says. I was gay all along.

He blushes.

Yes, and it was criminal, wasn't it, right up until the beginning of the 1970s, Jen says nodding.

End of the 1960s, Mark says and looks down at his own hands on the table.

I mean, you must have been quite a young man when all that was going on, Jen says in her sincere voice.

Oh, I was, Mark says. It's exactly what I was.

Everybody laughs.

It must have been terrible for you, Mark, Caroline says on the other side of him.

She puts a hand on his arm.

What was it like? she says.

Oh, it was all very jolly, Mark says. We all hid everything. All very exciting. Very stimulating.

I didn't know it was ever even criminal! Hannah says.

If they caught you it was prison. Or oestrogen injections, Terence says. That's what happened to Turing.

It's called cruising, not touring, Richard says, as far as I know, that is. I don't know. We'd have to ask the experts among us. Eh, Hughie-boy?

Caroline cuts in quickly and asks the Bayoudes did they call their daughter after the actress Brooke Shields.

Who's Brooke Shields? Hannah says.

You're too young to know, Jen says. She was an actress who went out with, what's his name, the royal, not Edward, the Fergie one, Prince Andrew, but when she was very young, much younger, she was associated with a seedy scandal when a rather dreadful filmmaker used her in a salacious film even though she was under-age.

It wasn't a rather dreadful filmmaker, Eric says. It was by one of France's best twentieth-century film directors.

Well, we've always disagreed on that, haven't we, darling? Jen says. He's always putting on things with subtitles. I look at it, and I think, *oh no, sub*titles. It's lucky we can all sit in different rooms in this house.

And no, the Bayoudes tell them, but they *did* name her after a film star, Louise Brooks, a star of silent film—

Who did Yorkshire clog dancing, we know, Hannah says—

—who was associated with playing roles full of free will, girls with an ability to survive, or with a profound nonchalance in the face of the horribleness that life can throw at a person, Bernice says.

After a brief astonished silence, Caroline, who is now also quite drunk, says: but then her name would be Louise, wouldn't it?

Louise Brook, Richard says. Didn't she win a British rowing medal in the Olympics?

103

Brooks, Terence says, not Brook.

I thought she was that nanny, the one who shook the baby in America, Hannah says.

Out of nowhere Caroline starts crying and laughing at the same time. She says she wants to make a confession. Her confession is that she's frightened of flying in aeroplanes. Hannah reaches across the table, knocks over an empty water glass and pats her hand. Jen starts shouting about CBT. Six sessions of CBT will sort you out, she says, only she shouts it, like a mad person, and she shouts it over and over, she has said it about six times, Mark thinks, either that or he is very drunk himself, which can't be possible since he's only had one glass and it was only half full. Hannah is shouting too, about how she has rights, and that one of her fundamental rights is the right to be able to take cheap flights, because her parents didn't have that right, and that flying doesn't harm the environment nearly as much as they claim. At this point, Hugo and Richard start free-associating a fantasy—Mark watches them slip into cahoots as if they'd not been being the least bit acrid with each other all night, as if cahoots is exactly the same as loggerhead—of filling the windscreen washer-bottles in their cars with urine, so that when they press the button to wash the windscreen the spray coming out of the nozzle and going over the roof of the car will cover any cyclists anywhere near the car with piss.

The Bayoudes exchange looks with each other over the head of their sleeping child.

I am competitive, Richard is saying, I'm not going to hide that fact.

Mark turns to look at Hugo. Hugo stares straight back at him, right in the eyes. It is the most lost look in the world. Mark thinks of Jonathan, and of the moment, after Jonathan had gone, that he understood the nature of Jonathan's love, when he'd sat one spring afternoon six months after the funeral and worked his way through the video footage Jonathan had taken of their lives together over twenty-five years, and found that whether it showed a lovely view looking out to sea on a holiday, or skimmed along a road out of a car window, or panned round whatever room they happened to be in, the camera eye always came to rest, in the end, for its final image, on Mark himself.

There is something heartbreaking, Mark thinks now, about video's inferior quality, something human and makeshift in the not-quite-good-enough that it is, the way it's all that remains, the way it makes what happened so much less. When they'd visited Rome and gone into the pretty little church, empty inside but with the queue of tourists outside it all waiting to have themselves photographed putting their hands into the Mouth of Truth, they'd found, in a glass case, a toothy smiling skull whose forehead was plastered with a name. S. Valentini. Wonder, Jonathan's voice says behind the image, as the image stays steady on the skull, if we *all* have our names in there written on us like that, on our foreheads, between the flesh and the bone. Then they both laugh, Mark heard his own laughter meeting Jonathan's. Then the camera eye, slightly shaky with laughter, comes away from the relic and round to rest on Mark, laughing.

Meanwhile Richard is demonstrating with his hands the goggles the police use to be able to see what the microdrone is seeing. Hugo puts his hands over his eyes too. Jen and Hugo, still with his hands over his eyes, start a conversation about democracy and internet porn. Mark feels queasy. He thinks about the couple of times he's brought himself off by watching the free porn on the net: two men on the steps of a blue swimming pool, three men dressed as soldiers in a toilet. Both times he had to go in search of something else on there afterwards to make himself feel less degraded. The second time he had simply typed the words *something beautiful* into the Google images box. Up came a picture of some leaves against the sun. A picture of a blonde photoshop-smooth woman and baby sleeping. A picture of a bird. A picture of Mother Teresa. A picture of a modernist building made of shiny metal. A picture of two people sticking knives into their own hands. Google is so strange. It promises everything, but everything isn't there. You type in the words for what you need, and what you need becomes superfluous in an instant, shadowed instantaneously by the things you really need, and none of them answerable by Google. He surveys the strewn table. Sure, there's a certain charm to being able to look up and watch Eartha Kitt singing Old Fashioned Millionaire in 1957 at three in the morning or Hayley Mills singing a song about femininity from an old Disney film. But the charm is a kind of deception about a whole new way of feeling lonely, a semblance of plenitude but really a new level of Dante's inferno, a zombie-filled cemetery of spurious clues, beauty, pathos, pain, the faces of puppies, women and men from all over the world tied up and wanked over in site after site, a great sea of hidden shallows. More and more, the pressing human dilemma: how to walk a clean path between obscenities.

Bernice is nodding at him, as if in agreement with him.

Oh God. Oh no. He thought he was just thinking but he has, it seems, actually been speaking out loud.

The merest opening of a common buttercup on a piece of wasteground in the light of an ordinary day, Bernice is saying, the mere blowing along a road of a piece of litter, is enough to dispel the so-called truth of every single thing online. But we're forgetting how to know what's real. That's the real problem.

How much of it has he said out loud? He can't be sure. Oh God. Did he say the word wanked? Did he say the stuff about the soldiers and the swimming pool? Oh God.

Bit of a Luddite approach, though, Jen says.

The internet IS real, Hannah is saying. You can't just say the internet isn't real. I have it in my house. That makes it real to me.

I refute the internet thus, Bernice says and knocks her hand into the neck of an empty decanter in front of her so that Jen has to catch it to stop it from toppling.

Hannah starts wailing that Bernice, because she has said the words contemporary and philosophy, is being superior and showing off. It is a fate worse than arty talk. Hugo and Richard are now making threats at each other about Damien Hirst's skull. It looks like a physical fight will break out.

Mark goes upstairs because he thinks he might be sick.

The bathroom is empty.

Through the open door of the room next to it, Miles seems to be measuring something by stepping and counting, stepping and counting. He looks charming, preoccupied. He sees Mark.

Seven steps long, five wide, he says.

Maybe Miles is a secret estate agent.

He has taken his knife and fork upstairs with him. He puts them on the sideboard, takes the salt cellar out of his pocket and puts it down next to them.

What are they for? Mark says.

Miles shrugs his shoulders.

Eating with, he says.

He presses the light switch, on then off. Both men laugh.

It's all sound and fury downstairs, Mark says. They're going to punch each other's skulls in any minute over whether Damien Hirst's skull means anything.

Miles shrugs his eyebrows and smiles a resigned smile.

And I think I might be sick, Mark says. Any minute now.

Miles nods. His eyes are kind.

See you, he says.

He means: see you in a minute, when you've sorted yourself out.

Mark goes into the bathroom. He sits on the floor until he feels better, less hot. Then he stands up and urinates. As he does, a whole childhood poem he didn't know he knew flows by itself through his head.

Fury said to a mouse, That he met in the house, "Let us both go to law: I will prosecute YOU.—Come, I'll take no denial; We must have a trial: For really, this morning I've nothing to do." Said the mouse to the cur, "Such a trial, dear Sir, with no jury or judge, would be wasting our breath." "I'll be the judge, I'll be the jury," said cunning old Fury: "I'll try the whole cause, and condemn you to death."

Like the tail of a creature; yes; the poem had gone down the page in the book shaped like the tail of a creature.

He'll tell Miles; Miles will be interested. Miles will maybe know what the poem is.

But when Mark comes out of the bathroom the bedroom door is shut.

For a moment he thinks Miles must have gone downstairs again. He turns to go himself. But then he stops. He stands in front of the shut door and puts his ear against it.

He goes downstairs. He stops before the dining-room door, which is half closed, and stands outside. In there they are talking about someone. There is a great deal of laughter, as if someone is the butt of a joke.

He listens. They are talking about Miles, maybe.

No, he's great, I mean, he's your stereotypical gay man, Caroline is saying. Your professional working gay man, I mean.

He didn't comment on my clothes at all. They're supposed to comment on your clothes, Hannah is saying. And he's not as neat and clean as they usually are. They're usually more pressed or ironed or something.

Loves his mummy, Richard says.

His mother's dead, actually, Hugo says.

That'll be why he's not so ironed-looking as he should be, Richard says.

Someone, Hannah, laughs.

How do *you* know about his mother? Caroline says.

He told me, Hugo says. She took her own life when he was a boy. Eleven or twelve.

They're not talking about Miles. *Took her own life.* It is a kindness in Hugo, to be so drunk yet to choose to put it as if he is holding it in gloved hands.

Sad, Jen says. That's very sad, isn't it?

She was some kind of painter, Hugo says.

House? Richard says.

Laughter, somebody, subdued.

He was brought up by an aunt, Hugo says. His father was away or not there, something like that, and he was brought up by an aunt after she, his mother, after she went. She was quite well known, well, she was after she died, I'd never heard of her. Faye or Faith or something.

You mean Faye Palmer? Bernice's low voice interrupts. His mother was Faye Palmer?

His second name *is* Palmer, Hugo says.

Oh, Terence says. Oh my God. One of Faye Palmer's sons.

He'd be about the right age, Bernice says. Oh, that's amazing.

Who's Faye Palmer? Hannah says loud and incredulous.

Faye Palmer, Bernice says.

The Bayoudes tell the table about Faye. Young. Jewish. Wildly talented. Hugely promising. Original. Seminal. Visual artist. 1950s. Strikingly beautiful when you see photos of her. You must have heard of her, they say, she's often referenced alongside Plath.

Oh yes, Hugo says, Plath, someone's wife, wasn't she, and completely brilliant, and insane as a nest of snakes.

Bernice describes Faye's most famous work, History Sequence 1 to 9, and how it begins with the faraway woman in the chair and, as you come closer, progress from canvas to canvas, you see that the woman is tied at the wrists and ankles to the chair, and then that she looks like she is crying, and then that what she is crying is blood, and as you come closer still you see that her eyes are a bloody mask.

Then you're right up against the face, up against the eyes, and you see that the eyelids have been sewn shut, with foul little bloody little black stitches, Bernice says. In number 8 there's nothing but these stitches in extreme close-up. It's like an abstract, but it isn't, it's painstakingly figurative. And then in the final canvas, she goes beyond the mask, right into the eye, and there's no eye in there, the socket is empty, there's a foul-looking insect and it's eating the lining of the socket.

Oh gross, Hannah says. Oh that's the grossest thing I ever heard.

It's true, Terence says. It's an image from reality. Somewhere there's a quite famous piece of writing by her, about what it means to have to bear the knowledge of inhumanity, having to

109

bear it communally—about how this thing really happened to a war prisoner, who'd had his eyes removed and then his torturers had sewn beetles into where the eyes had been.

Oh I'm going to puke, Hannah says, I really am.

And the big controversy after her death, Bernice says, was that she replaced the man to whom this really happened with what ostensibly, in her paintings, appears to be a series of self-portraits.

Oh, *ostensibly,* Richard says.

Bernice ignores his mocking. She goes on to tell them that this appropriating of history, the fusion of personal and historic, is the thing critics of Palmer's work still argue about most. In many ways, she says, a continuing tendency to dwell on the details of her autobiography, particularly on the fact that she committed suicide and the possible reasons why, has blocked the proper aesthetic reception of the work.

Oh, *aesthetic reception,* Richard says.

Shut it, Rich, Hugo says.

Why did she? Caroline says.

History Sequence 1 to 9, they're called, Terence says. You must know them. You will, you'll have seen them.

And how did she? Caroline says.

I'd know if *I'd* seen one. They sound really disgusting, Hannah says.

You'd absolutely know if you saw one in real life, Bernice says. You can't not. They're unforgettable. They're shocking to the core. But also, they're really shockingly beautiful.

No way, Hannah says.

They are, Bernice says. They just are.

You wouldn't take your child to see one of those pictures, though, would you? Jen says.

Our child sees worse things every day on TV, Terence says. She just needs to type a couple of words into a computer to see things every bit as bad, and, worse, to see them as if she's not really seeing them. Seeing a picture like one of Palmer's is very different from seeing something atrocious on a screen. There *is* no screen. That's the point. There's nothing between you and it.

And to leave a child, Caroline says. What a choice. It's unthinkable.

Unthinkable just to leave your own self. Think how robust your own heart feels, and your arms, and your legs feel, someone (it must be Eric) says.

Very selfish, Hugo says.

Most difficult thing in the world, Caroline says.

I'm amazed you've heard of her. I'd never heard of her, Hugo says.

But you've seen her, Bernice says. You will have. You've seen her without seeing her. She's hugely influential, she was hugely important in the ways artists, especially women, came to treat history and to examine how history had treated them. And you can see so clearly now too with hindsight, how they parallel Bacon, practically initiate the post-war self-infliction artists of the 1960s and 1970s, and even, in their colour planes, anticipate Hockney.

That's not possible, Bacon and Hockney together, Hugo snorts.

Trust me. They do. They do both, Bernice says.

Faye Palmer's son, Terence says.

Oh God, Jen says. Jewish. And I served him pork.

Bacon and Hock, Richard says. Ha-ha!

Yes but he *ate* it, Jen, Caroline says. He's probably one of the ones who don't mind what they eat.

Mark stands just beyond the door.

In his muscles he is thirteen years old and the hush is about to happen all over again, will happen in a moment's time when, small, thin, in the still-too-big blazer, he'll enter the prep-room full of boys at St. Faith's, and no longer be just the Jewish one, like Quentin Sinigal is the coloured one. Now that the inquest has been in the paper and everybody knows, he'll also be the one whose mother—like in the old joke about Jamaica, whispered behind his back for months and months to come (in fact there will literally be years of this whispering)—went of her own accord.

He glances back up the stairs. He can see the closed door.

The nice chap, Miles, is safe behind it.)

Say that a man is fully formed by not / just what's remembered also what's forgot Mark sat on the circular bench at the gate of the park. It was a warm October day. What would he remember from his visit to the Observatory today? A seagull had walked across the grass at the edge of the park on the tiny white table in the turret that's been curtained off to make the Camera Obscura. He'd enjoyed that somehow more than seeing a seagull in real life, he thought now, as he sat and watched another real seagull walk across a strip of grass right in front of him.

Say that the berries on a tree fermented / say that some birds ate them got drunk demented / couldn't fly straight flew straight into instead / wall of an office block and fell down dead / down on the pavement people undeterred / stepping over the mound of broken bird Mark sat on the bench on a Thursday in October in 2009. Forty-seven years ago today, to the day, he is standing in the lounge of Aunt Kenna's house. It is a couple of days since he was moved in. He has drawn the short straw. David got Aunt Hope, his father's other, nicer, sister, and was moved in to Aunt Hope's house on the other side of town a couple of days ago too.

Everything is so neat it's a kind of proof, though he's not yet sure what of. The sizes of the chairs in the lounge, new to the backs of his legs, are a kind of proof. The foreign fall of the cloth on the table is proof. The dark wood furniture in the room is proof. The wooden curve on the side and the top of that cabinet thing where Aunt Kenna keeps the drinks, and which gives off the smell of acridness and plush when you open it, which you can only do if Aunt Kenna doesn't know it's what you're doing, is proof.

His suitcase is in the spare room.

The note his mother left is in the suitcase.

In a house-move roughly seven years from now, when Mark will drop in to pick up the stuff that's still at his aunt's, and which his aunt has packed in bags for him, the note will get mislaid, and will be given away to a junkshop in the ribbing of what Kenna thinks of as an anonymous old suitcase. Because this happens at a time in his life when Mark is angry with his mother for doing what she did, he will decide not to go after it, not to go to the junkshop to try to find it again. By the time he is ready to want it again, the note, Aunt Kenna is dead and there's no way of finding out even which shop she gave the suitcase to all those years ago.

It says, in the dash of her handwriting, on a sheet of Basildon Bond:

> Button up your overcoat.
> Take good care of yourself.
> You belong to me.

That's all. Nothing else. It isn't addressed. His father doesn't know about it. Nobody knows about it. Mark found it on the desk of the open bureau, detached it from the pad along with the three sheets underneath which bear the imprint of the words and packed it without showing anybody.

Her writing is her.

Even the imprints.

He will never know whether this note was meant for him, or David, or for them both, or for nobody at all, just his mother scrawling down something she might want to think about later.

His aunt has an ancient pug called Polly. The pug's face looks ruined, melted. It looks like what Mark thinks the word tragedy would look like if it were a physical reality, a thing not just a word.

Right now the pug is sitting lumpy in the doorway, looking out on to the yard where Mark's aunt is what she calls *dealing with* a fledgling thrush which has fallen out of a nest, can't fly, and has been there, square, dense, idiot, all afternoon, on the cobbles.

There are lots of cats round here so his aunt is putting it out of its misery before a cat does.

But Aunt Kenna—, Mark said.

Aunt Kenna waved him away.

It was the pug found it first; Mark saw it circle the bird, curious, benign. It was so tired, the baby bird, of just sitting there on guard, that its eye kept lidding over.

Will the bird's parents, which are clicking and squawking above the yard, miss it when it dies?

Animals, Mark, have no use for nostalgia, Aunt Kenna says. It is not a tool for survival, my darling.

But Mark has seen the pug, on a walk, pick up a stone in its mouth and carry it for a little of the walk before putting it down, and then on the way back home again stop to find the same stone and pick it up to carry it some of the way back.

Forty-seven years later Mark could, if he'd chosen to, have called to mind the face of the pug, the dark of the lounge, the ebony cigarette-holder so often in the mouth of his aunt at this time in her life. But of this particular day, this moment, in this room with the resolute tick of its clock and the noise of birds outside, what did he remember?

Not a single thing.

Say that there is a heaven up above / say we survive the bumpy road to love Mark sat on the circular bench at the gate of the park. It was his day off. Twenty-seven years ago today, to the day, Mark is on a train coming south. He is thirty-two. His heart is high. In three minutes, according to his watch, the train will pull into Platform 8. Jonathan will be waiting for him at the head of Platform 8. Ten minutes ago, as the train reached the city's outskirts, Mark shouldered on his stripy cotton jacket, said goodbye to the American nun (!) in mufti sitting opposite him, with whom he'd had a long conversation about many things, including sunlight and Nicaragua, and began walking the length of each carriage all the way to the front. On his way through he carries out a little survey, for fun, of what people are reading on the train. A girl reading Women in Love. A man reading Zen and the Art of Motorcycle

Maintenance—still (!). A woman reading Death in Venice. A woman reading Heat and Dust. A man reading The White Hotel. A young man, very good-looking, reading a novelization of Chariots of Fire. A girl, looks like a student, reading Slaughterhouse 5. Now he's past the buffet, now he's through first class, where nobody is reading anything but the Daily Telegraph (!). Now he's as near the front of this moving train as he can get, and now he is pushing the window in the door down in the smell of diesel, watching the sun glancing off the deep blue of the moving side of the train as it pulls out of the tunnel into the light before the station, and now his hand is on the handle and pushing the handle down, and now the heavy door is swinging open and the train still moving and he sees him there and he jumps, hits the ground running.

Twenty-seven years later, this journey was lost to Mark. It was just one of so many mundane journeys they made, over time, towards and away from each other. He couldn't have remembered the details of this particular one, lovely though it was, even if he'd tried.

Time came and took your love away and now / say it's only a paper moon—and how / the ground beneath us melts away like snow / tell every little star I told you so Mark sat on the bench by the gate of the park and looked at his watch. But then again, this is what happens when, one Saturday night, he goes for a drink in the pub opposite the Turkish restaurant after a play, with a nice chap he's just met.

Mark: I've been invited to this dinner party next week.
Miles: But?
Mark: But, well, I don't want to go.
Miles: But?
Mark: But what?
Miles: Just but.
Mark: What do you mean, but?
Miles: Exactly what I say. Those sentences all sound like they have a but attached.
Mark: But?

Miles: Yes.

Mark: And would that but have one t or two?

[Miles smiles at him, shakes his head.]

Mark: Shame. Ah well. Right. Got that straight, then. So to speak. Ha.

Miles: So. You've been invited to this dinner party next week, *but* you don't want to go. You don't want to go, *but*—but what comes next? See?

Mark: I get it. You mean like a game.

Miles: I mean more than a game, I mean, like actuality, like how things happen. Like . . . I was going home, *but*, this man asked me to go for a drink, so here I am.

Mark: Is it always but? Can it be and?

Miles: Yeah, but the thing I particularly like about the word but, now that I think about it, is that it always takes you off to the side, and where it takes you is always interesting.

Mark: Like . . . this thing happened at the end of the play which threatened to spoil the whole thing—*but* . . .

Miles: See?

Mark: Ah. I see. You're kind of . . . amazing.

Miles: Ha-ha. *But?*

Mark: [laughs] What is it? All that grammar beaten into me at school, and I can't remember the name of the figure of speech for the word but. Preposition?

Miles: I'm not prepositioning you.

Mark: Ha. Damn shame.

Miles: I'm doing something much better. So. You've been invited to this dinner party, but—you don't want to go. You don't want to go, but—

Mark: But I can't really get out of it.

Miles: You can't really get out of it, but—

Mark: But I've just thought of a way to make it do-able.

Miles: You've just thought of a way to make it do-able, but—

Mark: But it depends on whether this man I've just met will accept the invitation and come with me.

Miles: [surprised] Oh. Oh, you mean me?

116

Mark: [surprised at himself] Yes. But—. Yes.
    [Laughter]

For every new bud there'll ever be / all the old leaves get shunted off the tree / say it's a kind of spooning—with a knife / this merciless merciful newness of life Mark sat, now, on the circular bench not far from the gate of the park. In a minute, he'd stand up and go and try the front door at the Lees' house again. Forty-six years ago, in the Easter holidays (when he is roughly the age of the boy who sheep's-eyed him earlier today up on the hill), he is "home" from St. Faith's and Kenna is at the dentist, and because she has a dentist she particularly likes going to across this side of town, she has left him in a greasy spoon until her teeth are done. Across the road there is an antique sort of shop and in its window is a golden-coloured, medieval-looking picture. Mark pulls his coat on and leaves the caff, crosses the road.

The picture is a holy picture, a religious picture, of two men. They are turned towards each other and a group of men is watching them. One has his arm, his hand, on the other's shoulders. He is looking at the man lovingly. The smaller of the two men is bending forward slightly. He is putting his fingers, his hand, right inside a wound in the first man's side.

Beautiful, a man behind him says.

It is the man from inside the shop. He has come outside and is standing next to Mark.

Mark says yes, he thinks it is really beautiful.

The man's name is Raymond. He's quite old, about twenty. He hangs a handwritten notice on the inside of the door. Back in 20 mins. He locks the shop up. Lunchtime, he says to Mark. Fancy something? He winks.

He takes Mark for a walk in a park Mark later learns is Greenwich Park. There, in the woody part, on a foggy day in London town, things come to a pretty pass. Somewhere between roughness and gentility the man, who is very beautiful, kisses him so thoroughly that when Mark gets back to the place he's supposed to meet Kenna an hour later he is flushed and new, a whole new per-

117

son, and all the way across town it is as if his eyes have changed, as if all the colours in everything he sees are golden and ancient and new. They get home and he goes upstairs. He is lying on the floor playing his records (there is that good-looking boy, John Allford, clever, in the form above him at St. Faith's who says that record is a word which means, in Latin, something which returns through the heart) on the little portable record player Kenna bought and lets him have on a Friday—or also when he is sad and needs to blot out the sad old songs with something more new, which Kenna understands, because Kenna can sometimes be very kind. He has his one ear pressed hard against the machine's speaker behind the little chainmail holes, and he leans to get the next record out of its paper sleeve ready to play it, Then He Kissed Me, and that's when he sees on it right there, the miracle, the word Greenwich, there on the label right under the word Kissed, and it is as if something somewhere has understood him.

LONDON AMERICAN RECORDINGS
Made in England
Then He Kissed Me
(Spector, Greenwich, Barry)
The Crystals

The song gives him an erection and then, when he takes himself in hand, a coming-of-age every bit as beautiful as the one he had in the park. He knows now what it means, to be bigger than yourself. Greenwich! England Expects That Every Man Will Do His Duty! The world is a bloodrush of rough harmony. Then it's over; the song, abrupt, dies away, fades to the noise of the needle on vinyl and it's gone. But he can lean over and do the thing with the mechanical arm so that the record will play over and over, on repeat, until you choose to stop, and you could even be dead and it would go on playing and playing.

Consider the fabric of things the vast / dustbin of detail who knows what will last / nothing left but rough wool skin moment touch / who knew so little would become so much Mark sat in the park. It is more

118

than fifty years ago. He and his mother are making a dash through London on a day when the rain makes the pavements greyer, the wind makes the litter more littery, a rough spring day. His mother's sleeve on her tweed dogtooth coat, the one with the big lapels, is turned back on itself at the cuff and the rough cuff is rubbing his wrist as they hurry along. The wisps of her hair beyond her hat are wet, pretty in the rain. She is telling him things as they walk-run, turning to tell him things even on the move and when they pass men the men turn their heads and look at her. Mark is proud. She is clever and quick, she is beautiful, his mother, she is like a bird both clipped and winged, and when she passes people notice, and when she laughs out loud in the street people stop and stare.

It's genius, old man, she says hauling him along and reeling off, like magic spilling behind her, like that dancer Isadora's scarves that streamed behind and caught in the wheel and killed her, rhymes by one of her favourites, he rhymes *sour* with *Schopenhauer*, *Freud* with *avoid*, *salmon* with *backgammon*, *civil* with *drivel*, *yes-men* with *chessmen*, *solemn* with *spinal column*, *Irving Berlin* with *pounding on tin*, he rhymes *word* with *absurd*, and *hurled* with *world*. Now Porter has wit, but is shifty, a little seamy, I know, and I couldn't not love him for it, Mark. But Ira, he's kind, he's always kind, and for genius to be kind takes a special sort of genius in itself, Mark old man, come on, we're late (they were always, she was always, gloriously, just a little late, it made everything worth hurrying for), and his brother dead, imagine, he must feel like half a person, imagine it, try, him still in the world and his other half, the tune half, gone so young, only a bit older than me, and I know you think I'm old, but I'm not old, old man. I'm not old at all.

His mother says the rhymes out loud in the street, in the rain, to the rhythm of her walk. It is because she loves songs. She does, she loves them. The bedtime stories she tells him, after David's been settled and she comes for the marvellous twilight time to his room, are all song-stories. She comes into the room and she sits on the bed and she says something like, are you ready? Then

119

I'll begin. Once a baby boy was born with no fingers on his left hand, imagine, just a stump for a hand. And when the baby had grown into a boy, the boy's mother encouraged him to learn piano even though he hadn't any fingers on that hand. And he got so good on the piano that when he grew up and was a man, he found he was a musician, and he wrote songs, and what's more, having a stump was an asset when people got drunk if he was playing piano in a bar. He not only played piano, he landed some great knock-out punches with it. The end.

Then, sitting on the end of the bed, she sings When The Red Red Robin, which is a song this man who only had half his fingers really did write. She sings it slow and lullaby-like even though it's meant to be fast, and then she turns out the light and leans over him with a kiss, and turns to go. One more, please, Mark says, please, when she's at the door. So she comes back and sits on the edge of his bed in the half-dark and she sings another song by the man with one hand. Side. By. Side.

But the Gershwins! she shouts now as she dashes along past the shops, pulling him in her wake, rain all over their faces and his bare knees numb with the rain, her hand holding his all paint and the smell of the stuff she uses to try and wash it off. In the rain, in the middle of dull Holborn, with the people and the cabs and the buses going past and the shabby weather round them, she is singing above his head and the words are about how they're writing songs of love, but not for her. A lucky star's above, but not for her.

What, if anything, did Mark remember of all this, more than fifty years after it happened?

He remembered the blur of a grey London day and his hand in his mother's hand.

He remembered she was wearing a coat whose cuff was folded back.

He remembered the feel of the cuff of this coat as they moved, as it rubbed against his wrist.

Say that the line we walk is very fine

Mark sat on the park bench, way in the future. Last week he'd read in the paper about the twenty-fourth copycat suicide in a French telecom company, where suicide was now being treated as a contagion.

What about that, then, Faye?

Say that the concept's part of our design

On the one hand, nothingness; on the other, birds that sang in their sleep.

On the one hand, nothing; on the other, a feeble attempt at it, rhyme.

On the one hand, nothing; on the other, but here's something, Faye, I read it in a book and I knew you'd like it. It's about the song called For Me and My Gal. It took three grown men to write that song. And one of the three was Jewish, well, maybe more than one was, I can't remember, but this one definitely was. And he fell in love with a girl and wanted to marry her, and she wanted to marry him too. So he takes her to the rabbi, to get married in the synagogue, this was in New York, and the rabbi says to her, are you a good Jewish girl, my child? and she says o yes, your worship, I am that, and he says to her, what was your mother's full name, my child? And she says, my mother's name was Emma Cathleen Bridget Hannigan Flaherty O'Brien, your worship. And the rabbi sent them away with a flea in their ear. So they went and got married at City Hall instead. Anyway, the girl's name was Grace, and Grace's favourite song all her life was this one her husband had helped write, and when she died he had the title of it engraved on her headstone. For Me and My Gal.

The end.

Nice one, Faye, what do you say?

Say that your own heart's keeping time for mine

He sat forward on the bench. He stood up. Half past four.

He left the park.

He walked past a pub, caught sight of his reflection in the glass of its window.

Old man.

·   ·   ·

121

The front door of the Lees' house was wide open. A girl with a clipboard and a man carrying a camera rig were standing in the doorway. The cameraman was gesticulating at a man in a van parked at the kerb. The girl with the clipboard was speaking to Jen Lee, who was also in the doorway and who, just at that moment, caught sight of Mark at the foot of the steps and looked away as if either she had no idea who Mark was or she was making it clear she didn't want to have to deal with him now.

Hello!

Mark looked down.

It was the child, the Bayoude child.

Oh, hello, he said.

I remember you, she said.

I remember you too, Mark said. Something happening?

It's Channel 4, she said.

Right, Mark said. How's your dad and mum?

They're very well, thank you, the child said. They got your nice card saying thank you for the book and everything. We have it up all the time, on the mantelpiece, in the front. It is an honour kept only for very special cards.

That's lovely, Mark said. I'm honoured.

Yes, you are, the child said.

Oh, hello Mark, Jen called down now. How are you?

She was free; the clipboard girl had come down the steps to the van and was unloading a heavy-looking tripod. The cameraman had disappeared, probably inside.

I don't think they'll need to speak to you, she said. I think we're pretty much giving them what they're after.

Good, Mark said. Well. I was just passing. I was just up at the park for the afternoon, and was just, you know, passing.

Right, Jen said. Well, if you'll excuse me. Lovely to see you. You do look well.

She went back through the door into the hall.

What did you do in the park? the child said. Did you go to the Observatory? Did you go to the Planetarium?

Yes to the first and no to the second, Mark said.

Were you at the Observatory all afternoon? the child said.

No, I spent some of it sitting on a bench talking to my mother, Mark said.

On the phone? the child said.

In my head, Mark said. She's long dead, my mother.

Oh. I knew that, the child said.

Forty-seven years dead last week, Mark said.

That actually happens to be longer than both my parents have even been alive, the child said.

Last Thursday, to be exact, Mark said.

That makes it sound like it was last Thursday that it happened, the child said.

In some ways it was, Mark said. Just last Thursday. Directly before the Cuban Missile Crisis. Ever heard of the Cuban Missile Crisis?

No, but it sounds serious, the child said.

Oh, it was, very serious, then, Mark said.

Mark took the folded pieces of paper out of his pocket, made sure the one he was putting back in was Miles's handwritten note, and held the magazine article out to the child.

Do you think you could slip this under his door for me? he said.

The child nodded, sure.

She ran into the house.

Half a minute later she skimmed out the front door and down the steps again.

They sent me out in case I disrupt the filming, she said. And I tried to just go up anyway but Mrs. Lee is sitting on the stairs and I couldn't get past.

Oh, Mark said. Well. It doesn't matter.

But I can give it to someone who can get it in for you later, the child said.

Great, Mark said.

And Mrs. Lee says to tell you they might want to speak to you after all, the child said, because when Celia, who is what is called the producer, found out you were here the night it happened she decided that therefore it would be an interesting angle.

I've no wish, Brooke, to speak to anybody about anything right now, Mark said.

Right then Celia the producer appeared at the door and stood there shading her eyes down the street, as if looking for someone. Mark turned his back, made a face at the child. The child nodded, jerked her head to show him which way to go. She ducked down a passageway to their right, into a break between the houses. Mark followed.

As they came round the corner and down the steps through the passageway the noise level rose. There were quite a lot of people standing around at the fence below the backs of the houses, and more people standing and sitting on the grass across by the modern flats. There were so many it resembled a local fête, or an impromptu protest or campsite. There were several different-sized tents pitched on the grass, Mark counted them. Nine.

The child introduced him to a Scottish woman who had, it seemed, been coordinating food deliveries to the window by means of an amateur-looking pulley system slung between some of the windows on the back of the row of houses. She shook his hand. She was very interested to hear that he'd been present at the original dinner party.

They've stopped feeding him anything but meat via the house now, she said. It's cruel. We had to do something. Finally he's eating fruit again, and fresh vegetables, thank goodness. People are coming here with things they've cooked, too, for him, but just in case, because you never know how folk are, we're only sending up fresh raw stuff or things we know are okay, things we can vouch for the safety of.

Mark looked at the rickety zigzag of the pulley system, and at the huge posters the other people living on the crescent had put up in their windows.

GO AWAY
THIS IS PRIVATE LAND
DON'T YOU HAVE
HOMES AND RESPONSIBILITIES

We tend to send the basket up at the same time every day, she said. You might think there are a lot of people here now, but last weekend at the one o'clock basket we had a hundred and fifty waiting to see the hand come out.

The one o'clock basket? Mark said.

Uh huh, Anna said.

She smiled.

Just the hand? Mark said. You never see his face?

He has the blind down low, see? she said.

She pointed at the window behind which, presumably, Miles was.

And at ten to one every day, Anna said, we get access to the upper flat next door, the people are very kind, the Gispens, there's Mrs. Gispen over there, look—

She waved, and a middle-aged woman leaning on the bonnet of a car waved back.

—and at one o'clock exactly we activate the pulley and swing the basket down and over, and he opens the window and puts his hand, his arm, out and takes what he wants out of the basket, Anna said.

Wow, Mark said. Who's paying for the provisions and everything?

When she saw him getting his wallet out she sent him over with Brooke to a teenage girl and a thin and beautiful older woman, both sitting on a rug on the grass outside one of the tents. Someone had pinned a piece of paper above the door of the tent with the words Smokers' Area on it; they were both smoking. They were interested to hear that Mark had been one of the original guests—even the morose teenage girl, who looked as if a state of being interested in things might constitute a severe life-change.

The girl's name was Josie, Brooke told him. She had constant access to the house. She'd deliver the note under the door.

Would you? Mark said.

Yeah. No sweat, she said.

The woman sounded very upper class. She introduced herself as the acting camp treasurer.

I've only £30 on me in cash right now, Mark said, but I can nip to a machine and get a little more, if that'd be a help.

The treasurer told him they'd had so many offers of donations recently that they were joking about getting a PED.

What's a PED? Mark asked.

Pin Entry Device, the posh woman said.

Chip & Pin thing, the teenage girl said flicking at the ashy end of her cigarette with a finger.

A small girl was kicking a football against a sign that said No Ball Games. A group of women of all ages were sitting in a circle, knitting round a camping stove. A good-looking man was cooking what looked and smelled like paella in a huge pan over another stove. Three dogs sat nearby, watching. A man came over with a tray of cups of milky tea and offered Mark one.

They're good as gold, the dogs, he said, though nobody seems to own them, and we get all manner of birds and squirrels, all from the park, I've never seen so much wildlife, even the odd parrot, and there's a fox that comes at night and all, pretty tame, and I've never seen a fox and dogs that don't go for each other's throats, but they haven't. Some of them, the more hippy ones here, say it's because Milo attracts animals to him, like St. Francis. But it's the cooking and the bin bags, I'd say. Beautiful, the fox I saw. A big red. Came right up to the edge of the grass.

Mark asked the man how long he'd been camping here.

Three weeks at the weekend, the man said. I was a day tripper for three before that. Then I thought, well, this is interesting, isn't it? I wanted to see what was going to happen. I was worried every time I went home that I'd miss something. What if something happened and I wasn't here to see it? So my son, that's him there, said, look, Dad, here's the sleeping bag. Don't know how much longer we'll get away with it (he nodded at the signs in the windows). It's not like we're noisy or anything. We're good as gold. They've tried to rout us three times regardless, twice with the police. But I'm here till the end.

Just one thing, if I may, Mark said. It's Miles, his name. Not Milo.

Yeah, I know, Anna's always going on about that too. But Milo's better, Milo's got something about it, hasn't it? the man said. It's catchier. It's catching on round the camp, Milo, where Miles sounds a bit, well, wet. A bit middle class, you know?

But his name's Miles, Mark said.

When the man heard that Mark had been at the original dinner party he got very excited.

Everybody'll want to know this, he said. It's like real contact. It's the one thing. I mean, we even sent him up a laptop in the basket one day, but he sent it back. Untouched. We're, like, starved, really. You're, like, one degree of separation.

He went loping off to gather everybody in the camp together to come and hear Mark tell them what it was like to really know Milo. Mark took his chance and headed back towards the passageway between the houses.

Best if you go the other way, the child at his elbow said, because the TV people are at the front of the house now, filming the parking spaces.

Mark waved goodbye to the man. Forty people waved, shouted happy friendly goodbyes.

He asked the child to take him to a cash machine. He withdrew a hundred pounds.

For the treasurer, he said. Or give it to that nice Scottish lady. Keep it safe. Ten for yourself for being the messenger, what do you say?

No thank you, Mr. Palmer, the child said. I'm not needing any money.

The child waved him down the escalator at the DLR.

Regards to your parents, he called up as he went.

Regards to yours too, the child called back.

But
(my dear Mark)
as promised
is very occasionally a preposition but is mostly a conjunction,
and the word conjunction, according
to my Chambers 21st Century Dictionary, means:
connection
union
combination
simultaneous occurrence in space and time
a word that connects sentences, clauses and words
one of the aspects of the planets, when two bodies
have the same celestial longitude or the same right
ascension
A conjunctiva is a [unreadable word] of the front of
the eye, covering the external surface of the cornea
and the inner side of the eyelid.
A conjuncture is a combination of circumstances,
esp one leading to a crisis.
But but?
And and?
(So simple.)
Conjunctions.

And conjunctions?
(So simple.)
The way things connect.

FOR

there was no more talking out loud now, and there wouldn't be neither, not for any money, not for anybody.

May Young was old. You'll always be "young" now you've married me, Philip had whispered in her ear at the altar, June 7, 1947. But she was no fool, she knew exactly how old she was. She knew it was January. She knew it was Thursday. She knew very well who the prime minister was, thank you very much. She knew plenty, no thanks to them. And here she was, in a bed that wasn't hers, now don't go getting ideas, she didn't mean anything funny by it, ha ha. She looked down and saw the thing, plastic bangle-shape thing round her wrist. 13.12.25. No date for the other yet. So there we are, chum. Proof. Still here.

But oh dear Jesus Mary and Joseph, was that thing there really hers, that old woman's rough raw wrist there, coming out of the end of the sleeve of a nightie May didn't know? Well, not intimately she didn't. Imagine not knowing the very clothes you're in. Finding yourself in pink when you wouldn't be seen dead in pink. Finding yourself in a colour you'd never've said yes to in a million. Not even if you'd been in the dark. Old age doesn't come its lone: old saying of her long-gone mother up with the angels since October '64. Well, no, mother, old age didn't come its lone, for look at this, it brought a whole other person with it, a stranger whose wrists were old, who wore pink when you'd never have chosen pink and anyone who knew the first thing about you would never have put you in pink.

Well, but it was sore enough, that wrist on the bed, to be her own wrist, no stranger's wrist after all, there where the plastic bit into it. That's how you knew it was you and nobody else, then, was it, when things were sore? She lifted a hand. Or, an old hand that looked like it belonged to some other body, an old body, lifted, and it *nearly* did what she asked of it, it wavered, it took its time about it, it felt its way, missed its target, came at it anew, if at first you don't succeed, and in the end it got one of its raw old red fingers in between the plastic that had her date on it and the skin under it and look! look at that! it was so tight! there was hardly room for a finger between this here and that there.

So it was no wonder it hurt like it did.

She did not say any of this out loud. She said it within the confines of her head.

The head has its confines. The head's got those all right, confines, *and* the heart. The heart has its reasons. That was a book, the what was it, name of it, the name of the book, the book that lay around the house for years, one of Eleanor's, it was Eleanor with her airs even when she was a child, liked all that royal and history stuff. It had a picture of the old duchess, the American, on it, the divorcée, some cheap thing. Not the duchess, the book. Though the duchess come to think of it had been a bit of a cheap thing too it was widely thought, and she married the king and he abdicated. They liked the Germans. They were right old German lovers, them two. Not that May had anything against Germans. On the contrary, she had met some when they came to the house on the exchanges with the school and so on when the girls and Patrick were young, and they had been very nice the Germans in reality.

The head has its coffins.

It's not the coff that carries you off, it's the coffin they carry you offin.

!

May made herself laugh with that.

136

Out loud?

No, it wasn't out loud. It hadn't been out loud, any of it. She could tell because of that girl.

What girl?

That girl there, the girl in the room, that girl sitting on the big raised chair the visitors sat in.

Who was she, then, that girl?

She wasn't family.

She was just some girl.

Even without her glasses May knew she didn't know her, couldn't place her face, not in a million.

Well, whoever she was she hadn't looked up, hadn't even blinked nor nothing and she would have looked up if May'd been spouting away out loud.

Good.

Though she might, the girl, be wearing one of the things they wear, in their ears, they all wear them now, so they can't hear anything but themselves and their insides, and even then they can't hear themselves think. And if she was wearing one of them things she'd not have heard if May spoke or laughed or did anything out loud, so it'd not make any difference whether it was out loud or no.

She was wearing next to no clothes, that girl. She was more skin than clothes.

May turned her head.

Outside the window it was snow.

They were all mad as foxbitten dogs, the girls of today.

It was proper snow, that.

It was real old-fashioned winter outside this room. These last days there was more often snow than birds in the sky out that window.

No one to love me and nowhere to go. Out in the cold cold snow.

May sang this inside the confines of her head in a pretend old crone of a voice.

That made her laugh.

She turned her head back from the window again.

No, she was not dead.

She was not dead yet.

Well, but we've all got to go in the end.

Well, but there's no getting away from it.

Well, what's for us won't go by us.

Well, Patrick held out the ten-pound note to me, out of his wallet, and I told him, I said, what would I be needing any money for? I'm on the last day of my holidays.

Well, that was the very last thing I said out loud, and the very last thing I ever will.

Well, these are my days of grace. And you don't get many of *them*.

Well, wish me luck as you wave me goodbye. No, not goodbye. Cheerio. The long cheerio. Not goodbye, May, Philip said when he was in here himself in this very pickle, and she'd been up doing the visiting and was about to get on her way home to pick up some things, pyjamas, clean things. Never goodbye, eh?

Philip was small against the pillows in the bed, and the man in the bed next to him couldn't pass motions, whined away in a high pitch behind his curtain while he tried; he was in real bad pain it sounded like. There was a chap the other side of Philip so thin he looked like a skeleton already. Across the ward there was a man who looked perfectly well. He was the illest of them all with something happening in his brain. Philip rested against his pillows and raised his eyebrows at her like a comedian. Then he reached up his hand to his mouth and his eyes and his nose to make sure his face was decent for her. He never liked to affront. He was a clean man. An awful lot of women ended up unlucky in their men.

May Violet Young (née Winch) (F) (84) (widow, husband dec. 20.7.99) admitted to IC 6/09 with general collapse / delirium / high fever / UTI, passed for rehabilitation 7/09 to Wd 7 then 8/09 down to Wd 5 (Geriatric) (slated for closure in 2/10 as per new NHS guidelines whereby future chronic-convalescence elderly: reallocation to community / family care). Post 7 months

UTI MRSA cycle: advisory meeting with NOK allocated "palliative care only" (though Mrs. Young was not aware this decision had been made for her, by her son Patrick Young, by her daughter Eleanor Bland, contact details for both on file, and by the sharp-nosed jumped-up peremptory little fellow who was the doctor, five foot five at the most, that was all, but whose mere appearance on the ward could make the nurses, the male ones too, scuttle about like a hutch of frighted chickens you could hear all the way down the ward.

Not that he scared May Young, she could see right through the likes of him, funny little chap who, in the very way he slammed his hand against the little plastic thing on the door with the stuff in it which gave out the antiseptic, made May Young want to say, at his disappearing back, in her most calm voice, foul words the like of which she had never said in her life, never even thought in her life, hadn't even known till then that she even knew existed).

Which was all proof, which all went to show, that May Violet Young (May Winch as was, till she married Philip that June day in '47, the river outside the church they got married in bright the length of itself with sunlight, and even the ruins themselves you could call the word beautiful then, with the grass growing and all the wild flowers nobody'd expected putting their pretty heads up all over the city) was not dead yet. She could prove for sure she was not dead yet because there, sweaty in the old claw of an old hand, whose old hand? *her* old hand, her own, go on, open it, proof: the balled-up tissue which held what she'd managed to get out of her mouth of the stuff they gave her to make her forget to remember the day, the month, the prime minister, make her drop her bowl with the custard in it, stuff which she had *not* swallowed, *would* not swallow, which she'd held under her tongue when the nurse, Irish-Liverpool, always a cheery word, gave her, and if it wasn't Irish-Liverpool it was Derek the male nurse, lovely boy from the Caribbean, with May nodding and sending them on their way with a friendly eye.

May was also not dead yet because she had seen the future,

and *their* future would not, while she had life in her, be *her* future.

Not Harbour House.

Well, she'd rather die, was the long and the short of it.

For in Harbour House (and even the very name was a lie, not even the ghost of a harbour anywhere near the place) she had, some years ago, visited a poor old lady. The poor old lady had been Mrs. Masters, and she was what you'd call a real lady, well-to-do, a long-time loyal client of Reading Flooring and Carpeting right from when Philip opened the business in '52. Philip had sold to her and through her to her friends too, for decades, the woven wool and rayon and nylon lines, the latex backing lines, linoleum lines, variegated yarn, the Danish, the short twist pile, deep pile, the cut pile lines, right up to the time of the hardwood and laminate. Thanks to Mrs. Masters, Philip had floored the quality's houses for years. Quality always brought quality with it. And Mrs. Masters was a fine clever lady, had been in Intelligence in the war.

May had sat in the Lounge of Harbour House with Mrs. Masters. She knew it was the Lounge because there was a sign, the kind you buy in Woolworths, stuck on the wall. It was cheap gold plastic and it said the word Lounge.

She had held Mrs. Masters's hand and had looked down as Mrs. Masters dozed, at the old lady's feet in their clean slippers on the carpeting of Harbour House.

The carpeting was an affront to those slippers. The carpeting was inadequate. It was patchy. It was none-too-clean.

In May's other hand she had a brochure she'd picked up at the front door. The brochure said that prospective Residents of Harbour House were *positively encouraged* to bring *one or two small mementoes* with them when they came, and that *the occasional (small) item of furniture* was also *permitted on request*.

Someone, just then, had put a hand on May's arm. May had looked up. A woman, not very old, maybe in her late forties and wearing a nice scarf, cashmere, asked her in quite a frank way if she wouldn't mind settling up.

May explained she was just visiting for the afternoon. She wasn't family or anything.

We accept Mastercard and Visa, the well-dressed woman said.

I think you'll find there's been some misunderstanding, May said.

Then the well-dressed woman took May by the arm quite firmly and led her through to Reception, pointing out where the décor had been done up and where it still needed to be done up and telling May how much the wallpapering had cost. At the front desk she took May's hand cordially, said goodbye, and then as she swept off up the stairs Harbour House's teenage receptionist had leaned over the desk, had made a face, had lightly touched her own forehead and had let May know that the well-dressed woman was an inmate (her exact word) who believed the place to be a guesthouse she'd run in her old life.

Ever afterwards May had berated herself for not having had the nerve to shout up the stairs after the well-dressed woman that she should sack that insolent receptionist first chance she got.

The longer-term outcome of it, though, was this. May would know she was dead for definite when she no longer remembered to think to herself: I would rather die and go to hell than wake up one day and find myself an inmate in that guesthouse of gone minds, gone things, bad carpets, furniture that needs permission.

For the well-dressed woman had been right about some things. There were things that did have to be settled up in a life. Mastercard, Visa, if only.

There was the rabbit. No amount of Mastercard or Visa would settle the rabbit May'd shot, got first time too, with Philip's old air rifle.

It was a wild rabbit that had taken to coming to visit the back garden. It wasn't even as if that rabbit was doing any harm. It sat and nibbled prettily among the flowers.

One day May had seen it there again and, without taking her eye off it, had stood in the kitchen and slipped off her shoes. She had backed away from the window and gone as quietly as she could through the first door, then the next door and into the garage. She'd persuaded the top off the rusty tin where Philip had kept the pellets. She'd cleaned the dust off the gun barrel with her apron and picked a fiddly pellet up and thumbed it into the little hole in the broken-open gun, then again with another, and she'd shut the gun and gone back through the house on quiet stockinged feet to the open kitchen window.

She held it, sighted it, pulled the trigger.

The gun didn't even kick. It was more a toy than a gun. But all the same the rabbit fell on its side, lay still on its side.

When she got her shoes back on and went out to look at it, it was still alive. She'd hit it in the fleshy part. Its furred back feet were neat one on top of the other. It lay in the soil of the flower-bed by the side of the lawn and it made no noise at all. It was as if it were dead. But when she looked down at it, it looked right back up at her, right at her with its brown eye in its head as if to say: well, you, you can just go and get lost.

You don't have to worry, Mum, Eleanor had said. They've recarpeted, it's the first thing I asked. They've actually recarpeted twice since the time of Mrs. Masters.

She meant well, Eleanor.

But May Young (who had stopped speaking out loud, and the blue of whose own eyes had iced over, the colour of them paler, behind a kind of frost on the day they'd told her, Harbour House when well enough, incontinent, probable onset of mild dementia, danger to self, the kind of looking-after that can't be done at anyone's actual home) thought to herself now that the leaving of life, when it came, might well be accompanied by a different seeing, maybe something akin to that rabbit's seeing.

That's what the babies did, after all, when they were born. They looked a look at the world as if they could see something that your own eyes couldn't, or had forgotten how to. That's what all three of them, Eleanor, Patrick, Jennifer, had done.

If the beginning was like that, chances were the end would be like that too.

Well, I'm in for it now, whatever it is.

Well, in for a penny, in for a pound.

Well, I wish, though, I really wish I hadn't done that thing to that rabbit.

Out loud? No. That girl who was in the room, whoever she was, hadn't moved. She didn't even glance up from her phone she was looking at or whatever the thing they all have in their hands and press the buttons on was. That was them these days, spending all their time looking up things on the intimate. The great-grandchildren, even, and them hardly past babies, spent their time on the intimate. It was all the intimate, and answer-phones and things you had to speak at rather than to. Nobody there.

Don't just say *nobody there* all the time when you phone, Mum, Eleanor said one day. Say, hello, it's me, then leave your message. It's distressing for us, it's distressing for the kids, it's distressing pressing the answerphone message button and hearing you on there, I mean seven times yesterday, and each time saying nothing but *the thing's not working* or *nobody there*. It's creepy, Mum. And the thing *is* working. Leave a message, like a normal person.

I say *nobody there* because when I phone up there's nobody there, May had said.

We *are* here, Eleanor said. We're just choosing not to answer the phone.

This beggared belief. What were phones for?

Why would anybody have a phone and then choose not to answer it? May had said.

Touché. That got her. Touché Turtle away! That was a turtle that used to be on TV, a cartoon with a French hat on like a musketeer that they used to watch, and Jennifer used to wear her old Wrens cap and play at being the turtle in the garden.

It's always Jennifer, was what Eleanor said once. She was angry. She was crying. This was years ago, ten years ago. May had made Eleanor cry by remembering something incorrectly. Eleanor was forty-five. She should have known better by then, a mother herself, with grown children herself, dear God and all the angels, than to have been standing crying at the sideboard about what got remembered and what got forgotten.

I know it was awful, Mum. I know how awful it was. But that time it was me. It wasn't her, it was me. It was me you painted with the paintbrush and the calamine. Nothing ever bit her. It was me who was always bitten. You said it was because I tasted so sweet. That's what you said at the time. Nothing ever bit her. It was always me who got bitten. I still get bitten. I still do. I'm still the one who gets bitten.

It was possible May had misremembered on purpose to annoy Eleanor. It was possible she knew exactly which child it had been, bare-backed, folded into herself like a paperclip on the little bed in the girls' room with the bites coming up red all over her shoulderblades and the tops of her arms, flinching away from the cold of the lotion on the bristles of the painting-by-numbers paintbrush.

That girl there on the chair looked to be about the age of Jennifer. She looked about the age.

Jennifer's dates: 4.4.63, 29.1.79.

They'd been watching an Alf Garnett film the night before on the TV. It had been quite a sad film for something supposed to be funny. Till Death Us Do Part. It was the film-length version of the TV programme. It was one of life's cruel ironies, is what Philip had said after, that that's what they'd been watching that night. January, taker of children into the ground. When she was two months shy of sixteen Jennifer's heart had had a problem in it that nobody knew about.

Such elegant narrow feet, she'd had. Like her father's feet. His feet, too, were narrow, that's where she'd got it from. Philip had had unexpectedly girlish feet, pretty feet.

Well, feet in the end all went the same way, six feet down, ha, and that was life.

You had to count your blessings, Philip always said. He always said it when he was disappointed. It was how you knew he was disappointed.

144

Well, it was all right for him. At least he had the words for it. May had spent the years considering the sharpness and smallness and perfection of the fingernails on the hands, the toenails on the feet of every grandchild born, with a sadness she did not have words for.

(Jennifer comes into the kitchen. She is eight years old and very angry. She is holding a book she's found in the pile of books on the table in the upstairs toilet. On the front it has a picture of a man on fire, his arms and legs stretched out inside what looks like a wheel of flames.

It is the most unfair thing I have ever heard of in not just the whole world, but the whole world and all the surrounding planets, Jennifer says.

She has been reading about people who burst into flames. The whole book is about people who suddenly burn to death there and then in their living rooms or wherever for no reason. Sometimes their legs and arms survive them and someone comes home and finds them in a pile on the carpet, nothing left of the main parts of their bodies but little heaps of ash.

Jennifer is near tears.

What if Rick was just playing football and kicking the ball and just as he was about to kick in a goal, just, out of nowhere—? Or Nor was doing modern dance like normal at the class on a Wednesday and then right in front of the big mirror, she—? What if Dad was fishing and he just, you know,—?

Well, then, the river would be the best place for him, May says. And it's not often you'll catch me saying that.

She puts down the iron and lifts Jennifer, who is clammy with anger, on to her knee on one of the kitchen stools.

But what if one day I came home from school, Jennifer is saying, and I went to make you a cup of tea, and then when I got through with the cup of tea, there was just a, a pile of ash on the chair, and there on the floor were your legs, and there on the arms of the chair were your arms?

Right. If this actually ever happens, May says, are you listening? These are my instructions. You are to just put the mug of tea in one of my hands there on the side of that chair regardless, have you got that? Because I'll be wanting that tea.

Jennifer nearly laughs. She is almost persuaded. Then she goes limp again on May's lap.

The water inside the iron on the ironing board makes a small impatient noise.

Jennifer, there is no way in a million you're going to burst into flames, May says.

It's not me I'm worried about, Jennifer says.

You've not to think about such things, May says. If you thought about such things you'd go mad. And the worst thing about worries is, they're contagious.

How are they contagious? Jennifer says.

What I mean is, if *you* worry, May says, then *I* have to worry too.

Jennifer looks desolate. She climbs off May's knee and goes and stands by the sink.

In the future, she says, I will keep my worries in the confines of my own head.

God and all the angels only know where she got that from. She is quite a child for the saying of things strangely. *It's my life too, you know,* is what she said in the middle of an argument they were having about breakfast cereal, and that was when she was barely four years old. May had had to turn round, turn away, so her child wouldn't see her laughing. And another time, last year, she'd just turned seven. *What if, when we're praying like to St. Anthony about things being lost, what if the being who hears us and sees us and helps us isn't St. Anthony at all but is Rascal the dog?* Recently too she's started refusing to take her mother's hand if they're crossing a road.

May pats her knee. Jennifer gives in, comes back and climbs back up. But her head is hot under May's chin, too heavy against her chest. The weight of her is sullen, maybe settling in for the afternoon if May's not careful.

The iron sighs on the ironing board again.

Could be quite good, mind you. If you burst into flames, May says.

Good?—if—? Jennifer says lifting her head.

Especially if you were on horseback, May says. You on that Shetland pony, what's its name, going over the jumps. You'll be all lit up like a bonfire on horseback at the Summer Fête at the Park.

Ha! Jennifer says.

Instead of the Hoop of Fire, May says, the police dogs would be wanting to jump through you.

Actually, Jennifer says, something like that would be pretty groovy.

She sits forward. But then she drops her head again.

What now? May says.

Because what if I was doing the jumping at the Fête and I looked up at the seats in the spectator stand for you to see me doing it, Jennifer says muffled against her cardigan.

Uh huh? May says.

And there was no you there, Jennifer says.

May nods.

Tell you what, she says with her mouth against the parting of her girl's hair. If I spontaneously combust I'll send my arms and legs by themselves to the park to watch you do it.

Finally she has made Jennifer laugh.

They'll need a seat each, mind, so that makes four seats. And you can pay out of your pocket money. That's only fair, May says.

Jennifer is laughing out loud now.

And I'm only letting you go to that Fête in the first place if you'll hold my hand when we cross the road, May says. And my other hand. And my arm. And my other arm. And my leg. And my other leg.

When Jennifer is properly helpless with laughter May shifts her legs like you do when you're playing the horsey game with a very small child, the bit where they think they're going to fall but know all the same that you've got them safe.

She catches her youngest at exactly the moment of letting her go.)

May Young eyed the strange girl there in the chair. The nails of both her hands were purple with varnish and far too long for properness. She was pressing the little buttons in the thing in her hand. It was as if the whole world was in thrall to the things. They all had them, used them as readily, as meekly, as May was supposed to take the stuff off the medicine cabinet. They swallowed it, hook and line. It was all supposed to be about how fast things were; they were always on about how fast you could get a message or how fast you could get to speak to someone or get the news or do this or that or get whatever it was they all got on it. And at the same time it was like they were all on drugs, cumbersome like cattle, heads down, not seeing where they were going.

The girl thumbed and fingered away at her own world in her hand like it didn't matter that she was in May's hospital room, or in anyone's hospital room, on earth, in heaven, wherever. It didn't matter where in or out of the world she was.

Maybe she was on a, what was it, scheme, a school scheme, the things they make them do instead of schoolwork, to visit people in hospital, to go and be visitors for people who got no other visitors.

But May had plenty of visitors. She'd no need for a girl on a school scheme. They were always endlessly coming, May's visitors, and standing about round the bed. She'd no need for strangers to do it too.

Maybe she was a friend of Patrick's girls and was doing a good turn for the Girl Guides, visiting an old person and getting a badge.

Maybe it was like when they came round singing to people in the hospital, like with the Christmas carols. Not just Christmas neither, because it was weeks after Christmas now and they'd been round again, they were round not that long ago singing their jolly song, on and on it went, interminable, about I am Jesus and they crucified me, and then they hung me up on a tree, all the details of the blood and the nails. It was January, nowhere near Easter. There was no excuse for it.

She lifted her hand and made to wave the girl away.

I'm not needing visitors, she said with her hand. You're free to go.

The girl in the chair saw May's hand move. She looked up from the thing she was holding in her own hand. She reached up to an ear and took the thing in her ear out.

Woke up, then, the girl said.

The girl spoke loudly and clearly.

May glared at her. She leaned forward. She wasn't some old lady who was always asleep with her mouth open, some old lady who couldn't hear.

She reached out for the jug and she didn't miss, she got it, by the handle.

Want me to do that? the girl said.

May looked her a stony look. The girl was clearly some kind of do-gooder, and if not, she was a thief. Well, May had no money in her purse. Her watch, in the locker, was worth next to nothing, £17 it had cost, at the airport once. The girl would soon find out there was nothing here for her to take.

May put down her hand on the wool blanket. It had the Kleenex with their medicine in it on the blanket. She opened the hand. She let the Kleenex go. The old hand lifted. It wavered towards the plastic tumbler. She got it. She brought it back to the jug and put the pouring place against its lip. She poured herself the juice. It went more or less safely into the tumbler. She reached and put the jug down, and not just down but in the right place.

Then she looked the girl in the eye.

That girl looked right back.

It is Mrs. Young, right? the girl said. If you're not Mrs. Young, tell me. I'm supposed to sit with a Mrs. Young.

She waved a piece of paper at May.

Please make sure someone visits Mrs. Young of twelve Belle-

ville Park, the girl said. If you're Mrs. Young, you took some finding, but we did it, we found you. That's if you're actually her,
like.

Now May Young knew who that girl was.

What Philip had seen, when it was his turn, was a man in a suit
standing at the back of the room. Hello, who's the chap? he'd
said, and May had turned and seen nobody there. May's own
mother had seen a man too. That man's back, she'd said. Where?
May and Philip had said, what man? May's mother was on mor-
phine. There, she'd said nodding towards the window, but he'll
not do any harm. May and Philip had looked. Nobody there.

So it was true. This was how it happened. They sent strangers,
not people you knew. They'd sent her a girl instead of a man in a
suit. They'd not sent Jennifer, because Jennifer wouldn't be a
stranger, but they'd sent her a girl the age of Jennifer.

May Young's head spun. There was no getting away from it.
Her number was up.

Ah well.

She closed her eyes.

Well, I can just go and get lost.

Well, it'll be nice to be accompanied, it will, to the other side.

Well, it's not so bad. There's fates worse than death.

Well, when your number's up, your number's up.

Well, call my number, St. Peter, and we'll see if it's Bingo we're
playing. House! As long as it's not Harbour House, dear God and
all the angels.

May Young breathed. She felt her breath move in her chest,
inside the awful pink below. She felt the long length of the deep
last breath she'd take. She breathed the length of it.

But then, the next moment, she breathed in again fine with
no problem at all.

Out. Then in again.

There was nothing wrong with her breathing.

She wasn't gone anywhere at all.

I'm dead but I won't lie down. Ha ha!

May felt immediately better. She opened her eyes fully. She

looked all round. There was no man in a suit anywhere in the room. There was just a girl. Right then the door of May's room began to open. A nurse! Quick! May sank back on to the pillows. She hung her arm over the edge of the bed so that the juice was near-spilling just in time. Irish-Liverpool came in. May Young was taking no chances. But the girl had seen. She'd reached to catch the tumbler. She'd watched as the nurse came in, and now she gave May a sly look.

May, you've a visitor this morning it seems! the nurse said. Another of the grandchildren.

The girl grinned at May. May looked at the Kleenex with the medicine in it, balled on the blanket. The girl saw her looking, turned to the nurse and smiled.

Yeah, she said. Just visiting Gran.

How are you doing today, May? the nurse shouted.

The girl reached forward as if to fold the blanket more neatly. She picked up the Kleenex. She used it to mop the little bit of juice that had spilled when May had slumped for the nurse's benefit, then she stood up and opened the big bin with her foot on the footpedal and threw it in. She sat down again.

What day is it today, May? Ah, is she still not talking to us? the nurse said. It's a pity. And isn't that lovely now, May. Just when you think you've met them all, there's more. Isn't life just a wonder of children and more children.

Lose your calm and you lose all. May let her head stay sagged and her eyes half shut. She made to nod like a person who had swallowed what she was supposed to would nod.

How was the bus, was it bus you came by? the nurse said to the girl.

She meant the snow.

The girl didn't say anything.

Not as bad as it looks out there, the nurse said.

She sat May forward and sorted the pillows behind her. She checked her for accidents. She announced to the room that May was clean, and that May was exceptionally good at keeping herself clean, and that it wasn't at all an easy thing to, and that May should be proud. She checked the clipboard at the end of the bed. She turned to the girl.

See if you can get her to talk, she said. We're all missing hearing her. I tell her all the time. We're all missing her wit about the place. And if you'd like to take her for a turn about the ward, or out and down to the café, just give me the nod. She's not been out of this room since Sunday. Do her good to see some different walls. Give me a shout and I'll sort out a chair and we'll lift her in and you can take her for a spin.

She was a kind nurse, Irish-Liverpool. She had the measure of the spirit of things. She knew there was more to an old body than an old body. But even so, May Young kept the sag in her jaw. She kept her head on its side. She kept her eyes half closed until the nurse, in a blur of uniform, went through the door and the door shut with a click. Then she waited another moment in case of anyone looking back through the little window in the door and seeing anything they shouldn't.

No, the nurse was gone, she could hear her, cheery down the corridor.

She shunted herself up the bed as best she could.

The girl watched her do it.

My grandad, the girl said. He had two strokes, one after the other, in six months. The second one affected his eyes, his seeing. So they said he wasn't to drive any more. We went to his house and my mum and dad took his car keys and they took the car out of his garage to our house, my mum drove our car home and my dad drove my grandad's car. Then my grandad was always on the phone shouting about how they'd stolen his car, sometimes in the middle of the night too he phoned about it. Then one day my grandad came down from where he lived in Bedford to where we live, we live in like Greenwich, he came by himself on trains and tubes and that, though he still wasn't supposed to be very well, I mean he walked with a stick and that, and he turned up banging on our front door with his fist though it's not like there isn't a bell, but he was like really angry, and he wouldn't come in, he stood on the doorstep all out of breath and held up this letter that said on it that he'd sat a test and passed it and he could drive if he wanted, and he put his hand out like this and demanded his car and his keys, and my dad just gave him them, there and then, and off he went in his car. And he drove it till he died.

And then after he died—this was like two years ago, by the way—we eventually found out he'd got this boy who's really good on computers to make up a letter, make it look like it was the kind of letter you'd get if you sat the test that said you could drive again. Like a really excellent forgery. The only reason we found out is because the boy came to my grandad's house when we were all there having the sandwiches and that, after the funeral. He lives across the road from where my grandad lived. He said my grandad paid him fifty quid which was ten pounds more than he'd asked for, and that my grandad had also said that if he died the boy could have his car for nothing for doing that letter. Then the boy put his hand out and asked my dad could he have the car keys. And my dad just went straight into the kitchen and took them off the hook and came back to the door and gave him them. There and then. And my mother was like furious. Don't suppose I can smoke in here, can I.

The girl stood up and went and had a look at the smoke alarm in the ceiling.

Could maybe get the cover off, she said. If it's worked by a battery.

She dragged the big visitor's chair over until it was directly under the smoke alarm. She climbed up on to it and balanced with one foot in the seat and another up on top of the edge of the high back. But because she was wearing boots the heels of which were like daggers, when one of the heels slid sideways on the cover of the shiny seat she lost her balance and toppled sideways off the chair, over the arm of it and on to the floor with her thin legs and the boots in the air.

How are the fallen mighty! May nearly said it out loud. She nearly laughed out loud. She pursed her mouth. She stopped herself. But the girl was a fine one, laughed at herself. She got herself up, dusted herself off, straightened what little there was of the daft little skirt and sat on the edge of the seat to unzip her boots. She was clearly going to give it a try again. She caught May looking at her.

A fall from grace, the girl said.

May liked that. She gave the girl a wink.

(May Winch is off-shift from the Mail Office and is at the Palace with some of the girls. They're watching the accompanying feature, a Gracie Fields. It's an old one, and people boo it to begin with since Gracie's recently taken herself off to America and people aren't very impressed with that. But it's a funny one, and soon people are laughing along regardless of the fact that Gracie's a bit of a runner-away.

In it Gracie is younger and wearing a big historical-looking hat. She throws an orange and it hits royalty by mistake. Then she argues with the policeman who arrests her, and she says to the policeman, *if you keep on talking to me like that I'll have to call a policeman*. Then the judge in court asks her did she think it was appropriate behaviour, throwing an orange at a person of royal blood. And Gracie says, *well, it was a blood orange.*

There's a dog somewhere in the theatre. It must have been smuggled in; dogs aren't permitted in the pictures. When Gracie starts singing a song and reaches a particularly high note this dog starts up singing along. AroooooOOOooo. Pretty soon the whole stalls is a riot every time Gracie hits the note and the dog joins in. Pretty soon it sounds like the people up in the balcony are rioting too.

The sound slows down suddenly and then stops. The film stops. Everybody shouts. The houselights come on. People are waving their arms about and shouting. The manager and the doormen walk up and down the aisles. There's a scuffle down at the front, then one of the doormen walks back up dragging two boys, one on either side of him, one by the ear, one by the back of the neck, then the other doorman carrying at arm's length a small wiry black and white Heinz 57 varieties mongrel, its tail going in circles like a propeller. The manager paces behind, ignoring all the eyes.

The place goes crazy with whistles and cat-calls. The chap sitting in front of May has turned to watch the parade go past up the aisle. Then his eye falls on May and her friends sitting there. He's in Air Force uniform, he's young. He's not bad-looking. He's with a girl but even though he is he still has a good look at all three of them and it's May that catches his eye.

His girlfriend looks none-too-pleased.

The film starts up again but not in the right place. The audience shouts and boos then settles down to the story anyway, a load of silliness about the prince of a made-up country giving up his kingdom to have a love affair with a barmaid who's a good singer. Gracie starts singing again and goodness knows what comes over May. It's as if she can't help herself. She knows she's about to do it, and she knows she's doing it only so as to annoy the snooty girlfriend. No other reason. No other time in her life so far has she ever been so bold and bad as she's about to be right now when Gracie does it, hits that high note, and May starts up a howl, making it sound as much like that little dog sounded as she can.

It's a split second before the roar of laughter shakes the whole place. Then everyone joins in. Soon the place is nothing but howling and yelping and laughter. May's friends are black-affronted. The girl in front is black-affronted. But the chap in front has turned again and had a long look, in the brightness that comes off Gracie on the screen, at May, who sits in silence at the centre of all the noise and roaring and whistling, smiles her pretty smile, then winks her pretty eye with all the knowing she has, at the silhouette of the boy who, she'll find out two nights later when she puts on her best dress, the blue and white one with the African trees and gazelles on it, and he's waiting there for her outside the Palace with the tickets for This Happy Breed already bought in his hand, is Philip Young, halfway through ten days' leave.)

There's an old song in May's head for some reason now. Sally, Sally, pride of our alley. That was what was her name, Gracie, Gracie Fields. And that was the thing about Gracie Fields, she defied belief, and then she showed you you'd been wrong ever to doubt her. You never believed she'd be able to hit that high a note. You could sense the note that was coming, the note that was meant to come, and you'd think to yourself there's just no way she'll ever reach that high, there's no way anyone could. And then she'd go and hit a note so much higher than the one you'd expected, like a whole ladder of notes higher, and you'd be left scoured like a clean sink by the highness of it. She was a classy one. She could sing like the women in the operas can. And she was funny too. There was the song she sang about the fly that washed its legs in a jug of beer and dried itself on a man's moustache, it was the fly's birthday in the song, and it took its lady friend to the Grand Hotel for a birthday treat. Oh, it was a funny one. There was a song about a clock that fell in love with a wristwatch and the wristwatch told him he was fast.

Sally, Sally up the alley, and there was Walter, Walter, lead me to the altar and I'll show you where I'm tattooed. We had fun, that was the difference between then and now. That was the intimate all right. I don't think I ever saw their father with his clothes completely off, and I don't think he saw me neither with mine, but we had the intimate all right, and we had fun. I don't see that there's so much fun in it, what I see of it now, May said in the confines of her head, not out loud, looking at that girl sitting there with the skirt that was barely worth the wearing. The girl was gloomy-looking now, for the alarm in the ceiling had defeated her. She picked at her purple nails. She got her little machine out again and picked at something on it. Oh they all think they're the first to discover it, they all thought, they were all convinced nobody'd known about it till *they* did, nobody could possibly know about it but them, with their flower-power, their nineteen-sixties with the flowers in the guns and their summers of love, as if all we'd had was winter, all we'd had was rations. Just very good at keeping it quiet, is what we were. We had to be. It was the way. Them with their jet-age.

There was Patrick, when it happened to him, coming home all doe-eyed and staring into mid-air over his sausages, then always in the shower and trailing the smell of that godawful after-shave all down the stairs, and going and standing breaking the rose off the stem out in the garden when he thought I wasn't watching, tucking the bloom inside his leather jacket for some girl and off he went to town, and Eleanor I knew about because she came home from college that time and she gave me such a warm cuddle, and it wasn't like her to take me in her arms like that, and I had a secret look at her and she had a shine to her so I knew immediately, and I *was* pleased for her, not that we could say any of it out loud, and not that I dared tell her father.

Not Jennifer, though.

Though what about him, that boy, that boy all along, the boy May couldn't look in the eye.

Even with all the years of that boy coming to see her and grow-ing into a man before her eyes, she could still see the boy in him.

But him turning up at the door every year couldn't help but mean another year had passed that May's own girl hadn't had.

The first year the knock had come at the door May hadn't let him in. The next year he did it again, same boy. That time May did let him in. She gave him a cup of tea. He always brought something. Chocolates, flowers, bulbs for the ground. Once he brought a little china figurine of a chaffinch. He'd noticed, maybe, how she liked them of birds, from the ones already in the cabinet. After he'd gone May had put it on the ledge at the back of the Hoover cupboard where she wouldn't have to look at it. Loyal as January. When he first came he had long hair, and a look about him of that boy who'd been in the film about Oliver, the artful one, not the little prissy one. They sat opposite each other, May and the boy, every year. He grew up, like her girl would have, before her eyes. One year he missed the day, but he sent a card from Canada written on in neat handwriting. Sorry I can't be there, kind of thing. It was the kind of postcard a man would choose, not pretty at all. On the front it said Toronto, above a colour photo of people walking in sleet, a snowy street of shops. Shops were the same the world over. But he'd paid for it so it would arrive at the house on the exact right date. It was nice of him.

One year, when it was nearly the day, she told herself she'd speak.

But when he came, she couldn't say anything.

All she could say was, Are you all right, then, son?

Fine thanks, Mrs. Young, how are you?

What else could he say? What else could they say?

I don't know how else, I don't see how else I could have been about it.

There had been nothing to do but put an extra biscuit on the side of his saucer, and tell him they were the luxury biscuits, and make sure he ate it, which he did.

She said all these things not out loud but in the confines of her own head.

For when May thought of her youngest child she saw her pure, fixed in time at the age of ten, no older, and enthralled thin-armed thin-legged on the rug in front of a brand new television watching her favourite programme in colour for the first time. Her favourite programme was full of clean untouched kids, shiny from being born well after the war, and they all lived in a scrap-yard full of old British junk and sang *see you next week* around the pole of an old London bus, and for the first time, a miracle, Jennifer saw the bus was bright red. For the first time the kids in her favourite programme ran about in unbelievable colour. They chased a little dog across a graveyard, they were trying to catch it for a lady in a sports car, and their colours were even more colourful against the graves and so on. The whole room smelled of new TV. Jennifer kept getting up and putting her nose to the place where the sound came out. *I'm just smelling what colour smells like.*

It was a blessing, thank God and all the angels, that Jennifer got to see colour before she went. Her brother and sister worked as a team for weeks, going through the new Radio Times every Thursday lunchtime at the dinner table and reading out the name of every single programme that had the sloped word *Colour* printed next to it; for weeks they did this, until May could stand it no longer and made Philip buy the new one, though the black and white one was still fine, went on working for years. But if Princess Anne was going to all the bother of getting married, the least they could do was make sure their children got to see history happen in colour.

All three of her children ran about in May's head in colour turned up too-high, on a throbbing green lawn bordered with throbbing yellow roses. They ran between the front garden and the back, appearing and disappearing from view like it was they themselves, running about like that, that gave grass and roses colour in the first place. It was a time when the smell of your clean child in your arms was a sort of dream smell, like when lime trees threw their scent ahead of themselves so you walked through it and by the time you reached the tree itself there was no smell left at all.

Jesus, Mary and Joseph, though, remember the smell in Patrick's house when he moved in with Ingrid! He must have no nose on him, Philip said when he and May came home from theirs with their own clothes all strange-smelling from the hippy burning sticks she had smoking away all over the flat. May had had to hang the clothes they'd been wearing out the back windows to air them and get the smell of it out afterwards. Ingrid was mad as a box of jackdaws, believed that God was in her crystals, and she kept them all arranged inside a cabinet. As if God was in a crystal and you should worship a bit of rock.

Well, there's definitely no God in that church you made us go to for years, Patrick said once.

Well, he was angry they'd been rude to his wife.

And he'd not gone to the church himself, not for years, not since Jennifer. Well, that was definitely understandable. I'd have believed in God if God'd done something about it, Patrick said.

159

But who or what lifted even a finger? Who sees the sparrow fall? Nobody. It just falls. She just went. Nobody saw. There's nobody there to see.

God is present everywhere, Mrs. Young, the young soft priest who'd just come to the church after the old Canon left, and who didn't know her from a million, said to her on the church steps. God is in everything.

Well, was God in the way there was no controlling your own bladder, your own bowels, any more?

Oh, it was blasphemous. She'd never get to the afterlife thinking a thought like that.

But was God in the way they told you *Harbour House, when well enough* so that you knew, by that, that something had made them blind to you? God was nothing more than a rhythm repeating itself in an old stone building. That's what God was in, if God was in anything.

Was God in the eye of that rabbit?

Well, you, you can just go and get lost.

Well, we're all just a heap of cut flowers on the ground at the end of the day.

Well, you can't make an omelette without breaking legs! is what Philip used to say.

Well, some go younger than others, it's true.

Well, I've had a much fairer innings than some that should've.

Was God in the eye of the January boy, the January man?

It was January now. It had been January for a few weeks.

May Young's heart gave a start. Then it went twenty to the dozen.

No, it couldn't be today, Jennifer's day, because the boy, the man, hadn't come.

But maybe he didn't know where she was. Maybe he had gone to the house and knocked on the door and found that no one was there, and had no idea where she was.

Well, he'd ask a neighbour, wouldn't he.

But what if something was wrong, something had happened to him?

No. If it was the day, she'd know, because he'd be here. He always came, without fail. Though just the once, he sent the postcard. But he always came. And he wasn't here.

But that girl was here, in the chair.

May levelled her gaze at the girl.

She needed her glasses.

She lifted her hand. The old hand on the bed lifted. She sent it towards the locker top, where the glasses were. But it missed, she knocked the hand into them by mistake, as well as into several get-well cards, and the glasses fell with the cards off the locker on to the floor.

She looked at the girl in the chair and she saw what youth was. It was oblivious, with things in its ears.

She lifted her hand. The old hand lifted and waved in the air.

The girl had her eyes shut.

May redirected her hand to the top of the locker. The hand came up against more cards from them all telling her to get well. It knocked them to the side. It found the box of tissues. It got its fingers into the open place, the hole where the tissues come out, and got a good grip on the box and got it over to the bed, there, and got an even better grip on it.

With all she had she made the old hand throw the box at the girl.

It worked! It hit her on the leg. The girl opened her eyes with a jolt and looked to see what had happened. She looked first at her leg and then at the box of tissues on its side at her feet and then at May in the bed.

What? she said.

May took a deep breath into the confines of her head. Then she did it. She opened her mouth. She spoke.

Look at all that hot water, running away like that.

It came out in a gravelly husk. It wasn't what she'd wanted to say at all.

Look at all the what? the girl said.

May tried again.

If someone had done the job right.

If someone had done the job, the girl said.

Wouldn't be happening.

Nothing's actually happening, the girl said. There's no water. I don't see any water.

May shook her head. The room swung.

They done the job wrong.

Okay, the girl said.

Terrible the waste.

The wrong things were coming out of her mouth by themselves. She shook her head at the girl again.

Okay, the girl said. We'll sort it.

Where's the cake?

You want a cake? the girl said.

You hold it and I'll cut it. Where's the plates? Where's the knife?

The girl put her phone thing down on the chair and went round to May's locker. She opened the doors and rummaged around. She took out a pair of shoes and put them on the bed. She took out a jar of sweets.

I don't see any cake. But I found these, she said.

She unscrewed its top. May opened her mouth like a child. The girl unwrapped a red sweet and put it in May's mouth.

May nodded.

The girl took one too. She took the sweets with her and sat down again on the visitor's chair. May sucked at the sweet. She nodded at the shoes on the bed.

Bad luck, that.

That was right. That was the first thing she'd said that'd come out right.

The girl got up, picked up the shoes again and put them on the floor under the bed.

I don't like pink.

The girl listened.

See, we were all supposed to hate her, think her a bad lot.

162

Because she ran away to America. But she had to, for her husband. In the war. Him being an Eytie from the Isle of Capri. And she didn't run away. That was a lie. She did her songs. She made a fortune. Enough money for a hundred Spitfires, they said! And the head German. The head German.

Like, you mean, Hitler or something? the girl said.

No, no. Weasel, he was. Little weaselly face. She was singing in France. The war effort. He gave the order, he said they were to bomb her hotel. Send a message. But they didn't get her.

Right, the girl said. In the war, yeah?

Yes, in the war! In Arras.

Is that a place? the girl said.

!

Ha ha!

The girl, amazed, sat in the visitor's chair and watched May laugh.

(May Winch is home on leave, cycling home in the blackout from the dance and there's no moon, but it's okay because she knows where the potholes are, it's like a game to miss the potholes and it's a game she's good at. But she rounds the corner on the stretch between the town and the village just past the crossroads where the signpost used to be and BANG the air itself becomes a wall, and oof she hits it, it all happens fast and slow, off the bike she comes and the bike goes one way and she goes the other, hits the ground side first, arm up to stop her head, then her knee and her thigh hit the road, and it takes her a jiffy to realize she's cycled into a warm flank, an animal, there, she can hear it go, it's run off too fast for a cow, must have been a horse, maybe a deer, the feet didn't sound like a horse, nobody's horse would be loose on the road like that. She sits herself up, feels her elbow, skinned, wet, bit of bleeding it feels like. She stands up, puts the weight on her knee. Fine.

She's fine.

She bursts into tears.

She walks the rest of the way home shaking.

It was the dark taking a shape, going solid out of nowhere in front of her. It wasn't like when the bomb hit the ball-bearing factory next door to the shop and she'd been blown across the room backwards and hit the wall behind her. That had been different. This had come out of nowhere and it had no sound, just the muffled thump of May being hit by the dark. The difference was that she'd just gone headlong with her eyes wide open into it, that she'd done it herself somehow, hit the dark.

When she gets to the fountain she gives her face a wash and dries it on her sleeves. At the front of the house she waits behind the hedge for a bit till she is calm, has sorted her face into the right face, for you need the right face to come into the house, for Frank, at sea, is already presumed, the word is, and has been for eight months.

Her mother comes into the hall. When she sees May her hands fly up to her face.

I'm fine! May says. Me and my bike hit a deer on the road. Fell on my arras.

That gets her upstairs without too much fuss, where she has a look at her elbow and her knee and they're not too bad.

The next day she's sore all over and the elbow is giving her gyp.

She walks back along the road and finds the bicycle, in the long grass in the ditch, and it's fine. She gets back on it. It goes fine, it's fine.)

He took me to London once, Frank did.

Who? the girl said.

On the Underground trains. The smell of all the dirty wool. I was only small, mind.

Right, the girl said.

I'm all washed up, me.

Seem like you're doing fine to me, the girl said.

Dog-tired. Been on the late shift.

Fair enough, the girl said.

But it's nice to be loved. Isn't it nice to be loved.

Telling me, the girl said and her face went sad.

The eyes of the men after war. Like rabbits in headlights. We all were. All them who never came back. All them going up into the air and then not coming down. A line through the name in the morning, Philip told me. And that was that. Well, we came through, Philip and me. And it was behind us, and we got married, got a family, got a new house, brand new. Never a house there before. Even the mud in the garden. Listen! Brand new mud.

But that girl sitting there in the visitor's chair wasn't listening, had a long face on her now. May lifted a hand. An old hand in front of her lifted in the air, wavered, then came down proper hard in a fist on the woollen blanket.

Cheer up, you!

(Jennifer comes into the kitchen. She is fourteen. She has the usual sullen face on. It is a summer evening and May is at the machine.

Jennifer, your shoulders, May says.

Yeah, because I'll need a straight back when we all die in a nuclear holocaust, Jennifer says.

May presses the pedal down on the floor and guides the material through beneath the needle. Now Jennifer has opened the cupboard, taken the top off a Tupperware box and helped herself to a handful of sultanas. At least she is eating something.

If you'd eaten your tea, May says. I need those for the scones.

Jennifer used to be so perfectly dressed. She used to be a model child. These days she is pale and thin with a miserable long face on her and wears such terrible old scruffy-looking clothes and leaves her hair a mess. May is forever telling her. Cheer up, you! It is her age. Also, she is hanging around with girls who are too old for her, the too-clever girls in the year above her at school, and spending far too much time with that boy, whose hair is too long and whose parents May and Philip don't know anything about. She is spending too little time thinking about school. You can't be a translator in Europe, which is where the jobs will be for people doing languages not science, without

165

proper qualifications. She is always going around the place with that boy, and if she's not with him then she's on the phone to him. She is fourteen. She is too young to have a boyfriend.

He's not my boyfriend, is what Jennifer says when May or Philip says this. He's my friend. I don't want a boyfriend. He doesn't want a girlfriend. We're friends.

She doesn't say it brightly. She says it darkly. She says everything darkly now, and she used to be so bright when she was a child. Her face has changed, got longer, hollow, as if adulthood has tried her on like a glove that doesn't quite fit yet, then pulled out of her and left her stretched out of her shape. Her shoulders are round because she never straightens her back. What she doesn't realize is that she'll never get on in life walking around with round shoulders.

Jennifer is behind May at the machine now, leaning with her back to the kitchen counter. She is wearing the terrible denim jacket. She swings herself up on to the counter like she did when she was a child.

If you scuff that cupboard, Jennifer, May says without turning round.

She can hear Jennifer's legs against the doors of the units. She's after something, that's for sure. Money? May ignores her. She presses the pedal down and pulls the material through. The cotton reel spins on the top of the machine. She puts the scissors down on the table with a slam and turns the leg of Philip's new work trousers round under the needle.

You know my friend, Jennifer says in one of the short silences between May's foot lifting off the pedal and pressing down on it.

What friend? May says.

He said this thing, Jennifer says.

May sighs.

He said when he was small, Jennifer says, and his grandfather was still alive, his grandfather would have him to the tunes off the soundtrack record he had at his house of the Mary Poppins film.

166

May presses the pedal down. The machine whirs. She takes her foot off again.

You mean, May says in the loud absence after the whirring noise, that his grandfather would have him over to listen to the tunes off the soundtrack record he had at his house of the Mary Poppins film.

She presses the pedal. The machine whirs.

When she takes her foot off again Jennifer speaks behind her.

Yeah, but that's not what he said, Jennifer says.

There is a silence for a moment.

He said it always started when the tune about I Love To Laugh came on, Jennifer says.

May presses the pedal. The little reel of thread on top of the machine spins like a mad thing. Jennifer slides off the counter and leaves the kitchen, swings out through the door with her hands in her pockets, whistling a tune. The kitchen door shuts behind her by itself.

May sits at the machine with her foot off the pedal and her head has something like a storm wind roaring through it.

When she next looks at the clock several minutes have passed.

She gets up from the machine and goes to the sink. She turns the hot tap on and she puts her hands under it. She leaves them under it until the water is too hot to keep doing it. She pats her reddened hands dry on a clean tea towel.

She goes to the back door and calls her husband out of the garage. Philip stands at the back door in the light summer dark. He sees her face and a look of alarm crosses his own. What? he says.

When Jennifer gets back in later that night from God and all the angels only know where, she is whistling the same tune she went out whistling earlier.

They see her through the window coming up the garden path, her hands in the pockets of the awful jacket, and they hear her come through the front door and make to go straight up the stairs.

Her father gets up and switches the television off. He calls her, asks her to come into the front room for a bit. She stops halfway up the stairs, then she turns and comes back down and does as they ask. Her father asks her to sit on the sofa. She does.

Why is the TV off? she says.

Is this about me whistling? she says.

Come on, *what*? she says.

They forbid her from seeing the boy again. Her mouth falls open. Then she says they can't forbid her because she and the boy are in all the same classes at school.

They forbid her from seeing him in the out of school hours. She shakes her head.

They forbid her from speaking to him on the phone. She says they can't do that, it isn't fair. They explain to her about trouble-making, attention-getting and lying. She crosses her arms and looks them both in the face and says they are being unfair. They tell her they are saying it for her own good, that people who tell manipulative troublemaking lies to cause a drama are not decent. She goes to say something but she decides against it. She stops herself. She stands up. She leaves the room, closing the door behind her.

May and Philip exchange glances. Philip gets up and switches the television back on.

May and Philip watch TV. Then they go to bed, when it's time to.

What happens next is that there is no talking to Jennifer for days. In fact, what happens is, Jennifer stops speaking. Jennifer won't speak. Morning, dinnertime, night, if she's in their company at all she sits insolent and silent.

Mealtimes are particularly difficult.

Then thankfully it all settles down a bit. Eventually it is like nothing ever happened. Nobody ever mentions it again.)

Nothing but shame, now.

What's a shame? the girl said.

What's a shame? May can't remember. All she can see in her head is a butterfly, but in the winter too, so no hope there, a butterfly out and about in winter's good as dead. What was a shame? She tried to remember. It must have been in the war, whatever it was.

A periscope on a torpedoed sub. It got dredged up, oh, forty years later it was. Covered in, in, that stuff that covers things under the water. Barnacles, you know, and the, the coloured stuff.

Like you mean coral? the girl said.

On the TV.

Wow, the girl said.

Oh the artfulness the sinfulness the wickedness of men. You'll fall and break your neck off the height of them boots, girl.

You're worse than my mother, the girl said, telling me what to do. And I don't even know you.

You've come for me. Eh?

I'm just here for the day, the girl said. You took some finding, but we found you.

The girl showed her a piece of paper with writing on it, but May hadn't her glasses and couldn't read the writing.

Uno Hoo.

What? the girl said.

Philip had bought May a camera for her Christmas once. It was the latest thing, a Kodak Disc, like a normal camera but a little round thing inside it instead of a spool. It didn't catch on; it wasn't long before it was hard to get the round things to take the photos on in the shops any more. But May still had it in its box in the top cupboard above the wardrobe. *Keep it alive. Keep it with Kodak.* Because it was a Christmas gift, it had a place on its cardboard box where you could write who it was to and who it was from. Next to *To* was May's name, in Philip's handwriting. Next to *From* he'd written UNO WHO, then crossed out with the pen the word WHO and written, under it, HOO.

UNO HOO in ballpoint now meant more to May than any camera.

Well, he went, and now it's me.

The door opened. The sharp-eyed nurse came in. This nurse

was the one who cleaned May too roughly. May slumped down just a touch too late, but this nurse wasn't a noticer, didn't notice a thing.

Visiting's not till two thirty, the nurse said to the girl. You're far too early. You'll definitely have to leave while we do the lunches in any case.

Okay, the girl said.

I'll show you where the day room is, the nurse said. It's at the end of the corridor, I'll show you in a minute once I've checked her over.

May winced.

Right, the girl said. No worries. Thanks.

The girl came forward with the box of Kleenex. She stood between May and the nurse and she took a tissue out. She wiped at the side of May's mouth with it, soft.

She speaking yet? the nurse said over the top of May's head.

Not a squeak, the girl said. She's pretty out of it.

After she said this she winked down at May like a pro.

Then the nurse went out into the corridor with the girl and the door swung shut.

Well, it's just what happens in a life.

Well, if I went to Harbour House, would Uno Hoo be what they call *a small memento*?

Them and their Harbour House.

Well, if they can't dispatch me to Harbour House, well, they'd not have cocked a snook at death then, would they? And then they'd be next. It'd mean they were next. Them next up. Next in line to the throne.

Well, they are.

Well, I won't slight them for their lack of kind.

Well, I wish them luck.

Well, truth's like the sun. Look right at it and that's your eyes ruined for life.

Well, it's time. It's time. It's time I upped and went.

. . .

When the girl came back in and no nurse with her, May sat up, ready.

Shoes.

What? the girl said.

Shoes.

You want your shoes? the girl said.

She bent down and picked them up from under the bed. May stretched out her arms. Two old arms stretched out in front of her. The girl put the shoes in the old hands. The old hands held them in May's lap, ready.

Come on.

Where? the girl said.

Come on.

You can't go anywhere like that, the girl said.

Where we going?

I'm only supposed to sit with you, the girl said. Nobody said nothing about going nowhere.

You've to take me.

Take you where? the girl said.

Not the Harbour.

Okay, the girl said. We won't go there.

Come on then. Where we going?

I don't know, the girl said.

You know.

I can't, the girl said. I can't do that. And what about your lunch? They're just doing the ward. It smells nice.

Well, after lunch then.

May was pleased about that. It was mince, it smelled like, today. The mince was good here.

After lunch then.

The girl went to take the shoes out of her hands. The old hands held on to the shoes as if the shoes were everything. May gave the girl a look so direct that the girl's face crumpled and changed.

Oh God. Okay, the girl said. We'll try. We'll give it a go.

After lunch. We're off.

171

Where, though? the girl said again. Where do you want me to take you? Home?

Where you come from.

Me? the girl said. Are you sure?

Never more sure in all my life.

The girl looked blank.

Then she got her phone thing out and fiddled about with it.

Hi, she said. It's me. All right. Yeah. Yeah, if you do too. Yeah, does that mean you're off then? Right now? Listen, that's great, because. D'you think you could do me a favour, can you pick me up? Yeah, ha ha. Brilliant. Yeah, but listen Aidan, not the bike today, can you bring the car? Just because. Uh. Uh huh. No, babe, listen. Yeah. Yeah, I'll send you the link. Well, whenever, really. Aw thanks, babe. Hour and a half. Right. I'll wait at, like. No, the door I came in is where the buses go to, it's where Accident and Emergency goes in, so just turn in there. Thanks. Yeah. No, I will, I'll be there. Okay. Love you see you wouldn't want to be you.

Not supposed to use them things in here.

Yeah but you won't grass on me, the girl said. You'll need a coat. Have you got a coat?

Anything but pink.

Do I tell the nurses we're going? the girl said.

Don't tell nobody nothing.

(Jennifer comes into the kitchen. She is nine years old. May is having a fly cigarette at the kitchen table since Eleanor, who is always going on about how smoking kills you, is out.

Mum, she says.

What now? May says.

No, listen. I need to ask you this question. What are human beings for? Jennifer says.

For? May says. What do you mean, for?

Jennifer hangs her weight off the door handle and swings off the door.

What's the point of human beings? I mean like what are we for? she says.

172

Um, May says. The point of human beings. Well. It's, it's for looking after each other. We're here to look after each other.

She is about to ask why Jennifer wants to know, but Jennifer is already gone, off through the door, already clattering up the stairs.

That night when May comes up to make sure the light's off in the girls' room, she sees a piece of paper on the top of the chest of drawers. It's in Jennifer's writing. She is always getting into trouble at school for her writing not being neat enough. May holds it up under the landing light and has a good look at it. WHAT HUMAN BEINGS ARE FOR. It's all right, the writing. It's not as bad as all that. And she gets good reports in all the subjects, so it's not as if neat writing is the be all and end all.

Then it is seven years later, a blink of the eye later. Jennifer has been dead one year exactly, to the day. May is in the kitchen holding a piece of paper with a child's handwriting on it. WHAT HUMAN BEINGS ARE FOR.

For having a good time RICK

For making the world a better place NOR

For looking after each other MUM

For building things that will last DAD

But because the thing she's holding in her hand, written in Jennifer's hand, is just a piece of paper in the end, nothing but a piece of paper, and because Jennifer's hand is what the word cold now means, and always will mean from now on, she opens the cupboard door. The top of the bin opens by itself when you open the cupboard door. Philip attached the bin to the door in a way that means it does this. He is handy about the house.

She folds the piece of paper again and she puts it in the bin. She closes the cupboard door and the lid, as she does, closes on top of the bin by itself.

Knock knock knock.

Someone is at the front door.

May answers it. She has to. Nobody else is in. It's a boy, standing on the doorstep. He doesn't say anything. Neither does she. They both just stand there. Then he holds something out for her to take and when she takes it he steps back on to the path. She steps back herself, on to the plastic runner over the carpet to keep the carpet good. She shuts the door.

She looks at what it is that's in her hands. It is a rectangular blue box wrapped in cellophane, a box of chocolates. Milk Tray.

She watches through the frosted glass in the front door as the blurred shape of him gets smaller, then disappears.)

I took her hand. It was cold to the touch. That was the worst, the very worst.

What's she saying? the bald man driving the car said.

She's just talking, the girl said. Leave her alone.

The girl was squashed into the back. May was strapped into the front. After Irish-Liverpool got her into the chair the girl had wheeled her down the corridor and they had both waved cheerily back at the nurses. Then the girl wheeled May straight into the lift and pressed down, and when the doors opened they went out past the place where the shops were and the people having the teas and coffees. The girl had taken off her puffy jacket then and had put it round May's shoulders and had run out through the main doors with almost no clothes on herself in the cold. She spoke on a phone. She lit a cigarette. She stood dancing from foot to foot out there. The cold came in round May every time the doors opened by themselves.

You'll catch your death.

Don't feel the cold, me, the girl said before the doors closed on her again.

The bald man wasn't wearing a suit.

Eventually he fixed the chair somehow on to the back of the car. He made a great fuss about it. He was an awful baby.

Can't see a fucking thing with that there, the bald man kept saying and squinting at his mirror when they were driving along.

She was in the hospital, Gracie, it was before she ran away to America, and she had a cancer down there, you know, nobody could say where, the place was not what you call mentionable, and she had to have an operation. And she nearly died from it, there was a fair chance she would. But in the newsreel she was there after it all, back on her feet, and she winked right at the camera filming her. Oh it was glorious. Right at the camera she winked. She'd come through it, she had. And there was one she did where she played a singer called Sal. That was where the song came from, the one about Sally. And in it she had to go to a posh party and sing to the rich people, you know, be their evening's entertainment. And she called the old rich woman Lady Tissue-paper, oh it made me laugh. And she taught this old rich woman to sing the words of a common song, and told her off for pronouncing the words wrong, oh it was so funny. I'll never forget it. And in it, I'll never forget this either, I'll remember it as long as I live, there was a girl in the story a bit younger than Sal, a bit naïve, and she was very poor, and her father drank, and his drinking and hitting her had made her act bad. Well, Sal, she let this girl come and live with her. Goodness of her heart, the girl had nowhere else, her father'd thrown her out, she was on the street if it wasn't for Sal. And the girl one day got angry with Sal all because Sal was kind to her. She started to act bad, break the plates and the little ornaments in the room. It's not like they were much. But they were all she had. And Sal stands in the room and watches the girl break all the precious cups and the things all round her. And she just says to her, you go right ahead, you break it. And here's my watch and all. You can have it, here, take it. Do what you want with it. Because I believe there's something that has been put in you by all that's happened to you and it's got to come out.

Doesn't half drone on, the bald man said.

Leave her, the girl said.

I went with Frank to the Palace and saw that one. My brother, Frank was.

Oh yeah, she was talking about him earlier, the girl said.

Did he lose his hair through carelessness? Here. You. Lose your hair through carelessness?

She means you, the girl said and laughed.

Me? the bald man said.

Like a convict. A concentrating camp, if you ask me.

It's the fashion, Mrs. Young, the girl said.

They were driving along the motorway and May was wondering which of the saints it was, she couldn't recall, the one who had carried the child on his back and walked across rivers and up and down mountains and kept it safe all the way, when she felt it happen, it all just slipped out without her being able to stop it.

Oh dear. Oh dear me.

The rich bad smell unfurled and filled the car.

Christ! the bald man said. What the fuck's that smell? What the fuck!

He swerved the car to the side of the road. He opened his door and jumped about outside the car in the sleet in the dark. In came the cold air round the smell.

Aw Christ, he shouted. Aw, my Mazda. For Christ sake, Josie.

The bald man cried. He stood in the sleet for a bit and he was crying. The girl reached forward to close the door because the cold was coming in and there was sleet on her jacket on May's shoulder.

Thank you, love.

Eventually he stopped the carrying on. He got back in the car. He shut its door and got it going again and pulled back out on to the motorway.

The roof above them slid back.

Close it, the girl said. She'll die of the cold. She's not well.

Yeah, well, what the fuck you think you're doing, what the fuck you're going to do with her anyway, I don't know, the bald man said.

The St. John Ambulance Portakabin at the crescent, the girl said. They'll clean her, they know about that stuff. Put the heating on. Aidan. Now.

And who's going to fucking well clean up my car, will the St. John Ambulance fucking Portakabin do that? the bald man said. Yeah, that's right, put on the heating and let the smell of her get right into the system so I never get rid of it. Fucking perfect. Thanks Josie. Thanks.

For all I know I'm dead and gone already.

Hand on my heart I wish you were. I wish you'd died before you put a fucking toe in my car, the bald man said.

Aidan, the girl said. She's old.

I'm not old.

I mean kind of relatively, the girl said. Aidan. Put the window up. Up.

I'll throw, the bald man said. I mean it. I'm going to throw.

It's only a stupid car, the girl said.

And where's she going tonight? the bald man said. Where are you going to put her? Who's going to take her, state she's in?

You're such a selfish wanker, Aidan, the girl said.

It was cold, when I took it, her hand. But she was a bold true girl when she was here, and she whistled away. She whistled away like a trooper.

You tell him, Mrs. Young, the girl said.

In the city the bald man parked and got out. He went to the back of the car and rattled about a lot. Then he came to the passenger side and threw something on the pavement that made a crashing noise when it hit the ground. He opened the door and stood well back. The wheelchair was on its side at his feet.

I'm not touching her, he said.

I'm going home for a shower, he said.

Don't phone me again, you, he said.

Thank Christ the seats are leather, he said.

The girl went somewhere while the bald man stared at May in his car in disgust.

Cheer up, you.

And you can shut your mouth, the bald man said.

Married, aren't you? Wife doesn't know, does she?

The bald man turned his back on her.

Just a kid. I know your type.

He didn't say anything. He stood with his back to her, tapping his foot on the pavement. The girl came back with two big men she'd found in a pub, one on either side of her. Neither of them was wearing a suit.

Phaw, one said and stepped back. Somebody's coming up roses and daffodils.

Told you, the girl said.

Careful, the other said as he lifted May out. No, I've got her, I've got you, love, no worries.

A while since I've been in a big man's arms.

The man holding her laughed.

A pleasure, darling, he said.

This man put her in the chair and the two big men went back to the pub. They crossed the road waving, laughing at the bald man and what had happened to his car. The bald man slammed the car door shut and locked the car with a key that made a beeping noise. He went without forgiving.

Known a couple like him in my time.

Bet you have, Mrs. Young, the girl said.

You be careful round him.

I can handle myself, the girl said. Don't you worry.

May sat in the sweet smell of May. She could feel herself all down herself, cold now, very unpleasant, all round and down her legs. The girl pushed her along the dark pavement, round a corner, and the road turned into a crowd. There was a great noise and a great smell of food, and there were people all over the place, standing and sitting around even in this cold. There were stalls, places you could get things to eat. It was like a circus, or a hanging. The place was mobbed. People standing in a queue parted for them so they could push through; the girl laughed and told May the queue was for the Portaloos.

Well, I don't need to go, now.

This we know, the girl said.

Where are we?

Greenwich, the girl said behind her.

Oh.

You said. You wanted to come, the girl said.

Did I? It's the Greenwich Fair, is it?

Could call it that, the girl said.

The girl pushed the chair up a ramp into a big hut with heaters in it. Oh, it was warm! A woman wheeled her through the back and there were sinks, with taps and all. There was hot water and things for cleaning people up in this hut. It was marvellous what was possible in a hut these days, and a kind woman washed her down with a showerhead and towelled her dry and there was baby powder too, in a cupboard in the hut. When the girl came back she'd brought blue pyjamas, with trousers, and a jumper and a coat and things.

Cut this thing off my wrist, will you, girl?

The girl found a pair of scissors and she cut the plastic thing with the date of her birth on it off. That felt better, it did. Then the girl wheeled her back through to the door of the hut where there was a chap sitting waiting. He was an older chap but he was quite a looker. He wasn't wearing a suit.

This is Mark, Mrs. Young, she said. He's the one who found you. He's going to take you to his house for tonight and make sure you're okay.

Not Harbour House.

She's scared of boats, the girl said.

I'm not scared of boats.

The man shook her hand.

Careful where you touch. Couldn't keep it in.

Understandable, the man said.

You're nice and clean now, the girl said.

The man was going to take her somewhere warm. It would be a pleasure, he said. He said he'd pick her up at the main road, if the girl, he called the girl Joe, would have her ready waiting at the kerbside so he could just duck the car in quick.

The girl wheeled May back out into the great crowd, through all the people. It was a great celebration. It was just like after the war. The girl stopped the chair and came round the front and bent down to fix the scarf round May's neck, make sure the hat was properly on.

What's it all for?

God, you smell loads better now, she said. You actually smell positively nice.

If it's got to come out it's got to come out. No stopping it.

The girl turned with one arm round May and pointed above the crowd, up at the backs of the houses.

See those windows? See that one in the middle? He's in there, she said.

The man in the suit?

He's not in a suit, not as far as I know, the girl said.

Well, I'm not dead yet, then.

You said it, the girl said.

<u>For 29 January</u>

Dear Mrs. Young,

I'm sorry not to be there in person this year, I'm in Canada on secondment and won't be home in the UK again till the end of February.

But am sending this card to say hello.

With best wishes.

I hope you are well.

Miles

fact is, London might not always be here! There have been times in the history of London that London practically stopped existing! Brooke stands next to the Shepherd Galvano-Magnetic Clock. She holds her sides. It is what you do when you are getting your breath back. Then she feels her jeans pocket to check for the Moleskine book. Moleskine books are notebooks that were famously used by famous authors like Ernest Hemingway and Bruce someone. She can feel the edge of the sticker Anna stuck on its cover. The word HISTORY is in her pocket. That is quite cool! For example there is when Queen Boudicca burned London to the ground which was to do with a tribe called the Iceni tribe and the uprising they were part of. If you were being witty with words that is what you could call what Brooke just did right now when she ran up the slope: up-rising. To be more literal she did it a moment ago and it took under a minute yip yip! Brooke Bayoude Fastest Runner In World Coming In Well Below 60 Second Mark. You can leave the word the out of Fastest Runner In World and in other places because it is a headline kind of thing and people will understand that the word the is there even if it isn't actually there. It means the word the is implied. But it would obviously have been a lot faster than 54 seconds if she hadn't had to dodge a lot of people. A lot of people have decided to visit the Observatory today due to it being the Easter holidays. The Shepherd Galvano-Magnetic Clock is a slave clock. A slave clock is a clock driven by a master clock, whose mechanism is elsewhere from the slave clock. The Shepherd Galvano-Magnetic Clock also has 23 hours marked on it instead of just the normal 12, like it is a double-length clock plus an 0 at the top where 12 midnight and noon would be, to make 24. It means that sometimes it is actually nothing o'clock. Nothing o'clock! What time is it? It's a quarter past nothing. It's half past nothing. Doctor, Doctor, I think I'm a clock. Well, don't go getting all wound up about it. Joke from the days before watch batteries and digital. Brooke's own watch is new. It is a Me To You watch. The picture on it is of a bear holding out a flower so that every time you look at the time it is as if the bear would like to give you the flower. It was from her mother and father on her birthday and it came with an actual bear that has been made to look like it is old though it isn't, it is new with a pretend patch sewn into its face with big stitches. This is because old-looking things are more lovable. The bear is called Tatty Teddy. 54 seconds is Brooke's first up-slope score (according to the watch) since she became ten. She has been ten for one day. She became it on Sunday 11 April. Ten on eleven April twenty ten. It will be particularly good next year because she will be 11 on 11.4.2011! Last year at school Brooke told Wendy Slater that there is a whole other range of numbers other than the usual ones that come after twenty-nine, that go twenty ten, twenty eleven, twenty twelve, twenty thirteen. Wendy Slater believed her and *altered her homework accordingly* is what the letter home said about it THINK YOU'RE SO CLEVER Brooke's class has had Mr. Warburton as its teacher now for two years. *There is no doubting Brooke's intelligence. Her verbal dexterity is notable and she is wonderfully imaginative and of course we do not have a problem with that or either of these things. But sometimes her infectious imagination can be vertiginous for her peers* THINK YOU'RE THE CLEVEREST vertiginous: makes you feel dizzy.

But the fact is, Greenwich, right now, with all the buildings down there that people come here specially to look at, and the towers that are from now, and the old buildings that are histori-cal, was once, way back in time, quite bustling and so on exactly like it is bustling today. But then out of nowhere and in a way no one could have predicted it all just stopped being bustling, not just when Queen Boudicca set fire to London and burned it down, but also when the Roman Empire began to not be an empire. Then, for some reason that is historical, London stopped being a port that was important—ha! the im*port*ant *port* stopped being im*port*ant. Greenwich was very im*port*ant back then, historians know now, because it had a temple and a shrine and so on.

The fact is, they found a coin and an artefact, or artefacts.

The fact is. The arte-fact is. Brooke bends down to do up her lace. The arty-fact is, there was a picture of a man's head on the coin, and it was one of the things they found that prove that a Romano-British temple was here once. The picture is of the head of Flavius Constans who was an emperor and the coin is dated the year 337 and then the history of Flavius Constans is that he was murdered in the year 350 which is actually only thirteen years after his head was on a coin! So people in authority should be more careful because having your head on a coin doesn't mean you are immune to history like people are immune to things they have been inoculated against by a doctor. Just because someone is in authority, for example in charge of you, and can get you by the arm when no one will know so that your arm afterwards really hurts, and shout in your ear, so loud so that it feels like a slap and your ear can feel the words in it for quite some time after, it doesn't mean history won't happen back to them.

The fact is, when someone shouts like that at you it is like a passenger-carrying hot air balloon filling with the hot air that's supposed to send it into the sky but instead it is being inflated dangerously fast inside a very small room so that its sides and top press against the walls and ceiling which means that either the walls and ceiling will have to give way or the balloon that is your head will explode. The balloon that is your head is metaphorical. This does not mean that it is not real. It is just a way of saying something that is difficult to say.

(Brooke's mother and father called her through to the kitchen. Her father was standing by the window, holding the two letters. Her mother was sitting at the table. She patted the chair next to her, which meant she wanted Brooke to come and sit there. Brooke stayed standing where she was at the door. She looked down and at the same time sideways at the letters out of the slant of her eye, because it is possible to look like you are looking down but actually be looking up. She could see the school letterhead on the top of one of the letters. Brooke, her mother said, we can sort out whatever it is if you tell us but we can't if you don't. We're not angry, her father said, we'd just like to know why. Brooke shrugged one shoulder then the other. Later, her mother took her in her arms and sat her on her knee. I know something's wrong, she said, I know my girl and I know when she's sad, we can't have this, your father is very worried. Brooke didn't say anything. Later, her father took her for a walk down by the river. Want to go through the tunnel? he said. Brooke shook her head. I thought you liked the tunnel, her father said. Brooke stared at the slapping brown surface of the water. It shifted about like thousands and thousands of little shoves. You've got to start behaving better, her father said, your mother is very worried, all this not coming out of your room, not turning up at school, where do you go? what's the problem? You can tell me. Her father looked at the water too as he said it. Then he said, or you can maybe tell your teacher, if you don't want to tell me THINK YOU'RE THE CLEVEREST WELL WAIT AND SEE MISS CLEVER-CLEVER WHATEVER YOUR STUPID NAME IS BECAUSE BEING CLEVER IN MY CLASS IS ALL VERY WELL BUT IT MEANS NOTHING IN THE REAL WORLD WHICH YOU'LL FIND OUT THE HARD WAY YOU'RE A LITTLE PIECE OF NOTHING YOU LITTLE PIECE OF SHIT then her father said, okay, imagine it isn't me asking you. Imagine you are here with your-self, only yourself is my age, she's old and wise and not nine any more, and imagine that you can say anything you like to yourself, about anything, and if you imagine that, then what would be the thing you would most need to tell her? Then there was a long time when nobody said anything. Then Brooke said, Dad? Yes?

her father said and his face was waiting and serious. I think actually I *would* like to go through the tunnel after all, Brooke said. Her father nodded. He took her by the arms and he swung her into the air and carried her into the tunnel dome. They went down in the lifts. There weren't very many people in the tunnel because it was the middle of the afternoon. He and Brooke did the whistling thing, where one of you goes way ahead of the other and then listens for the really good way that whistling sounds bouncing off the tiles down there, which is especially good when you can't see the person who's whistling or tell what direction the whistling is coming from. By the time they got to the other end and went up in the lift and patted the old one-eyed dog that sits on the grass at Island Gardens and looked at the view of the buildings and so on from the other side of the river, her father had forgotten what he was asking on the other side before they came down into the tunnel. So it was okay.)

So. So the fact is, at the end of the 4th century Greenwich was covered in the kind of plant life and so on that grows over the places no one goes to or uses. Probably there was a lot of ancient wildlife which came when that happened, the equivalents of frogs and hedgehogs and the kinds of things that come and inhabit wild places like on Springwatch on TV. On that programme they tell you how to make a wilderness in your garden so that live things will come and visit it or even decide to make their homes there. Some of them can be quite rare like the bird that is called a willow warbler which used to be widespread but now there are hardly any. But the point is, places that right now right this minute are places people go to in London and do not think twice about being in, can seriously just *disappear.* And if it could happen then it could happen now or any time, because there is a historical precedent, which is not the same as President Obama which is a different spelling though also a precedent of president at the same time! which is quite cool and witty when you think about it THINK YOU'RE THE CLEVEREST

the fact is, actually, it is okay to be clever. It is more than okay, to. It is cleverist, to be. Brooke Bayoude: Cleverist. CLEVERIST.

So all these people here today looking at Greenwich, London, and thinking that history is past and over, that all it is is grass mounds in the ground where the Anglo Saxon men were buried once with all the shields and the music of the spears, should look again. Just look! It is called the Observatory here after all! ha ha! There is a picture of a man at the front of the telescope book at home. The man who is from the year 1660 has his whole body covered in eyes that are open. There is an eye on his foot and an eye on his knee. There are some all up his leg and his arm, and one on his shoulder, one on his wrist and one on his hand. The hand with an eye on it is pointing at the sky, where another hand, without an eye on it, is coming out of a kind of cloud of light and words are coming out of the fingers of the upper hand. The upper hand! Joke. The man who is looking at the word-hand has open eyes on his stomach even. The eyes cover him like butter-flies would if butterflies ever landed all over you all at once. Imagine if your whole body *was* covered in butterflies and the butterflies were eyes, opening and closing their wings like eyelids and all seeing at the same time at different heights and angles. Would we see things from all their different sides at once? Would that make what we see have a different dimension inside our brains? In that telescope book there is also a picture of a Green-wich pensioner sailor from the old days hiring out his telescope to people and underneath the picture it says that probably the people are so keen to look through it because he has it pointed at Execution Dock. Because people actually paid money to a pensioner sailor to watch somebody be executed through a tele-scope! A person on Execution Dock would probably be being hanged, not guillotined, because the guillotine was not used in England although there was a way to execute called the Halifax Gibbet in England in history which was a bit like the guillotine. The point of the guillotine was that it was used so people would have a clean and quick death. It was popular in France, and 16,500 people were historically executed on one in what is now Europe where you go on the Eurostar to, in the 1930s and 1940s, though not since as far back as 1967 when the last person was guillotined somewhere. Brooke can't remember where. She will have to check her facts. The problem with reading facts on the internet and sometimes in books, is that sometimes you might not be reading the true facts.

The fact probably is, a man was sent to prison in France for slapping the face of the head of a person who had just been beheaded to see if the face was still alive after the head was cut off!

The fact probably is, too, that in Halifax you could be sent to the Halifax Gibbet if you stole thirteen and a half old pence, and Halifax is not very far from York, where there is a house where a lady lived who was pressed to death by big stones. Brooke knows this because she has visited the lady's historic house where there is a museum.

But the fact is, how do you know anything is true? Duh, obviously, records and so on, but how do you know that the *records* are true? Things are not just true because the internet says they are. Really the phrase should be, not the fact is, but the fact seems to be.

The fact seems to be, someone tried to blow up this very Observatory right here in 1894! It is a fact, apparently, that he didn't damage the Observatory but instead he just blew his own stomach out right here in this park! There was a hole where his stomach should be and one of his hands exploded off, when the bomb exploded in that very same hand he was holding it in, well, the moral of the story is, don't hold bombs in your hand, duh obviously. In fact a two inch piece of bone from inside the hand was found near the Observatory wall after that man died but the Observatory itself was not damaged by it or anything. Brooke puts her hands where her own stomach is and feels for what she can't see inside herself. The man was apparently still alive when the people found him, and he could still speak apparently. Doctor Doctor, I feel a little empty inside. Doctor Doctor I really need a hand. !!! No, but it will have been really horrible. That man, therefore, could have literally actually in reality basically reached his own hand through the hole in himself and out the other side (meaning the hand he still had, obviously, not the one that got exploded off). So that is what history is, people and places that disappear, or are beheaded, or get damaged or nearly do, and things and places and people that get tortured and burned and so on. But this does not mean that history is not the unseen things as well. As an example of this: from up here you can see some of Greenwich—but not all of it. You can't see all the people who still don't know what in fact in reality has happened, still waiting there outside for Mr. Garth to come out or not come out. They are invisible for the simple reason that the place and the people are behind the trees and buildings so you can't see them from here. It is a matter of perspextive. You can't see the theatre, or even its roof, where the man called Hugo who was there the first night Mr. Garth shut himself in is doing the monologue. A monologue is a play with just one person in it. The title of the actual play is Miles To Go Before I Sleep, because Miles is Mr. Garth's first name, although all the people outside call him Milo. It is meant to be about Mr. Garth and what is happening inside the room.

(The man called Hugo was sitting there on the stage when the audience members came in and sat down. He sometimes waved to them and sometimes acted like they weren't there. When the play began, you couldn't tell that it had begun, and then suddenly it just had. He did a lot of talking to himself and to the audience about how he had shut himself in the room because he wanted to be an actor and be on TV and the Stage but he had Failed in his life. There was a lot of sitting in the play, and some standing up, and then sitting down again. He sat on the bed and spoke, and then he stood behind a chair and spoke, and then he sat on the chair and spoke, and then he sat down on the floor and spoke. There was a great deal of speaking. He had pretend long hair and a pretend long beard like a wizard. He did not look anything like Mr. Garth. Brooke and her mother and father went on Friday night. It was an Alps of boredom. Brooke fell asleep in the second half. Then Brooke and her mother and father were on their way out of the theatre and they met Mrs. Lee who goes to see it every night and matinee because she has something to do with it. She told them for ages, again, about how realistic it all was and how she went and stood on the stage sometimes before or after the audience was allowed in and imagined she was in the actual real room in her house, and sometimes she could actually believe that she was, that's how real it was. She told them again how the people doing the play even sent to Amazon.co.uk to get some of the very same DVDs that were in the actual room, with the same pictures on the covers, to make it be true and lifelike. He doesn't look anything like Mr. Garth looks in the room, Brooke said. Well, none of us knows for sure, do we, Brooke? Mrs. Lee said, and the performance, every night, virtuoso! Mrs. Lee shook her head as if there was something she was looking at that she couldn't believe. It was kind of you to put the tickets aside for us, Brooke's mother said, especially with the run being sold out like it is. Then Mrs. Lee spoke some more about how the play was transferring soon to a real theatre. This *is* a real theatre, Brooke said. You enjoyed the play, didn't you? Mrs. Lee said to Brooke. I found it weary, stale, flat and unprofitable, Brooke said. Mrs. Lee laughed. A bit over her head, Mrs. Lee said over Brooke's head to Brooke's parents. It is so not over my head, Brooke said. We all enjoyed it very much, thank you, Brooke's mother said. We certainly did, Brooke's father said. Then the Bayoudes said goodbye to Mrs. Lee and left the theatre. They stood outside and waited to cross the road. Virtuoso, Brooke's father said. Virtue so-so, Brooke said. Her parents laughed so much that she thought about saying it again but people tend not to laugh so much the second time you make a joke. It wouldn't be virtuoso of her if she did. It would actually be a bit virtue so-so if she did! Why is the theatre always sad, Brooksie? her dad said taking her hand as they crossed the road. Joke or do you really mean it? Brooke said. Joke, her father said. I give up, why is the theatre always sad? Brooke said. Because the seats are always in tears, her father said. It was a good joke when you knew that it was about the other spelling of the word tears: tiers. Tiers: rows of seats on a slant.)

The fact is, Mrs. Lee's husband isn't living at the Lees' house any more. Josie Lee has to go to Bloomsbury to visit him since that's where he's moved to. Hugo who is in the play now lives in the Lees' house because it is so close to and handy for the theatre. Is that a kind of history too? She will write it in the Moleskine. But history usually only records the Abbots and Kings and the Dukes and so on fighting over who gets to own a park like Greenwich Park and who gets put in jail because someone else wants what they've got so just sticks them in the jail and leaves them to rot and goes and takes it. But that doesn't mean we shouldn't record all the histories. On the contrary.

(Take One-Tree Hill, for instance, Anna said when she gave Brooke the Moleskine for her birthday. Look how many trees are really on that hill. Lots more than just one tree. Look at Queen Elizabeth's Oak. We all know the story, or we can find it out really easily if we don't know it, about how it was already old and hollow when Queen Elizabeth the First sheltered under it when all of a sudden she was caught in the shower of rain. And we know that it only finally fell over about twenty years ago, when the people who decided they were going to conserve it stripped off all the ivy then found out, when they did that, that it was that ivy that had actually been holding it up in the first place, and then while they tried to fix it into place forever with a piece of metal they knocked the tree completely down by mistake. Ha ha! Brooke said and Mr. Palmer laughed too. They all laughed for ages. It was funny. What if Queen Elizabeth the First had been there and had seen those things happen? Off with their heads, probably! But think of all the other trees in the park too, Anna said. They all have histories.)

The fact is, every tree that ever lived or lives has a history just like that tree has. It is important to know the stories and histories of things, even if all we know is that we don't know.

The fact is, history is actually all sorts of things nobody knows about.

(One evening about suppertime Brooke was worrying about what would happen if the walls and the roof just fell in, the ceiling just collapsed on top of you. Instead of worrying, she took the book down off the shelf, The Secret Agent by Joseph Conrad. It was about Greenwich and the man blowing himself up in the park! Then Brooke found this thing: from p63 to p245 in this particular book there were pencil circles round certain words. Ostentatious. Transcendental. Ergo. Maculated. Physiognomy. Propensity. Pensively. Finessing. Brooke went through to the kitchen. Why did you put circles round some of the words and why did you choose these particular words to do it to? she asked her father. Her father was doing something with a packet. What words? he said. Brooke held the book up open at page 63. Her father put the spoon and packet down and flicked through the book. Interesting, he said. He looked inside the front of the book and showed Brooke where someone had written in pencil the price £2.50. Yep, he said, it's second hand. Second hand! this was funny. First: because of the clocks and watches at the Observatory in the museum which have second hands, and second: in a sort of weird way because of the man with the hand that exploded off his arm. First hand. Second hand. It'll be whoever owned that book before us, he'll have done it, her father said. Yes, but it could have been a girl or a woman who owned the book before us, Brooke said. Very true, her father said. Which do you think it was? Brooke asked. I don't know, her father said, there's no way of knowing. There must be a way of knowing, Brooke said. She did a little dance leaning on the table. Her father gave her back the book. He began reading the side of the packet, which was something to do with rice. Unprecedented. Intimated. Brooke went back through to the front and sat on the rug and made a list on a piece of paper of all the words with pencil rings round them. Pristine. Unscrupulous. Then she went back through to the kitchen. What shop did this book come from? she asked. Her father was looking worried at the cooker. He always got rice wrong. I don't know, Brooksie, he said, I don't remember. That was unimaginable, not remembering where a book has come from! and where it was bought from! That was part of the whole history, the whole point, of any book that you owned! And when you picked it up later in the house at home, you *knew*, you just *knew* by looking and having it in your hand, where it came from and where you got it and when and why you'd decided to buy it. But dad, why do you think a person who first owned this book would have circled these exact words? she said. Her father was holding a saucepan under the tap but not turning the tap on. Hard to say, he said. Augment, Brooke said. She flicked further through the book to find another one. Emulation, she said. They're easy to say. Her father laughed. No, I didn't mean it literally, he said, I meant it's hard to say why he, or she, did it. Ah, Brooke said. Maybe the person was circling the words he or she didn't understand or know the meaning of, her father said. Yip yep, Brooke said, that is a possibility. She went back through to the front room. She climbed up on to the sofa, balanced on her knees on its high back and reached down the big dictionary. Expedient: suitable or appropriate. Coruscation: glittering, a sudden flash of light. Augment: to increase, make larger. She knew already what lucid meant. Then she looked at the list of words on the page to see if the person who had circled them was maybe making a code out of, say, their first letters, because the book after all was about spies and spying, at least this is what it said in the writing on the back cover that it was about. Tempppf. Or maybe the code was hidden in their last letters. Lodyyyyg. That one looked a bit like the language called Welsh.

But the fact was, in reality, it was a mystery as to what had happened with this book and why. It was something Brooke would simply never know and she simply had to settle for that fact, her mother told her a couple of nights later when she was in bed and thrashing about and pulling up all the covers, and couldn't sleep at all for the very much wanting to know. It was her third night of not getting to sleep because of it. It was nearly 2am. Count backwards from five hundred, her mother said. Count sheep. But it wasn't that kind of a not-sleeping night. It was a different kind of not-sleeping from the kind where all the dead people from history line up instead of sheep, looking with sad long faces and queuing for miles and miles at a gate too high for them to jump over, so many there's no way you could count them. Queuing for Miles! it would have been good if all these people went and queued outside Mr. Garth's window and not at the end of Brooke's bed! all the people who died in Haiti when their houses fell on them, just collapsed out of nowhere, and all the people who died in the tsunami, who got swept away, children as well, and the people whose aeroplane crashed into the sea, and the boy who was ten who was executed because he stole a loaf of bread because he was hungry, and the boy who was stabbed to death outside a school just because he was black, and the girl whose body was dug up in a back garden who had been murdered by the man, and all the people killed in the wars in Afghanistan and Iraq and Darfur and Sudan, and they were just the ones at the front of all the people who had died when they weren't meant to in all the other historic wars, and even the children who had died because they were being made to work in factories or clean chimneys in Victorian times or who were executed to death for things like stealing less than fourteen pence. You don't need to say executed to death, her mother said then, because to death is implied in executed. Her mother was getting impatient. But the Secret Agent awakeness about the words was a much more annoying kind of awakeness. There was no one to say sorry to in the Secret Agent awakeness. The person who somebody should be saying sorry to was Brooke! for making her not be able to know what the answer to why the words were chosen was! Brooke had to decide, her mother was saying now, again, that if she wanted to read that book and not be annoyed by the not-knowing, she would either just have to persuade herself, right now, to put up with the not-knowing, or she would have to make the active decision to rub out the circles that made the words stand out for whatever their unknowable reason was, and then she'd be able to read the book without it annoying her. Brooke put her head under the pillow. It defeats the purpose, she said under there. She wondered if her mother could hear what she'd said from under the pillow. Her mother was saying something. Brooke couldn't hear properly. She took the pillow off her head again. My special eraser from the office tomorrow, her mother was saying, the really good one, will that do? Thank you, Brooke said. It will have to do. Her mother kissed her goodnight and switched off the light and drew the door over. But inside Brooke's head what she thought as she closed her eyes knowing she would not sleep, was: it will not do. She opened her eyes and saw the ceiling above her.)

The fact is, Brooke is the six hundred and seventy-fifth person clicked into the Observatory today by Mr. Jackson with the people-counting clicker which it is his job to hold. Sometimes when Mr. Jackson is in a bad mood he won't tell you which number you are. Today he is in quite a good mood. Well, if it isn't the London Eye, he says. Where've you been? I haven't seen you in weeks. It is quite busy here today, Mr. Jackson, she says. School holidays, he says. Tends to have that effect. You're number 675 since my shift started. Brooke says goodbye and thank you. Then she weaves in and out through all the people who are taking photos of things and past the place where the Flamsteed Well was.

The fact is, the astronomer called Mr. Flamsteed dug a hole that went directly down into the ground 40 m, which is a really substantial depth, and lay on a couch down there to look up at the stars because he thought going as deep down as possible would be a good way to see as high as possible. But it was very damp down there so it was not an ideal way to do it. Brooke passes the last remaining bit of the Herschel Telescope, which the Herschel family all sat inside one New Year because the telescope was actually big enough for them to sit in, because the astronomer called Mr. Herschel believed that the bigger the telescope the further up *he*'d be able to see. When the family of Mr. Herschel's ancestors sat in there because the telescope was now no use to anyone and was dismantled, there was actually enough room for them to eat their New Year supper and then they even sang a song inside the telescope! Which is quite cool. Looking through a telescope that big would be like looking at the sky through the Greenwich Foot Tunnel. Telescopus: far looker CLEVEREST when they first invented them people were pleased because it was an invention that would be really useful in wars, like CCTV now CLEVERIST this is Brooke's name in Morse code: Dash dot dot dot. Dot dash dot. Dash dash dash. Dash dash dash. Dash dot dash. Dot. There is a multiple of dashes right at the middle of Brooke's name. How do Vikings send secret messages? By Norse code. Brooke dashes past the pretty bushes and up the steps and in through the place they sell the guidebooks. The girl called Sophie who works behind the counter waves hello and shouts, where've you been? It's been so long! We were beginning to think you'd moved away! No, I still live here, Brooke shouts and waves back. The woman Sophie is working with does not smile because she is one of the kind of people who don't talk to children. It is a quite good museum as museums go, though the museum in York, which is near the town where Brooke used to live, has actual old streets downstairs in it with shops with things from the past for sale in them and horses that were once alive. There was a young lady of York. Whose pet pig was made into pork. Though she cried, oh, you've minced 'er! They still all convinced 'er. To eat up her pig with a fork. That is one of the limericks she made up with Anna and Mr. Palmer on Friday morning sitting on the wall, the day Anna gave her the Moleskine a couple of days before her birthday and wrote the word History on the sticker in her really nice handwriting. Thought that would cheer you up, Anna said. And I'm officially assigning you the job of Historian. The history of their limerick writing that day is that it was much harder to get Greenwich to rhyme with things but in the end the limerick about it was funnier because of that. There was a young lady of Greenwich. Whose dad said be home before tenich. When she missed the last bus. Her dad made such a fuss. She was never allowed out againich. Mr. Palmer is really good at limericks. Mr. Palmer and Anna have gone now. You won't miss us, Mr. Palmer said. You'll be back at school in a few days. Today is Monday, there are six days of holiday left after this day THINK YOU'RE THE CLEVEREST LITTLE PIECE OF it means Brooke will wake up with hope in her for six more days. And when she goes back anyway things will have changed and she will not be cleverest. She will be *the* Brooke Bayoude, Cleverist.

The fact is, it is Spring and a lot warmer than it has been though it is still quite cold for April. Brooke wonders if the old lady who died in March is cold in the ground, or if Spring coming means it will be warmer for her down there. But that thought is a lot of nonsense because dead people are dead and can't feel. It is funny peculiar to think of her down there wherever it is that they put her in the ground in the town she lived in. The people came to take her to a hospital and she died in the ambulance on the way. Money doesn't matter, she told Brooke one day. She was holding Brooke's hand. It was when she still recognized Brooke. It was before she stopped being able to recognize people. All sorts of things we think matter don't, she said, so long as you don't wake up in the morning with no hope in you. Now Brooke has the note that Mr. Garth passed under the door which meant Mr. Palmer went and found the old lady's house and asked the neighbours where she was and they said hospital. Brooke got the note from Josie Lee, who Mr. Palmer gave it to, and is going to conduct an interview with Josie to ask her about when she went to the hospital and everything, because it is part of the history of what has happened, and then Brooke will write the record of it. It is a historic document. It is dated December 29 2009. It is sellotaped across two pages of the History Moleskine and Brooke has left blank pages round it. It says in Mr. Garth's writing: *Hello. I'm hoping it will be possible for someone to visit and sit with Mrs. May Young, 12 Belleville Park, Reading, for some of the day on 29 January, on my behalf. Very grateful for your help. Thank you.* Brooke also has the very first historic note Mr. Garth pushed under the door. It is not dated. *Fine for water but will need food soon. Vegetarian, as you know. Thank you for your patience.* It is on the first page of the Moleskine. She has all the The fact is notes. They are not dated either. She is going to sellotape them in. In a minute she will go and sit somewhere and look through the book and choose exactly which page the sellotaping-in of them will start.

The fact is, the Morse code for Mr. Garth is — — • — • /— — • •

— • — • — • • • • *and the Morse code for your first name Miles is*
— — — • • • — • • • • • •

    The fact is, there was a London Bridge first built in 1176. It took 30 years to build it. It lasted until 1831. It was over a thousand feet long

    The fact is, a light year is the distance that light travels in a year

    The fact is, that the sun will definitely die and there is nothing we can do about it, but it will not be for quite a while yet and definitely not in our lifetime so there is no point losing sleep over it

    The fact is, the moon is 238840 miles from the earth

    The fact is, the Hubble Ultra Deep Field telescope can reveal stars in a sky when it looks to the Naked Eye like there are no stars in it

    The fact is, the Hubble Space telescope was launched in 1990. It is made of a tube that has a mirror at each end

    The fact is, there was a telescope maker in history who was a woman her name was Mrs. Janet Taylor

    The fact is, the author of the book called Robinson Crusoe had a brick factory where bricks were made that were used in the bricks that made the Greenwich Hospital

    The fact is, the atomic clock that has replaced all the clocks at Greenwich doesn't keep exact time because it still loses a second every 20000000 years

    The fact is, that the plaster they used in building St. Peter and St. Paul is partly made of horses hair

    The fact is, there were whales that got stuck in the harbour in Greenwich in 1273 and in 1658. A fisherman threw an anchor from his boat at the one in the 1600s and it went right through the whale's nostril

    The fact is, bats always fly to their left when they fly out of caves

    The fact is, rabbits like to eat liquorice

    The fact is, deer know about weddings and about who you will marry

The The fact is notes are all in her own handwriting except for the one which is in the shape of the paper plane and is addressed to Brooke. Anna looked at it before she left and she said that it was definitely Mr. Garth's writing, though Brooke could pretty much tell from the other notes. It is totally the wrong size for sellotaping into the Moleskine and might need a book or a place of its own in which to be kept. Anna left this morning and so did Mr. Palmer, but they said they'd be back again and they would want to read the final history when she was finished it and they gave her their email addresses. What do you call a Scottish cloakroom attendant? Angus McCoatup. Joke. Anna is from Scotland. The photo queue out in the Observatory yard, for people who want a picture of themselves standing on the Prime Meridian, is pretty long today. Is the Prime in Prime Meridian the same Prime as the Prime in Prime Minister? The election of the new government is next month so all the news and papers are about who looks best on the TV. All the candidates say that they are the man who will win. Even so, nobody knows who will win. The future can't be seen, not even at an Observatory. Observe a Tory! Joke. According to her mother, the Tories, who have not been in the government since way way back in the twentieth century before Brooke was born, are something to do with history repeating itself. Brooke stands with the toes of both feet on the less visible piece of Meridian, behind the silver structure thing. There is a lot less courtyard space on the east side of the Meridian than there is on the west. I am on the border, she tells herself. She imagines a man like the one at the airport when they came back from the conference her mother was at in Rotterdam, who asked them to step to one side, then to step into an office, and who left her, her mother and her father there in the bare office with the cameras in the ceiling, the table and two chairs (although there were three people including Brooke, though she is a child and so possibly did not fully count) and the screen thing that looks like a mirror but which is a secret wall people can look at you through, and they had to wait for two hours and forty-five minutes and were then let through and were never told the reason why they had to wait. There. She has done it. She has stepped across and hasn't needed to show any proof of who she is! And again. She has stepped across again and no one has even noticed. She can do it again, and again, back and fore. She is invisible. She is a Free Agent. She jumps over the line from side to side. A lady in the queue laughs at her and films her on a little camera. Then she gives Brooke a thumbs up, as if the film she has taken is a really good one. Brooke waves at the lady. She imagines herself on one side of a border waving and laughing at the people on the other side of it. They are the people who can't and aren't allowed to cross it. Then she puts a foot on either side, straddles the divided world. Roll up! See Divided World Held Together By Small But Impressively Strong Ten Year Old Girl Brooke Bayoude Speedy Enough To Run Up Observatory Slope In Under 60 Seconds! That is a sentence full of implied the's. Roll up: a kind of cigarette that Josie Lee sometimes smokes. But it is also a phrase people used to shout in the olden days to make people, for example the public, be interested in coming to see something fascinating and maybe pay good money. Roll up! See executions of people who are not yet dead! Then Brooke sees a man over at the Talking Telescope fishing in his pockets for a coin for putting into the slot. Roll up! See Man Saved From Wasting Money In Talking Telescope By Speedy Ten Year Old Brooke Bayoude! She is over there in a ji (a ji: less than half a jiffy). Excuse me, she says. The man stops. He turns and looks at her. I just wanted to let you know that the Telescope is a bit truculent and will sometimes eat your money and then not actually speak, Brooke says. The man looks at her like she isn't there. He puts the pound in the slot as if she hasn't spoken. He presses a button. The Talking Telescope voice that comes out is the German one. Brooke is polite. She waits till the voice ends. Then she says: In my opinion you were lucky this time. The man steps down from the little footplate and goes off towards the shop. Possibly the man doesn't understand English, though that is very unlikely since German people can mostly speak English a lot better than English people can speak German. Possibly he did not recognize the word truculent and was therefore put off the rest of what Brooke was saying. Truculent: Brooke can't remember exactly what it means. She draws an imaginary pencil circle round it in her head to remind herself to check later. The Talking Telescope's German voice is male. Its French voice is female. Its English voice is male. Is France more female than Germany and England, or was there only a lady French speaker there and no men who could speak French the day they were doing the voice recordings? It is much more worth it putting money in the machine which gives you a printed-out certificate that proves you stood on the Prime Meridian and says the date and the time to several digits for example, if it was 14.29 when you stood on it, it would say 14.29.1234 on 12 April 2010, so that you know the fraction of a second pretty exactly, and also you have something you can take home with you and you can even write your name on in the space left for the name above where the certificate tells you about the crosshairs of the Great Transit Circle Telescope and Longitude 0°. *That* is what Brooke calls worth it. Whereas even though it talks in all those languages, all the Talking Telescope tells you about in its languages is stuff you can see really obviously with your eyes without needing a telescope to. Then it even tells you to go and listen to the other Talking Telescope round by the statue of General Wolfe. It is a waste of money just to be told to go and listen to another Talking Telescope which also tells you to go and listen to *this* one in the Observatory yard tell you to go and listen to *it*! Brooke puts her eye to the dark little circle which only lights up if you put in the money, and then only sometimes. I SEE NO SHIPS. That was what Admiral Nelson apparently is reputed to have said historically when he put the telescope to his blind eye and because he did the English won the battle. That was shortly before Nelson died on the deck of the ship and said Kiss Me Hardy to Thomas Hardy the famous author. When they brought Admiral Nelson's body back from the battle in a barrel of brandy or another drink like brandy, there was a queue of people to see him lying in a state and the queue was probably about the same size as the one outside the Lees' house watching Mr. Garth's window. The Milo Multitude, her mother calls them. The Milo Masses. Newspapers call it Milo Madness, Milo Mania, Milo Mayhem. Brooke doesn't think she is in any of the photos the newspapers have printed, though there are some people in some of them that she recognizes, also on the Milo footage on YouTube of when the blind in the window moves a bit and of visitors' Milo Days Out there are loads of people she knows. Roll up! Roll up! Come And See Invisible Man In Room!

The fact is, ha ha! all those people outside the house and watching YouTube and reading the papers or looking on the net don't know what the fact about Mr. Garth really is.

(They're back again, then, her mother said on Friday afternoon when you could smell the smell of people all crushed together again and hear the noise as you came towards that part of the town. Her mother sighed. Why did you sigh? Brooke said. I feel for them, her mother said. For all of them together or for each and every one of them singly? Brooke said. Sort of both, I think, her mother said. Then she said, you're feeling a bit better yourself, aren't you? What I am feeling is irrelevant, Brooke said, but if you *are* feeling for all those people, that is an astronomical amount of feeling. It is an Alps of feeling, her mother said, and what you are feeling is never irrelevant, and I feel an Alps of feeling about that too. There was a bit of shouting from the Milo Masses: Milo, Milo, Never Come Out! Milo, Milo, Never Come Out! and Milo, Milo, Come Out Now! You Are Needed Here— And How! The two shouts mixed into one single noise, like the noise of a small football match. Her father was in a bad mood that day because he had looked up the news online and had read the word Entertainment, and then underneath there had been a piece of news about people digging in a forest for the body of a woman who has gone missing. This had put him into the bad mood. He kept saying the word Entertainment, like the word made him feel sick. Then he said again, like he is always saying, how he felt the Milo Masses were here because TV and the internet were full of nothing but humiliation. God, her mother said, one cheers up then the other goes down in the dumps. I can't win. All those people, her father said. It's terrible. They're here because they feel so disenfranchised. What is disenfranchised, again? Brooke said. It means you don't have a vote, her mother said. So all the people outside the house outside Mr. Garth's window feel like they are not allowed to vote in the election? Brooke said. I kind of mean it more metaphorically than that, her father said. As if *metaphorically* they are not allowed to vote in the election? Brooke said. Exactly, her father said. Mum, Brooke said. Uh huh? her mother said. What is metaphorically, again? Brooke said. An Alps of feeling, her mother said, that's metaphorical. To describe something indescribable you sometimes translate it directly into something else, or join it with something else so the two things become a new thing, so an Alps of feeling lets you know the size, the huge amount, as big as a range of mountains, of the feeling. But it doesn't mean it isn't a *real* feeling? Brooke said. Sometimes, her mother said, it's the only way to describe what's real, I mean because sometimes what's real is very difficult to put into words. Brooke memorized the word. Metaphorically: another way of describing what's real.)

The fact is, today the crowd outside Mr. Garth's room was so big that it was the kind you can get carried along by in a direction you don't really want to go in. Roll up! Come And See What Can't Be Seen! The people sitting and standing and playing the guitars and eating their lunches on the big plastic mats that stop the grass becoming mud are back. The foodstalls are back. The Milo Merchandise stall that Mrs. Lee organized is back, with the T-shirts and badges and flags saying MILO-HIGH CLUB and SMILE-O FOR MILO ;-), and the Milo Little Ponies for if people bring children. There have been flashing cameras at night for the last few nights, but the crowd has been being good because the police always move in if the crowd is too rowdy. There were TV cameras there this morning because there are two more women who are claiming to be Mr. Garth's wives, though there are always people pretending to be Mr. Garth's wives, and after they'd been filmed having a fight about who was the real wife the two wives went walking round the crowd arm in arm. There are TV cameras most days now. There are cameras from America, and there were some French TV people who came for the debate they had before the last time the police moved everybody on, when France was saying that France had a person who had shut himself in first, before Mr. Garth did, so Mr. Garth wasn't the real original. Also the Psychic who wears the hat and gives people the Milo Messages is back. The people who light the candles and tie ribbons and teddy bears and other things to the fences at the bottom of the gardens under Mr. Garth's window are back. The people with the banners that say Milo For Palestine and Milo For Israel's Endangered Children and Milo For Peace and Not In Milo's Name and Milo For Troops Out Of Afghanistan are back, and probably the man dressed as Batman will be back too who tries to get up on to the flat roof and put his banner up under Mr. Garth's window. The lady will probably definitely be back who goes round asking everybody how much of Jesus do you need to see to believe in him and who gives out the leaflet with a picture of lambs and the rainbow and the children holding hands. She is always telling people they will die and go to hell unless they do as she and Jesus say. She is always asking Brooke will Brooke help her give the leaflets out.

(Be polite but demur, Brooke's mother said. Mum, Brooke said, if you can demur. Uh huh? her mother said. Her mother was frowning. She was working at her computer in her office, doing admin, which is short for administration, which is short for migraine-stimulant. She stopped typing and looked up, looked over at the arch of the window where Brooke was pretending to tightrope-walk the edge of one of the big stones in the floor. Then surely you must also be able to mur, Brooke said. I mur with you about that, her mother said. Brooke curled on the flagstones laughing at the word mur. Her mother came over and tickled her until they were both lying there on the old stone floor, laughing helplessly. You and me, her mother said when they got their breath back, we just made up a word. We so did, Brooke said. Her mother sat up, nodded, ruffled Brooke's hair, got up off the floor and went back to the admin of phil and lit.)

The fact of the matter is, Brooke spoke to a lady this morning who had paid the Psychic man the £30 for her special channelled message from Mr. Garth in the room. Brooke asked the lady what her special message was. The lady smiled a smile like she knew a secret. She said she couldn't possibly tell anyone what Milo had meant to say only to her. Then Brooke asked her was she sure, could she know for sure, that the message came from Mr. Garth *in the room*. And the lady said she was surer of that than of anything else in her life. But that lady doesn't know. That lady has no idea, like everybody else way way out of the loop, because first, everybody who knows anything knows that Milo isn't Mr. Garth's real name. And second, anybody who is anybody in this history knows what the real fact is about Mr. Garth, the one that was making Mrs. Lee cry on the stairs yesterday because all the badges and the T-shirts and the caps and key rings and the inscribed Easter eggs that she organized and invested thousands and thousands of pounds in will soon maybe not be worth money any more.

(No one must know, is what Mrs. Lee said yesterday when they found out. Josie Lee went to get her a Valium. What do you give an elephant who's cracking up. Trunkquillizers. Joke. It happened yesterday morning. Brooke went in and Mrs. Lee was crying on the stairs. Brooke went all the way up the stairs. The door to the room was open. So Brooke gathered up the The fact is notes, they were all piled neatly up on the sideboard under the clean knife and fork and under them all was the paper aeroplane with the story on it that begins The fact is, like it is a kind of The fact is note! and with Brooke's name there on the wing of it when she turned it over. She could not see, anywhere in the room, the story she did for Mr. Garth and put under the door on Friday lunchtime, about the journey through time (at the end of which Brooke has given it two endings so there is an alternative). But there did not seem to be any other bits of paper left in the room. Brooke put the ones she'd found, which were hers because she wrote them in the first place, and the plane which Mr. Garth made and wrote on, which was hers to take because it is addressed to her, inside her jumper and tucked her jumper into her belt. Then she came back down the stairs and stood behind Mrs. Lee, who was crying like anything even though she could go and stand in the real room now any time she liked. No one can see by looking, can they? is what Mrs. Lee was saying. No one can tell from the outside, can they? she said wiping her eyes, taking the glass of water and drinking it so fast that she nearly choked.)

The fact is, Anna knows. Josie knows. Mr. Palmer knows. Brooke knows. Mrs. Lee has sworn them all to secrecy but it is the kind of secret Brooke decided she could tell her parents, so Brooke's parents know too. But if all the people outside knew, it might make them feel even more metaphorically like they can't vote in the election. Plus, Mrs. Lee is not the only person who will lose money and maybe some people will lose their jobs because of it, like the Psychic, who has been giving out messages as usual all day yesterday and all morning today like nothing has happened, to all the people paying him, all the people queuing outside his tent with the sign on it which says Personal Messages From Inside: £30.

The fact is, the room is completely totally empty and nobody is in it!

The fact is, Mr. Garth has gone.

History Of What Brooke Bayoude Thinks About While She Runs Across Park Towards University: Brooke is thinking about a joke about Madonna taking her babies that she has adopted from Africa to Oxford Street so they can be reunited with the clothes they made before she adopted them. It is funny, the joke, when you think about the babies shaking hands with say a cardigan with no hand in it, or a blouse giving the babies a big hug because it is so long since it saw them, but it also makes Brooke feel strange in her stomach. It is like the feeling when she reads a book like the one about the man in the park with the bomb, or thinks a sentence, just any old sentence like: the girl ran across the park, and unless you add the describing word then the man or the girl are definitely not black, they are white, though no one has mentioned white, like when you take the the out of a headline and people just assume it's there anyway. Though if it were a sentence about Brooke herself it would have to add the equivalent describing

213

word and that's how you'd know. The black girl ran across the park. It is like in Harry Potter where it says about Angelina that she is a tall black girl and that's how you know that fact. On the internet it says on one site that there is a reference to a character being black in one of the first Harry Potter books and that this was edited out of the UK copies of the book but left in the copies of the book that got sold to readers who bought it in America. But that fact might not be true, because it is only a fact on the internet.

But the fact is, I am Hermione too, Brooke thinks as she runs across the grass.

The fact is, I can be Hermione if I like. I can even be old-fashioned characters like George out of the Famous Five. I would not want so much to be the one called Anne. I can be Bobbie in the Railway Children book, though they went away from London and I have come to it, but I can still be her if I want, and work out how to stop the train accident from happening. I can be Cinderella. There is more than one tree on One-Tree Hill! The girl ran across the park. Girl Runs Across Park! The girl is Brooke Bayoude, Cleverist. *The* Brooke Bayoude. I can be Snow White if I like and duh obviously I would never be stupid enough to eat the apple, no one would. I can be Anne of Green Gables. Her hair can be the colour of mine if I like.

The fact is, in history a man went down in a kind of machine he invented called a bathysphere to see what colour it was under the sea. There was only one colour, and it was blue. The man wrote about it and he sounded like it made him be very depressed that there was only blue under there. But now they have lights they can take underwater, though before it would have been candles and obviously that would never work. Imagine walking into the sea with candles! Ha ha! But with the lights that they can take underwater nowadays the fish are all darting about in their real amazing colours, orange and yellow and cyan. Brooke Bayoude runs through the gate of the park and down the street. She is running into the past. She is on her way to the place where the man is about to lower his bathysphere into the water. She will shout, Stop! She will say, Look, I've brought you these. They are From The Future. Try going down with these fixed on to the front of your bathysphere and see what you will see! It will be like bringing to under the sea the light there is when you go through the railway station at St. Pancras whose roof is all made of iron and glass, and wherever you are going, even if it is nowhere, just to one of the shops to buy a sandwich, the way the blue of it comes in from above makes you look up really high at the roof and then makes you look again at everything else beneath it.

History Of Education Part 1: Brooke runs past the Stephen Lawrence Building. It is a building named after a boy who was historically murdered. If something is in the past, can it still be in the present or not? It is a philosophical question. If you travelled to the past to make the future better, would you actually be able to? She runs past the library, which has the plaques built into the wall inside where all the people paid money to buy "beds" for old retired sailors, because a lot of the university was once where the old sailors who had served their country well at sea came to live when they were old and had no homes, if they had not actually died in wars. The plaques are not really beds, they are nothing like beds, they are just plaques, dedications, like for dead people. They says things like: Hamilton Canada bed. Lloyds Bank bed. Lloyds bank rupt! ha ha! Joke. One of them is from a man's mother, in memory of him. It says he died in HMS Pathfinder in 1914, which was historically the first year of one of the World Wars. One plaque says this thing: "They were lovely in their lives." It means the dead people. The dead people were lovely in their lives. She runs past the building her mother's office is in. Her mother's office is a room where a sailor once slept! More than one sailor, to be precise. Outside above the doors to the corridors it says, painted on the stone in the arch, things like Britannia 46 Men or Union 46 Men, which means 46 men could fit into the number of rooms there. Outside in the corridor of the philosophy department there is a little table, and someone has put some good things for playing with on it, like a plastic rabbit standing on top of a drawing of a spiral and a game called Fuzzy

Philosophers where you can use a magnet pen to drag iron filings and put hair and a beard on a bare face. She passes the path you take if you're going to the Painted Hall. In the Painted Hall there is a painting on the ceiling of a lady who is meant to stand for Africa and she is very pretty and on her head she is wearing a hat shaped like the top of an elephant's head. Joke: a man is standing in the middle of the road. He is spreading elephant powder around. A policeman comes up to him. The policeman says: Excuse me, what do you think you are doing? The man says: I'm spreading elephant powder all over this street. The policeman says: There aren't any elephants around here. The man says: See? You can't beat elephant powder. She runs past the huge globes on the top of the main gate of the university. They look like they are wrapped in string, like huge balls of string. But actually the string is meant to be longitudes or latitudes, or trade routes maybe, or maybe it is trade roots, Brooke will ask.

(Mum? Brooke said. I'm really really busy, Brooksie, I'm really having to concentrate, her mother said. Her mother had her worst face on. She was doing an application about funding. What is the application you are doing about? Brooke said. Um, her mother said. It's for a project we're calling Tecmessa. Teck mess a, Brooke said. Uh huh, her mother said, she's a character from tragedy. Tragic application, her father said. It's about which you would choose, her mother said, if you had the choice of these: you can enjoy a really lovely treat yourself, but because you do someone else somewhere will have to suffer. Or: you can choose to suffer with somebody who's also having a really difficult time, but because you do, the suffering will be easier for that other person. Okay, Brooke said, can I have some time to think about it before I have to decide? Definitely, her mother said, much better to think about it than not. How long have I got? Brooke said. Ha ha! her father laughed from the sofa, that is the question! And, mum? Brooke said. Mm hmm? her mother said with the leg of her spectacles in her mouth. Did you hear about the optician's son? Brooke said. Which optician? her mother said. He made a spectacle of himself, Brooke said. Ha ha! her father said. Oh for

God sake, her mother said. Terence, I need to work, take this child out. Brooke, I need to work, take that father out. But mum, but can I just ask this one thing? Brooke said. *What?* her mother said. What's a slave clock? Brooke said. Her mother sat up. Then she sank back into her chair. A slave clock, she said. The Shepherd Galvano-Magnetic clock is apparently a slave clock, Brooke said, but what I want to know is, what exactly is a slave clock? Oh, her mother said, a slave clock, well—. And what I also want to know is, if something is in the past, Brooke said, can it still in any way be happening now? Is the past present in the present, her father said, and is the past present in the future, good questions, Brooke. They're philosophical questions, her mother said. Are they? Brooke said. Is a rose red in the dark? her father said. If a tree falls in a forest and there's nobody there to hear or see, does the bear excrete in the woods and is the Pope a National Socialist? Oh God, her mother said. Now, don't go bringing God into it too, her father said, cause then we're really into a whole other World Cup match.)

History Of Religion: Brooke waits at the lights and then crosses to St. Alfege's, which is said out loud like St. Alfie's, regardless of how it looks when it is written down. Philosophy is actually quite easy. She will perhaps study it when she is at university, if she does not become a person who sings in musicals like on Over the Rainbow on Saturdays on BBC1. She runs round to the front of the church. The door is open. The church is empty. Inside she looks up, like she always does, at the painted wooden unicorn rearing his front legs. Unicorns are imaginary. She looks at the picture of General Wolfe in the window. He was something in a war. Then she goes to the table with the historic photocopy on it of the Viking axe head which was once found in the Thames and is from the 11th century, and is now in the British Museum. That makes the British Museum kind of like a sort of river too, full of things that have been found like that in, say, real rivers. The axe head is supposed to be like the one—in fact it might even, it is actually possible, be *the* one—which a kind man who had been baptized by St. Alfege used to kill St. Alfege after a Viking brained him with the head of an ox and pretty much killed him, just not outright. So the kind man hit him in the head with his axe. *Moved by piety to an impious deed* is what it says on the bit of paper under the photo of the axe. The axe blade looks really blunt and rusty. What happened was: Alfege was a man who decided he didn't want any wordly possessions so he went into a monastery in the 11th century. But the monastery was too full of wordly possessions so then he became an anchorite in a bath, or maybe in Bath. Whichever, so many people came to ask him things, because he was so religious, that he stopped being an anchorite and founded a monastery of his own, and once on his way to somewhere in Italy he was attacked by robbers but the robbers while they were attacking him heard that their village was burning to the ground, and it only stopped burning when they stopped attacking Alfege. Then he was Archbishop of Canterbury (like the author Samuel Beckett who was stabbed to death on the altar) and he converted a lot of Danes. Some of the Danes he didn't convert took him to Greenwich as their prisoner and they put his feet in irons, the historic kind not the clothes kind, and locked him in a cell full of frogs which was apparently geographically right here where this church is now. The story goes that he conversed with the frogs and the frogs spoke back to him miraculously as if they were all old friends. And even though he could miraculously communicate with frogs and even though he could miraculously burn down places and also miraculously cure a lot of bad stomach problems the Danes had, the Danes still wouldn't let him free unless someone paid them a lot of money, and no one, not even one of the people who had come to speak to him for advice when he was an anchorite or anything, would pay his ransom for him, so one night the Danes were having a feast and they started for entertainment just throwing the bones they were eating at him, and one of the bones was the whole head of an ox. But after he was dead, he carried on causing miracles, like if a dead stick was stuck in the ground and sprinkled with his blood, then the stick when you looked at it the next morning would be covered in leaves. There is a book in this

218

church over by the organ keyboard for people to write things in. Today it says *Please help dads friend Tim rest safely in hevean because my family and I miss him much Thanks God Amen. God, please pray for my mum and close friends, for them to stay healthy and be happy Thank you for all the nice things happening in my life. Pray for me to stay in good health thank you. Sat 3rd Dear God—Please help MARIO RINGER be calm / patient whilst he is at home awaiting for his broken ankle (which has been pinned and plated) to be mended Thank you.* There it is, the pencil lying longways down the middle of the pages. It is a red one and it says on it Longitude 0° 0 00. It is one of the kind they sell at the Observatory. Brooke knew a pencil would be here. It is why she came into the church. There is nobody else in the church. She is just borrowing it. She turns while she is putting it in her pocket and pulling her jumper over the top of it and pretends while she does this that she is looking at the famous keyboard which is in behind glass or perspex so no one can play with it. It is called a console. This is funny, if you think of a computer console, and also because of the word that means make people feel better. She reads the history of it next to the console on a notice: *This eighteenth-century console came from the organ when it was rebuilt in 1910. Experts believe that some of the octaves of the middle of the keyboard are almost certainly from the Tudor period and therefore likely to have been played by Thomas Tallis and the princesses Mary and Elizabeth when they were living at Greenwich Palace.* Brooke can imagine them really easily. It was before the Princess was the Queen and wore the red wig and had rotten teeth that went black, and wore so many jewels that she could hardly walk. It is from when her hands were small and were young hands. It is quite easy to imagine her. What is much harder is to imagine all the hands of all the people who will have played this console but who the notice doesn't mention. There must have been some. Brooke imagines just anybody's hands playing on the old yellow keys. She imagines wrists on the hands, and then if it is a lady she imagines a sleeve of a dress, blue, and if it is a man a sleeve of a jacket, brown and tweedy. Then Brooke imagines the Queen, but alive right now, and really young. She has just run across the park

219

and sheltered under a tree because it was raining. It was just any old tree. Now her sheltering under it has made it historic, and all the paparazzi people come up from the Lees' house where there is no point in them being any more, and take photos of it and of Walter Raleigh putting his coat on the puddle for her and her stepping on it, they make her step on it several times over so they can get the best photo. Now the Queen is sitting in front of a screen. There are a lot of courtiers asking her things and she is ignoring them because she is in the middle of playing Call Of Duty. She is aiming her gun at a window and looking through the telescopic sights. That is like Amina, the girl in the year ahead of her at school who everyone knows came from a warzone and is way Christian, and says she became it and believed in God the very moment a bullet that was fired at her missed her. When she talks about it happening she draws a line in the air close to her head for where she felt the bullet go past her. From the moment it missed, she says, she has believed in God. Well duh. But what Brooke wants to know is what about the people who *were* hit by bullets and died? Does that mean that God didn't like them? Or that they didn't believe in Him or It? Or that they believed in the wrong God? Or that they did believe but that God just decided against them? What do the dead people feel about believing in God? But that is just a lot of rubbish because dead people can't feel or believe anything. They are just dead, like the old lady, in the ground, or some are ashes if they have been cremated. Brooke leaves the church, past all the stones with the dead people under them in the ground not having to believe or feel. She will bring the pencil back when she is finished using it. She walks past Straightsmouth, then stops. Would it be best to start writing the History Moleskine here or down nearer the River Thames? Which would be the better historic place? The pencil says on it This pencil is made from recycled CD cases NMM London 2007. It was made when she was still only seven and still went to school in Harrogate, not here.

History Of Education Part 2: There are six days left, after this day today, of Easter holiday LITTLE PIECE OF it is okay. It is still quite a lot of days.

(Wendy Slater was writing out project stuff with her Hello Kitty pen. The Hello Kitty pen was a very short fat silver-coloured one with a little Hello Kitty head on a chain fixed to its top, but because it was such a funny shape and a bit difficult to hold, because it made you wrap your whole hand round it, it was making Wendy Slater's writing look retarded. She's writing with a vibrator, Jack Shadworth said. Chloe and Emily laughed like mad. Brooke thought up a good rhyme. Wendy Slater writes with a vibrator. But she didn't say it because it would make everybody say it, and that would end up with a lot of everybody being cruel to Wendy Slater and because rhyme makes you not forget things easily people would remember to be cruel for longer. You don't know what a vibrator is, Josh Banham said to Wendy. Yes she does, Brooke said. No I don't, Wendy said. More boys gathered round, Daniel and Thomas, and Megan and Jessica came over from the library shelves too. You don't know either, Josh said to Brooke. Duh, obviously I know what a vibrator is, Brooke said. She turned away from the laughing, back to the book about Flight and the page about the Montgolfier Brothers, who believed they had invented a new gas whereas the fact was, they had just discovered heated-up air. She was no good at drawing hearts. She could cut very straight with scissors, but not snap her fingers. She didn't have a Facebook page. She had a weird accent. She didn't talk like or sound like the other girls, any of them. Everybody knew she didn't even have an ordinary mobile, never mind just a phone that wasn't an iPhone. Wendy Slater was still asking everybody what a vibrator was when Mr. Warburton came back into the room. He heard Wendy and then pretended he hadn't. He winked at the boys and then at the girls like Simon Cowell on Britain's Got Talent when he gives the person on the stage in the theatre a wink if he's liked them and they're going to get through to the next round. Brooke saw his glance go round the class and allow everybody not to like her. She looked hard at the picture of the first Montgolfier balloon, blown about by the wind high above the crowds in the streets in France. Everybody in the room knew, though nobody would ever have dared say it, about Mr. Warburton not liking Brooke. She looked at the wildly blowing-about balloon in the picture. Last year a plane going from Brazil to France just fell into the sea by itself in a storm, just right there into the sea, and all the people on it drowned. In the paper a Science Correspondent said that modern jets should be able to withstand any storm.

The fact is, Brooke stood in her parents' bedroom at 5am in the morning, with the light coming under the blind. She had not been able to sleep. She had got out of her own bed and come through. Their door had been a little open. It did not creak. Her mother was lying on her side, facing away from her father. Her father was lying on his back. Her mother's arm was flung over her father's stomach and side. Her mother's breathing was steady and quiet. She couldn't hear her father's breathing, but could see his chest moving under the cover so he was definitely not dead. They looked really happy asleep. Brooke thought what she would say instead. Who invented fireplaces? What is the world's most dangerous cake? There was Brooke's father, over by the window in the kitchen with the two letters in his hand. *Over less than 80% attendance concerns over Brooke's truanting behaviour no doubting Brooke's intelligence however conduct leaves a great deal to be desired* is what the letter from the head said. There was her mother patting the chair next to her. Tell us. CLEVER-CLEVER CLEVEREST. Alfred the Grate. Attila the Bun. Right, Mr. Warburton shouted. Project books away. History charts out. Daniel. Give out these photocopies. Thank you. A vibrator, Brooke said to herself under her breath to nobody, is a thing which vibrates.)

The The fact is notes will all go *here*. Brooke is sitting on one of the wooden benches near the river along from the place where you go down into the tunnel and she is counting the blank pages in the History Moleskine. The The fact is notes will go after the note about being vegetarian, which came first in real time, and then there will be the note about Mrs. Young, and then the The fact is notes. The the! It is funny to say two the's. So there are times you don't need a the at all, and there are other times you need more than one the. There are sixteen of the the the the the—! so many the's all said together sounds like a car that won't start—there are sixteen The fact is notes. That will need thirty-two pages or sixteen double pages. And then the piece will come which she will write down for historic records about visiting Mr. Garth on Wednesday, and that will take up a page or maybe two, so probably (she counts the pages) that will be on *this* page, and then the fact that Mr. Garth has left the room will need to be written down *here*. And then that will be the end of this history, at least the bit that has Mr. Garth actually in it. Though it might be a good idea to leave some pages blank at the end in case there is anything else that happens, in case the history isn't over. There are definitely enough pages. There are loads. She keeps her finger in the right place in the book and she gets the pencil out. She starts at the top of the page, in her best handwriting. *On Wednesday 7th of April Two Thousand and Ten at about half past two pm 1430 in 24 hr time Brooke Bayoude went in and sat in Mr. Garth's room after she knocked on the door and said would he like a cup of tea and he said he would. The tea was Marks & Spencer's Earl Grey tea the one that comes in a black box. The Milk was Skimmed kind. Brooke Bayoude made the tea in the Lees' Kitchen. On the way up the stairs she did not spill it on the stair carpet. When she gave it to him he did not want sugar which was just as well because she had not brought any up stairs. Mr. Garth was very well and Brooke Bayoude said it was nice to see him and he said it was nice to see her. Brooke Bayoude asked him if he remembered her and he said yes he did. He told her some good jokes including the one about the grandads and grannies and there was also another astronomically long joke which was a variation on the Knock! Knock! kind of jokes, about "will you remember" see later in History). Brooke Bayoude then asked Mr. Garth if he would like a biscuit because she knows where they are kept in the Lees' Kitchen. Mr. Garth Declined. Then the time for the visit alas was over and Brooke Bayoude said goodbye and Mr. Garth did too and they shook hands. Brooke Bayoude then closed the door after her and took the mug down stairs she washed it out at the sink and did not put it in the dish washer because the dish washer was full of Clean things. It was the mug that has the picture on it of a tiger which Mr. Garth drank out of on that historic day. Brooke Bayoude dried the mug and put the mug back in the cupboard.* She reads over what she has written so far and then checks to see if she is keeping her lines level. It is not too bad for it being blank paper, it only slopes a bit at the ends where the writing has to get smaller to fit the words in, which is only natural. She reads through it again. When she gets to the last line she crosses out the word historic. It does not need to be said, because it is implied, being in a book with the word history on the front. Then she thinks she might like to say it even though it is implied. Then she is glad she has written in pencil so she can decide about the word for definite later.

(Brooke Bayoude Ten In Four Days' Time Fastest Runner Up Stairs In World got in the front door when the cleaning lady who comes on a Wednesday was just leaving and was loading her things into her van and Brooke slipped past her and in the door while it was still open and ran up the stairs really fast as befits a so fast runner. She had the latest The fact is note to deliver. It had actually been weeks since the last one. Brooke had not been feeling like delivering anything to anyone. But then she had seen this fact on an antiques programme on TV and had thought it was a very good one and should maybe be shared. She stood at the door and took the note out of the front pocket of her jacket and unfolded it and was about to bend to slip the note under the wooden door when she said this, out loud, to the door, just, like, said it. Listen do you want to know a joke about a door? Then the voice from inside the room said the words why not. Okay, right, Brooke said. What prize did the man who invented door knockers win? The voice didn't say anything. (The voice was Mr. Garth.) Do you give up? Brooke said. I give up, the voice said. The no bell prize, Brooke said. Then the voice said: Knock knock. Who's there? Brooke said. Toby, the voice said. Toby who? Brooke said. Toby or not Toby, that is the question, the voice said. Brooke

224

really laughed because it was about Hamlet. Then she started to tell a knock knock joke herself, but when she said Knock knock, the voice answered Come in. So Brooke turned the handle and the door opened. It's not locked! Brooke said. Mr. Garth was sitting on the exercise bike with one foot on a pedal and one foot on the frame. It hasn't been locked for months, not since last summer, Mr. Garth said, but nobody's knocked on it till now. I brought you a note, Brooke said. Good, Mr. Garth said, is it a fact is note? I wondered where they'd gone. What's the fact today, then?

The fact is, a mystery clock is an old-fashioned sort of clock that seems to go by itself on its own without seemingly needing any winding or ever being looked after by anyone. Mr. Garth read it out loud off the piece of paper. Yes, that's a good one, he said, thank you. Thank you for sending me all the facts over the weeks, I wondered who it was that was being so kind as to think I would want to know things. I thought that you would need to, while you were in here, Brooke said, in case you were a bit bored. It's like a newspaper getting delivered, but better, Mr. Garth said. I appreciate the time it took to find the facts and write them down for me. That's all right, Brooke said, it didn't take very long. It's what I like about handwriting, Mr. Garth said, that it is about time. How do you mean? Brooke said. Well, Mr. Garth said, it takes time to write things down, put one word after another. And also, the letters you sent me are in your handwriting, which is like sending me an exclusive artefact that nobody but you could have made, so, thank you. That's quite cool! Brooke said. Though there's one fact in particular I did want to ask about, Mr. Garth said. Mr. Garth got off the bike and went over to the chest of drawers thing and looked through the pile of The fact is notes and held one up. This one, he said, *The fact is, deer know about weddings and about who you will marry.* I'm pretty sure it is a fact, Brooke said, it's what it says in that song. What song? Mr. Garth asked. The one about knowing where you're going, Brooke said. I don't think I know that song, Mr. Garth said. Brooke sang it for him: *I know where I'm going. I know who's going with me. I know who my love*

225

is. And the deer knows who I'll marry. Mr. Garth started laughing. No no, I'm not laughing at you, he said in the middle of the laughing, you sang it really beautifully. It's just the thought, the thought of a herd of deer standing on a hillside knowing who we'll marry. He laughed a bit more then he wiped at his eyes. Oh dear, he said. Oh God. You've actually been in here for a very long time, Brooke said. It's very small for such a long time, do you not want to come out of here? Could I? Mr. Garth said. I don't see why not, Brooke said, I mean, I think so. What I mean is, it's not as if there's very much a person can do to keep himself or herself occupied in here. Oh, I don't know, I've been pretty busy, Mr. Garth said and he showed her how many miles he'd done on the exercise bike speedo, which said 3,015.78 miles, so that meant nearly 3,016. Yes but this bike was in the room before you came into it and there must have been *some* mileage on it already, Brooke said. I swear to tell the truth, the whole truth and nothing but the truth, Mr. Garth said, there were six and a half miles on it when I first sat on its seat, I cannot tell a lie. Then Brooke said, that's funny, you've done all those miles, and Miles is also your first name, Miles by name and miles by nature! It's true, Mr. Garth said. His cuffs were frayed and there was a tear in his shirt at the hem. I'm a vegetarian too now, Brooke said so he wouldn't think she was judging him for his clothes being a bit torn, because she was pretty sure he noticed her seeing that they were. Then she asked him if he would like a cup of tea. I would really like that, he said, I haven't had a cup of tea in months. Do you want to come down to the kitchen while I make you one? Brooke said but he said no, I'll just stay here if you don't mind, but thank you. Will I shut the door? she said and he said yes please. But when she came to the top of the stairs with the mug of tea he'd opened the door again by himself and he was actually standing in the open doorway, he was actually almost in the hall. He was looking a bit tired. Behind him she could hear all the noise of the people outside. It sounded funny in the stairwell now that the door was open. They went back into the room and Mr. Garth just kind of stood with his arms at his sides. Brooke said, will I shut the door again? and Mr. Garth nodded. Then he sat on the bike again and held his tea in his hands with his arms on the handlebars and Brooke sat on the floor and told him about the time she and her mother and father had gone to Greece and stayed in a hotel apartment place on an island and about how the old man whose family owned the apartment place would always sit outside right next to the main road all day on a white plastic chair, and that he always said hello when they went past to town and came back from town. But this one day we went out in the morning, Brooke said, there was this dead dog in the road that had been hit by a car, and it was quite a big dog. And the man was sitting there watching the road, only now it was as if he was watching the dead dog just lying in the road right in front of him. So he maybe even saw the dog get hit, but now he was just sitting and watching, I mean, why would he not take the dog off the road and put it at the side, even, so it wouldn't keep getting hit? Because when we came back from the town and from going to the supermarket the dog was flattened right into the road in some parts of it like its legs and tail. It is weird what people do. Yes, Mr. Garth said. It's very mysterious. Mr. Garth spoke very slowly. I mean, I know the dog was obviously already dead anyway, duh, Brooke said, but it is kind of horrible to think of it getting run over and over again by all the other cars all day. And what if it was a dog he knew? I don't mean his own dog, I mean like if it was a dog he had patted or that he knew the name of? Mr. Garth nodded and shrugged. He took a sip out of the mug and he flinched. Oh! I forgot if you wanted sugar, Brooke said and jumped up to go and get some from downstairs. I don't, but thank you very much indeed, Mr. Garth said, it is really kind of you, but I think I was just surprised at it being hot. Brooke sat down on the floor again. Am I talking too much, she said, because I have been known before now to talk too much? No, Mr. Garth said. Please keep talking to me. Okay, Brooke said. Sometimes I have this dream, do you ever have the dreams that mean that you don't know whether you're asleep or awake in them? Yes, Mr. Garth said. I often have dreams like that, tell me your dream. Are you sure? Brooke said, because sometimes it can be very boring to listen to people's dreams, at least that is what my mother tells my father at breakfast sometimes. I'm not bored, Mr. Garth said, and I will tell you if I am. Okay, well, there's this dream, I had it like weeks ago, like it was ages ago back when I was only just nine, Brooke said, it's a historic kind of dream, and there is a boy in it and it is back in history except I am there too, and he is the same age as me. He is dressed in torn clothes, much much more torn than yours are and much dirtier like he is a very poor person from the past, and he is standing like with a crowd behind him, like the crowd outside your window kind of except in historic clothes, and behind the crowd, what the crowd are all looking at, there is like a stage with a tall post with a rope on the end of it and the rope has a noose on the end. And then the boy comes up to me and he holds up a loaf of bread and he says, look, and he points over his shoulder at the crowd and he says, they're going to execute me to death because I stole *this*, and he holds up the loaf. I was hungry and I took it, he says, and now look, it is not fair that this is happening. Then I woke up, and then I couldn't get back to sleep, do you ever have that kind of dream? Not exactly the same, but I think that's a very healthy dream, Mr. Garth said. Do you? Brooke said, because I mean when I woke up I knew it had happened, and if it was real it had happened way back in history and there wasn't anything I could do, and even if it hadn't happened in reality and was only happening in my dream I still couldn't stop it from happening. I think, Mr. Garth said, that the boy in your dream simply wanted you to agree with him that what was happening wasn't fair. It really really wasn't, Brooke said. No, Mr. Garth said, it wasn't. Then he said, that was a very clever dream you had. Yes, Brooke said, but maybe is it too clever? No, Mr. Garth said, not at all, there's no such thing as too clever anyway. Brooke looked round the room and wondered if maybe it would be a good place to come on the days when she didn't go to school. Then she asked Mr. Garth did he really think there wasn't anything wrong with being cleverest. Top of Mount Cleverest, Mr. Garth said. Brooke laughed. Then Mr. Garth said really slowly:

the fact is, that at the top of any mountain you'll feel a bit dizzy because of the air up there. Cleverness is great. It's a really good thing, when you have it. But there's no point in just having it. You have to know how to use it. And when you know how to use your cleverness, it's not that you're the cleverest any more, or are doing it to be cleverer than anyone else like it's a competition. No. Instead of being *the* clever*est,* the thing to do is become *a* clever*ist.* Then Mr. Garth told a great knock knock joke where what you do is you say knock knock and the other person says who's there? and you say Granny, and the other person says, Granny who? and then you say again, knock knock, and the other person says who's there? and you say Grandad, and the other person says, Grandad who? and then you say knock knock, and the person says who's there? and you say Granny again, and you keep going exactly like that, saying Granny and Grandad for a few more times, and then you say knock knock and the person says who's there, and you say Aunt, and the person says Aunt who? and you say Aunt you glad I got rid of all those grannies and grandads. Brooke laughed until she nearly choked. Then she said, the thing is, I can see the point of a joke, and I can see the point of a fact, but what is the point of a book, I mean the kinds that tell stories? If a story isn't a fact, but it is a made-up version of what happened, like the one that is a book made up about the real man who tried to blow up the Observatory, I mean, what is the *point* of it? Mr. Garth leaned his head on the handlebars. Think how quiet a book is on a shelf, he said, just sitting there, unopened. Then think what happens when you open it. Yes, but what *exactly* happens? Brooke said. I have an idea, he said, I'll tell you the very beginning of a story that's not been written yet, and then you write the story for me, and we can see what happens in the process. Okay, Brooke said. That is a really interesting idea. Yes? Mr. Garth said. Okay. Here goes. There was once a man who lived in a small room and, without leaving that room, managed to cycle his bike three thousand miles. Do I have to remember it exactly word for word, Brooke said, or can it be approximate? It can be as approximate as you like, Mr. Garth said. Yeah but the thing is, Brooke said, if I write it, you have to write one too, where I get to tell *you* how to begin. Okay, Mr. Garth said, it seems only fair. It's a deal. What's my beginning? I think it is an idea rather than a beginning, Brooke said. Okay, Mr. Garth said, I'm all ears. All ears! That was funny. Brooke told him about the picture of the man in the telescope book who is all eyes. Is that my beginning? Mr. Garth said, a man covered in open eyes like butterflies? No, Brooke said. This is it. You have to imagine that if you were sitting there where you are, on the bike, and also here in the room with you was another version of you, like, say you but three or four days before you were ten years old, I mean if it was nearly your tenth birthday. I mean if you were in the room and you were exactly the same age as me, and at the same time you're in the room too, old like you are. I mean older, because you are not old like old people, but you are quite old. I get it, Mr. Garth said. I see, myself then and myself now, yes. So if that really happened in reality, what story would you tell your self and what story would your self tell you? Brooke said. Mr. Garth closed his eyes for a bit of time. Then he opened them very wide. Nearly your birthday, then? he said. It is on Sunday the 11th, Brooke said. I'll write it for you for your birthday, Mr. Garth said, but you'll need to bring me some blank paper, can you? Yes, Brooke said, and would you like a biscuit too, the thing is I actually know where Mrs. Lee keeps them. No, Mr. Garth said, I don't need a biscuit. But I can have one, Brooke said. Yes, Mr. Garth said. Thank you, Brooke said. She went down the stairs and into what was Mr. Lee's study before he moved house to Bloomsbury. There were still things and furniture and so on waiting for him to come and collect them. She found A4 paper in the photocopying tray on the desk. She took two sheets because she didn't know how long or short the story would need to be. Then she went into the kitchen and opened the cupboard door above the microwave and climbed up on to the unit next to the waste disposal and opened the plastic box and took one of the teacakes out and put the lid back on the box and the box back exactly where it had been, as if no one had touched a thing. And anyway an adult had said it was okay, so she could.)

The fact is. The fact apparently is. The fact seems to be. The story goes. Once upon a time a man threw a clock out of an upstairs window. Why did the man throw the clock out of the upstairs window? So he could see time fly. But that joke isn't altogether a very good one, because to be true it should really end like this: so he could see time fall. Brooke turns to the very back of the History Moleskine, which is where she's decided she'll put the really good joke Mr. Garth told her after she came upstairs with the paper for him. She writes across the top: *Joke Told By Mr. Garth to Brooke Bayoude Wednesday 7th of April at about 3.30pm or 1530 in 24 hr time.* She underlines this. Then she writes the following.

Mr. Miles Garth—Will you remember me in a months time.
Brooke Bayoude—Yes
MG—Will you remember me in 6 months time.
BB—Yes
MG—Will you remember me in a years time.
BB—Yes
MG—Will you remember me in 2 years time.
BB—Yes
MG—Will you remember me in 3 years time.
BB—Yes
MG—Knock knock
BB—Who's there
MG—See you've forgotten me already.

It is funny sitting here today and wondering where Mr. Garth has gone. He could be anywhere! It is funny thinking of all the people who are watching the window, and of Mrs. Lee going in on Sunday herself to the room and moving the blind a little bit and then jumping away from the window because of the excited noise her just moving the blind a tiny bit made the crowd make. Mrs. Lee had completely stopped crying after that and had come out of the room looking quite happy and making everybody swear all over again on their lives that nobody would tell anybody Mr. Garth was not there any more.

But the fact is it would be amazing if Mr. Garth was, right this minute, standing outside in the crowd himself and looking at the window he is meant to be behind. And imagine if he saw the blind move with everybody else and it was meant to be him moving it!

(What are you doing, Brooksie? her father said on Thursday night. I'm busy, Brooke said. She was on the rug with her back to the radiator. Doing what? her father said. I'm writing a story, Brooke said. What are you doing, Bernie? her father said to her mother. Leave me alone, I'm proofing these exam papers, her mother said. Her father picked a piece of paper up off the table near her mother's hand. Her mother tried to catch it as he took it. He danced across to the other side of the room. There's nothing good or bad but thinking makes it so: Discuss, he said. I wish they'd not used that as the Hamlet question, her mother said, it'd be such a good first-year philosophy general question. There's always next year, her father said. Next year, yes, her mother said, remember to remind me, Brooke, to use that quote next year. Okay, Brooke said. Her father picked up the copy of Hamlet her mother was checking things in and flicked through it. "As the indifferent children of the earth," he said. Ha—as if there's any such thing as a single indifferent child of the earth. Who is it says that, again? her mother asked. Rosencrantz says it, Brooke said. Uh . . . you're right, it is, her father said. She's right. How does she know that? She's a genius. She takes after me. What are you writing about, spawn of Terence Bayoude? It's about a man in a room who stays in the room and never leaves it but in that room he has, like, a bicycle, and he cycles three thousand miles on it, Brooke said. What a turn-of-the-century-sounding story, her father said. Like Mr. Garth? her mother said. Sounds more Kafkaesque to me than fin de siècle. Fin de cycle!

her father said. Is someone making him do it? her mother said, is it, like, that he has to provide electricity for the whole building by going round and round like a rat on a hamster wheel in a cage? No, Brooke said. He quite likes doing it and nobody is really making him do it. And though he doesn't ever leave the room, all the same he cycles through Greenwich when it is nothing but a forest, and he cycles up a mountain to the summit, where he learns how to breathe even though it is difficult to there, then he cycles through time past the Queen who causes the uprising and burns London down, past all the people building it up again and past the Queen who is sheltering under the tree in the rain, and he gets off his bike and he takes his mac off and puts it over a puddle for her. What a gent! her father said. Then he cycles so close to the cell window in a prison that he can hear the original frogs talking to the original St. Alfege, Brooke said. What are the frogs saying? her father asked. They are talking in their own frog language, about the weather, and how difficult it is to have frog-spawn, and what an interesting experience it is to grow legs when you start off without any, and how nice and damp it is in the cell and how glad they are that they're there, although they are sorry for him, because he is clapped in irons and not a frog like them, and they answer his philosophical questions with their croaking, Brooke said. But St. Alfege can understand them. And he tells the man on the bicycle what they are saying. What's going to happen in the end? her father said. I don't know, Brooke said. But what I want is the bicycle to be able to go across all the rooftops in London at the end, but I don't know how to get it up there to do that realistically. It sounds like those frogs could talk the legs off a donkey, so maybe they could talk the wings on to a bike, her father said. Yes they could, Brooke said, that is a good idea! But it is no good, because the thing is I also want the story to be true and factual as well as a made-up thing. So you want miraculous talking frogs *and* realism, her father said, a story with more than one ending, maybe. She means she wants a work of the imagination that's simultaneously rigorously true, her mother said without taking her eyes off her work. See how our daughter takes after me. On the contrary, her father said, she takes after me, she is writing a story with some subtlety, very unlike the ones your mother was championing to me last night. Her father started poking at her mother like he does to make her ticklish. Very unlike what exactly? Brooke said. Terence, I'm trying to work, her mother said but she was laughing. Your mother and I were having an intellectual discussion last night about turn-of-the-century manhood, her father said. It was because your father was annoyed that I was watching a film called Ronin on TV and that I wouldn't put it off and come to bed, her mother said. It was because your mother said that being blown through the wall by an action hero or, in this case, stalked within a hair's breadth of your life round a dark parking lot by a man with a gun, was so exciting that she couldn't come to bed till the film was finished, and when I said that I would tell all her students and work colleagues and employers that she prefers, as examples of turn-of-the-century manhood, Arnold Schwarzenegger and Al Pacino to Proust's Swann and Joyce's Bloom, she got quite violent with me and even started hitting me quite hard in the chest area, her father said. If only you were a real man, her mother said, and Schwarzenegger isn't even *in* Ronin. Yes, but he's big in A La Recherche, her father said, and one can only thank the great writers for giving us such good role models. Sylvester Swann. Leopold Schwarzenegger. Robert de Bloom. Both her parents were laughing. Brooke looked up from her piece of paper and watched them throwing the words for birds and flowers and Hollywood actors at each other like they were throwing little rocks wrapped as presents. She looked round the room at all the books on all the shelves. A closed book on a shelf sat there quietly, not saying anything. Her mother was shouting about Wesley Snipes. Her father was holding up his hands and laughing. Do you two want to know a really good joke? Brooke said. Go on then, her father said still looking at her mother with love. Yes, her mother said still looking with the same pleasedness at her father. Then they both turned at once and looked at Brooke. Okay, Brooke said. There was once this man. Which man? her father said. I won't tell you it if you are stupid with interruptions, Brooke said. Okay, okay, her father said, go on. There was once this man, Brooke said, who wouldn't stop singing. Is this joke about your father? her mother said. *Don't* interrupt, Brooke said. Very sorry I'm sure, her mother said. Come on. Go on. Okay, Brooke said. Well, this man just sang all the time. Eventually it made them so angry at him singing all the time that they told him he was going to be put in front of the firing squad if he didn't stop. But he kept on doing it. So the soldiers arrived with the guns, and the man was led out to be executed and tied to the stake and a blind-fold was put on him. And the captain said, you can have one last request. So the man said, okay, as my last request I'd like to sing a song. Permission granted, the captain said. So the man began singing. Nine thousand nine hundred and ninety-nine green bottles. Hanging on the wall. Brooke's father laughed. Her mother laughed. Good one, her father said. Not bad, her mother said, I've heard worse.)

The fact is, imagine. Brooke closes the History Moleskine and stands up. She looks at her Me To You watch. It is 4.16 pm, or 1616 in 24 hr time. Imagine if all the civilizations in the past had not known to have the imagination to look up at the sun and the moon and the stars and work out that things were connected, that those things right in front of their eyes could be connected to time and to what time is and how it works. She puts the Moleskine in the back pocket with all the The fact is notes folded inside it. She takes the paper plane out from inside the front of her sweater. It is a bit crushed, but it will probably still fly and she has refolded it now three times and it is not too worn, and anyway if she unfolds it again and then forgets how to refold it, the story comes with instructions as to how to do it properly. So she can easily unfold it and read the story on it and then fold it up the same again. In her own story for Mr. Garth, in the first ending, the man on the bicycle has learned from frogs, who know how to develop into frogs from tadpoles, how to transform his bicycle into a Montgolfier balloon, a kind of balloon which did actually exist in real fact, and then he cycles into the cloudy sky over the rooftops of London, even past the big gold clock Big Ben itself which is further down this river if you go on the boat, and on TV they show the film of him they took from the security cameras as the bike disappears round the river bend. In the second ending the exercise bike became a real ordinary bike (that is the only imaginary thing that happens in this ending) and the man just carried the bike through the door and down the stairs and out of the front door and on to the pavement and got on it and cycled out into the road and away among all the other people who are the general traffic of the city of London. Holding in her hand the plane that says on the wing of it in Mr. Garth's writing

to:

<u>the</u> *Brooke Bayoude*

Cleverist

she runs across in the sun to the railing. She climbs up and leans over it to see the river. The Thames is brown and green today. It changes what it is every day. No: every minute. Every second. It is a different possible river every second, and imagine all the people under the water walking across to the other side and back to this side in the tunnel right now, because under the surface there is a whole other thing always happening. Brooke looks down at the water then up at the sky, which is blue with clouds today. Then, with the historic river flowing at her back, Brooke sits on the little bit of wall below the railing. She unfolds the piece of paper in her hands and she reads again the story written on it.